THE
WOUNDED

AND OTHER STORIES
ABOUT SONS AND FATHERS

IAN GRAHAM LEASK

For Ken
Best Wishes,

[signature]

28 April, 1993

NEW RIVERS PRESS 1992

Three stories in *The Wounded and Other Stories about Sons and Fathers* appeared in slightly different versions in the following publications: "The Anobiid" in *Stiller's Pond: New Fiction from the Upper Midwest* (New Rivers Press) and "The Wounded" and "Daddy's Eyes" in *Inroads*.

Among the numerous friends and family members who have so wonderfully supported him in this project the author would particularly like to thank C. W. Truesdale, Susan Welch, Robert Cowgill, and Ann Pedersen for the editorial suggestions on some or all of these stories; Lon J. Lutz for his hospitality and companionship at 1101; and for correcting his French and German in "Hesta's Tale," Martine Planeille and Christa Tiefenbacher.

The publication of *The Wounded and Other Stories about Sons and Fathers* has been made possible by generous grants from the Arts Development Fund of the United Arts Council, the First Bank System Foundation, Liberty State Bank, the Tennant Company Foundation, and the National Endowment for the Arts (with funds appropriated by the Congress of the United States). New Rivers Press also wishes to acknowledge the Minnesota Non-Profits Assistance Fund for its invaluable support.

New Rivers Press books are distributed by:

The Talman Company   Bookslinger
150 Fifth Avenue   2402 University Avenue West
New York, NY 10011   Saint Paul, MN 55114

The Wounded and Other Stories about Sons and Fathers has been manufactured in the United States of America for New Rivers Press, 420 N. 5th Street/Suite 910, Minneapolis, MN 55401 in a first edition of 2,000 copies.

This first one is for Jean Moriarty.

CONTENTS

THE WOUNDED

She woke and found him not beside her.

It was unusual. Henry's clothes – the threadbare gray cardigan, old woolen trousers, white shirt – were not draped over the chair. His cigarettes were not on the bedside table. She listened. The house was still, not a sound, and neither could she hear anything outside; there was just her own breath and the buzzing in her ears.

Her watch said two o'clock. She yawned and the yawn produced a roar in her ears as if someone held sea shells over them.

How stupid of me, she thought, he must be waiting up for the boy. She lay back and pulled the eiderdown up to her chin. Every Saturday for a month the boy had been coming home later and later; for the first time in her life she thought Henry might be truly worried about him. Last week was the worst so far. She didn't know how to handle it, he was just a boy and he came home drunk, very drunk, paralytic.

Alone with him next morning at the kitchen table, sipping tea, he told her – it astounded her that he remembered anything at all – that his so-called friends had sent him home in a taxi and given the driver the wrong street number, so he was dropped two hundred yards down the road. He tried to explain to the driver but he couldn't make his mouth work. The driver pulled him from the car, saying, "Come on, you disgusting slob, get out of my car," and left him lying in the gutter. He crawled home. Glaring into his tea, the boy said, "I'll find that bastard and rip his face off."

She had replied that if he ripped the face off everyone who told him the truth he'd be doing a lot of ripping. That put him in a big funk. He went out and slammed the door.

No, she'd never forget that night: she and Henry were watching a late night television show. It was an awful sound, hearing the front gate bang back against the wall – when you live with drunks, sounds like that have their own unmistakable grammar – Henry turned down the volume of the television. Standing in the center of the lounge, they heard the slow progress of a half-conscious body, dragging itself along the path. Then came a thump against the door which made the windows rattle.

Then, after a minute's quiet, an unearthly animal-like wretching in the porchway, followed by the clatter of scattered milk bottles.

She never saw Henry's face with such a look of horror. With melodramatic coincidence, the grandfather clock in the hall struck midnight. He put down his whiskey glass and went to open the front door. The boy tumbled in, filling the hallway with the smell of beer and vomit. His knuckles were split, his face bruised – he'd been fighting again.

She helped Henry get the boy into his room. They pulled off his clothes and got him into bed. She bathed his face with a flannel while Henry went to get the bucket, just in case he wasn't finished being sick.

The boy hiccoughed and moaned, thrust his head from side to side on the pillow. Sighing, Henry sat down on a stool beside the bed, and with his left hand, palm up, took hold of the boy's right hand, rubbing his thumb over the split and bloody knuckles. She stood beside him, looking down. She knew she shouldn't have said it, she knew he was already thinking of it, she knew he was in agony, but she said it anyway:

"You know this is all your fault, don't you?"

Henry turned his face up to her: she'd never seen the blue of his eyes seem so pale. After all that she'd been through over the years, after all the wasted words, it made her sick to see him so sorry for himself. Pathetic, she thought, bloody pathetic. Then he looked back down, and closed his right hand over the boy's fingers.

She said, "I'll bring in your scotch."

"No, Judy," he said. "A cup of tea, that's all."

She knew she shouldn't, but she said:

"A cup of tea? Well, certainly. A little late though, isn't it?"

Henry put his forehead onto the pile of hands and closed his eyes. His shoulders shuddered in a series of quiet spasms. The only time she'd seen him weep was when he was dreaming, which he did often, but this was different. She left the room, swinging the door so that it closed itself as she walked away. When the door was closed, she tiptoed back and listened to him crying. She made him a cup of tea then went to bed. Henry stayed up all night, holding the boy's hand.

2

She thought: what a lot of things the poor devil must have thought about.

Yawning, she got up from the bed and put on her dressing gown and slippers. She went downstairs, looked in all the rooms. He'd left the kitchen light on. Two-thirds of a bottle of Black and White stood on the counter. The dog was gone, too. She looked outside and saw the parked car. The boy was still out.

"Guilt," she said, "he's walking off some more guilt."

She used the toilet and went back to bed.

She woke and found him not beside her.

Something had woken her, her blood was in alarm, but she didn't know what.

A clatter on the kitchen floor — scissors, it sounded like. Sitting up, she said, "What on earth is the fool playing at? I hope to Christ you haven't polished off that bottle. Please God, don't let him be stinko, not tonight."

She heard the old dog, walking calmly on the parquet flooring of the hall; it shook itself awkwardly — this alerted her to the fact that rain was patting against the bedroom window. She turned on the light. She thought she heard Henry's voice, but it could've been her own thoughts echoing in the silence. If he was stinko at least he wasn't shouting.

She thought perhaps the boy had come home and they were having a chat. They had never really had a good talk, only rows; Henry never talked, he lectured. And the boy was now too much of a know-it-all himself not to insist on his own opinion. Of course, Henry thought no one of sixteen should have an opinion. Neither of the fools had learned anything from having drunks for fathers.

The way his liver was, Henry wouldn't live much longer; his lungs were bad from smoking; his heart was suspect: it was essential for the boy's future that Henry make an effort to communicate.

She listened. Indeed, there were voices, murmuring.

She wondered what they were talking about.

She switched off the light and tried to sleep.

Suddenly she thought: they're talking about me.

She sat up, turned the light on, and said, "They better not be talking about me."

She put on her dressing gown and slippers and quietly crept downstairs. She'd give them what-for if they were talking about her.

The kitchen light was on; Henry moved around rapidly in there. The boy's clothes were outside the kitchen door, thrown in a wet pile against the wall. The grandfather clocked ticked softly. Restless and whining, the old black dog wandered into the lounge and back into the hall. She hurried forward and stood in the doorway.

The kitchen table was pulled into the middle of the room and on it lay her son, dressed only in white underpants and blue socks. He was lowering the whiskey bottle after having taken a swig. He stared vacantly at the ceiling and said:

"This isn't working, dad. I can feel."

Blood was smeared over his torso, and lines of it, burgundy colored, as if

3

dripped from a paint brush, ran along the linoleum from the back door to the table. The massive expanse of his right rib cage faced her. Henry was bent over the boy's left side, attending to something.

Her hands covered her mouth, all sensation left her face, and when sensation returned, it was in the form of prickling skin, all over her body. Henry looked at her across the boy's chest. He looked down again, saying:

"Now don't make a fuss. It's imperative that you stay calm."

"I'm not making a fuss," said the boy.

"Not you, fathead, your mum."

"Oh, good old mum's arrived," said the boy, glancing at her. "All right, mum? I'm afraid I was involved in a bit of an altercation, a fucking great frac-arse." He took a long swig from the bottle.

"Altercation?" said Henry, "This was very nearly an alteration, old chap."

The boy laughed, slurring, "I'm sure that was their intention, father-man, old dad-dads, old baldy." Then he winced with pain.

"Don't do that, son. It makes the blood run."

She wasn't going to faint, she fought it off. She came around to the left side of the table and looked at the wound. It ran diagonally, an oozing jagged rip, from the top of his hip bone to his bottom rib. At its deepest, white fat globules showed against the torn red insides of the boy's flesh. Henry was sewing up the wound with white cotton that he'd boiled in a saucepan. He'd smothered the wound in iodine.

"Why didn't you call me?"

"I know how to do this, it's under control. I didn't want to worry you until the worst was over."

"How very considerate of you. Why didn't you take him to the hospital? This isn't a battle station, you know. The war's over."

"It was the dog that found him," said Henry, starting to sew the last part of the wound, the deepest part. "He sniffed him out. We went up the alley behind the cinema and the dog found him in among the dustbins. I knew it was him."

"But I don't understand, why you... "

The boy banged the base of the bottle on the table:

"No fucking hospital, do you hear me, bitch! No fucking hospital. Dad'll do it, let dad do it for once."

The house echoed with the boy's shout.

"Don't do that, son. It makes the blood run."

She took the sponge mop out of the cupboard, wetted it in the sink, and cleared blood off the floor.

BOMBAY MORNING

The monsoon was late.

The heat hadn't allowed the *burra-sahib* to rest properly and he'd been sweating and shivering through distorted visions of his life. When he dropped into sleep the dreams were vivid but unmemorable, and the borderland between sleeping and waking was all hallucination. The pain ended when his father shrieked "Harry!" with murder in his voice, making Henry open his eyes.

He was still alive. Heartbeats thumped in his ears, and the room swarmed with hovering and darting hummingbirds. For a while he could see the inside and outside of the bungalow, and, clinging to the walls like wet gems, were thousands of brightly colored scorpions. There was malaria in his blood; he always had the impression that his veins were filled with red pepper, but despite the fever he began to see his real life again. Iona was long gone. The war had been over a long time and he wasn't on a plank in the North Sea being hunted by black sharks, he wasn't being dive-bombed by red-eyed ravens.

He found himself trapped by the dead weight of the girl who lay across him. He didn't want to wake her because she'd want to make love and he didn't feel up to it — his neck ached, his mouth was sour, he felt nauseated.

He was safe inside the mosquito netting.

The hummingbirds and scorpions vanished.

Beyond the mosquito netting at the foot of the bed, he could see the white framed window, the curtains only half pulled, breathing in and out with the slight breeze. After the high cockalorums of last night neither he nor Jamila had been

5

capable of drawing the curtains, so that now hot light flooded rudely into the white room; with it came the odor of disinfected excreta and the early morning scent of the seasonal flower beds that had long ago been laid out in the garden by Iona. Yes, she was in England now, cool England, and he could scarcely imagine what her life was like there.

On one of the twin dressers, the one left of the window that used to be Iona's, was a framed picture of the two of them taken in about 1935. She sat on his lap, smiling. They were in the high-backed wicker chair that was at this moment, a decade and a half later, placed in the corner, close to the right side of the bed; and on it lay his tennis whites, neatly pressed and folded by Bagwan. Even through the netting he could make out how the two faces in the photograph signaled the lives beneath them: she, dark-eyed and frivolous, forever on the edge of laughter, a typical thirties' "fishing fleet" girl who had come out to India to find herself a husband; he, with that nasty close-set hawk's gaze – intellectual and lethal – and that caustic, slightly crooked smile. It wasn't long after that that he went in the navy and fought the war; even then, at thirty, the libertine in him had gained the upper hand.

Most mornings were like this.

Hung over, he'd lie in bed and, with disgust, see the past again. But he didn't think of himself as a bad man, he was a decent chap inside. He just always ended up doing bad things, hurting people. He never seemed to get anything legitimate going and, in the mornings, the future frightened him; it seemed like an impenetrable sea mist.

He could smell booze in his sweat.

The girl smelled of masala. Her face rested in the cavity between his neck and the pillow; he could feel her soft, barely discernible breath against his collar bone. Her long oily hair tumbled about his chest. There was soft black down in front of her ear, her childish front teeth dug into her bottom lip, and where he so savagely bit her neck in the night there were raised purplish abrasions. He had felt great love for her the night before. He was looked down upon by the European community for keeping her, but the India of his youth was gone and would never return, so what did it matter? He would've fought them all on principle last night; he would've given his life. Now he simply felt ill and nothing much mattered at all.

He wanted to call Bagwan but was afraid of the girl. Sometimes his plumbing didn't work when he'd been drinking heavily. It was embarrassing, and she was sure to start crawling all over him as soon as she woke. She was so small and light, almost like a bird, but, perhaps because of her inexplicable devotion to him, a passion had been released in her which he hardly thought possible in a human being. Certainly, he had experienced nothing of the kind in his marriage.

The left edge of the bed was five feet from the door. It was possible that Bagwan would be reading on his *charpoy*, awaiting his employer's pleasure; such diligence took place only during periods of intense loyalty that were impossible to predict, and were, like Jamila's love, inexplicable.

Gently, Henry called, "Bagwan, are you there?"

The vibration of the words pained his temples.

No answer came.

He looked at the photograph again. He had never needed to worry about waking Iona. She had cured hangovers by wrapping a pillow around her head and sleeping till noon. She was the one who hated being crawled all over, especially toward the end. Losing Iona was the first unredeemable defeat of his life. She took young Alec with her, but that was no great matter for she had long since poisoned that relationship, and the boy would be better off in England now. There was no excuse for the way he had treated them, no excuse at all. And here he was, alone with the consequences, riding out time among the last echoes of a lifestyle that would never return.

His own last days were on his mind, too. Someone was trying to kill him. It was probably Jamila's brothers whose honor was now ruined for eternity by her love affair with an infidel. They shouldn't have been surprised for this was part of the new India: everyone was to have freedom. But he'd been making mortal enemies all his life, and, according to his state of mind, it was possible that these enemies had come together and were conspiring against him. He was lucky to escape the sting of a tiny, lethal scorpion that someone slipped into his jacket pocket at the club; he'd been shot at one morning during a tennis match, and could still feel the thud in his feet as the bullet kicked up a chunk of clay inside the tramline; an attack by thugs outside his warehouse at the docks had made it necessary for him to kill a man.

He hissed: "Bagwan, I want you."

There came no response.

Beyond the window, over the fence in the street, two men squabbled in Marathi, something about a job having been improperly executed – a typical argument. Five years ago they would have kept their voices down. This was still a secure suburb, housing the remaining Europeans, *box-wallahs* mostly, and the Indian professional classes who moved into the bungalows vacated after independence. But the noise, dust, and filth were encroaching; squalor, disorganization and corruption bounding back – the Garden of Eden gone to seed. It sickened him; he had always believed that the great umbrella of his own people kept the sun from scorching India, and now that they were gone, everything was hotter and sadder.

"Pssssst, Bagwan!"

Henry's immediate priorities were a glass of scotch, a cigarette and a wash. The sickness would abate with a drink, his rising irritation could be stemmed by a smoke, and the strong native perfume of the girl could be soaped from his skin. He lay sweating, naked but for his watch, while the irritation spread in him. Because Bagwan was currently in a rebellious mood he would probably be sitting in the kitchen, as far out of earshot as possible. The rebellion, no doubt, was caused by his disapproval of Jamila; he would be stubbornly sitting in the kitchen, smoking stolen cigarettes and reading one of those laborious Victorian novels he was so fond of haggling over at the bazaar; if he had to move for something it would be as quietly as a cat.

The thought of this made Henry's irritation peak and he sat up so sharply that the girl flew off him. He ripped aside the mosquito netting.

"Bagwan!"

The girl, smiling, uncoiled and yawned. Her eyes opened, the long black lashes blinking, and her hands began loving him, the soft ochre palms stroking his chest and shoulders, and, whispering his name, she kissed her way down his ribs to his hip bone. He watched her for a second, wondering if something would move in him. It didn't and he pushed her away.

"Bagwan, you bugger, get in here."

The night before he had let Jamila drink too much gin. This extroverted her, brought out the actress, and she pretended to be a slut, an officer's *ramjani*. This excited them both. She was a great mimic of accents and actions, gained from the films she was so utterly addicted to, and after they'd made love she entertained him by mimicking pompous and deluded *memsahibs* as they waited for drunken, whore-mongering husbands to return from the hills. Then she grew serious, and bitterly mimicked her own mother's pious look while being made love to.

"Oh, Harry," she said now, slithering back to him, "some love for Jamila?"

He said, "Not now. *Howa-khana* time."

Then he put his head out of the netting:

"Bagwan, *tum soor ka butcha*, what the bloody hell's going on?"

Bagwan burst in, out of breath, and the girl slid under the sheet.

"Where the bloody hell have you been you black bastard, you pox-ridden son of a bitch, you pig-descended child molester!"

Bagwan smiled, wobbling his head, "Bagwan thanks the *sahib* for the colorful early morning insults."

"You can take your wit, Bagwan, and stuff it up your skinny Hindu arse. I want scotch and cigarettes — fifteen seconds."

"Yes, *sahib*. Thanks awfully, *sahib*. Please repeat the order."

"Bagwan, you bastard. I'll have you hung by your balls if I don't get a smoke immediately."

"Most immediately, *sahib*. Bagwan is very protective of his balls." And he backed out, making a calming gesture with his hand.

Laughing, Henry said, "Why have I put up with him so long? He's not even like a servant, he's more of a clown with his ridiculous diction — he's a parody of a houseboy."

The girl was on the move again. "Harry, Har-ree..."

"Once," he said, "many years ago now, I caught Bagwan looking in a mirror

8

and reciting ridiculously formal sentences from Galsworthy — in the voice of Charles Laughton, would you believe? It was quaint at the time. He's become rather a fixture, hasn't he? I suppose life without him would be impossible."

In Henry's ear, the girl said, "Sack him, he's a thief."

"Whoever would hire the pedantic wretch?"

Jamila got on top of him.

He pulled her face close to his, "Look, I'm not in the mood yet, do you understand?"

Her eyes misted over, she was a debutante from the Home Counties, in love with Laurence Olivier: "Oh Harry darling, how I adore you . . . "

"Oh for Christ's sake. . . I'm surrounded by bloody lunatics. . . Bagwan!"

"Coming, *sahib*, coming coming, please to keep hair on head."

Just as Bagwan backed into the bedroom, using a teapoy as a tray on which wobbled a bottle of Black and White, a jug of water, a glass, a packet of Players, a box of matches and an ashtray, there was a distinct movement taking place in Henry's plumbing.

"*Sahib* better get up soon," said Bagwan, "tennis match with important local official at seven o'clock sharp. Bagwan is pleased to advise that you drink plenty of water with your scotch."

"Yes, yes, I know, you alliterative savage."

"Thanks awfully for that fine insult, *sahib*. Shall I get rid of the *ramjani* now, so you can smoke in peace?"

The girl, who had covered herself with the sheet, shot up in the bed. Her eyes glared and a string of Urdu explicatives rattled and hissed from her mouth. Hands on hips, head waggling, Bagwan waited for her to finish. Then he jabbered back at her, his teeth showing, his eyes wide and angry. Then they both shouted at once, glaring and gesticulating. The girl was so furious that she stood, completely uncovered, in the middle of the bed with her arms flying. Not once did Bagwan look lower than her mouth.

Henry poured himself two fingers and drank it off. He poured himself another, this time adding a little water, then he lit a cigarette and sat back, fascinated by the decibel level.

His lack of reaction finally wore them down and they stared at him, puffing and indignant, with wild expectant expressions. The girl pulled the sheet around herself.

Pouring a third drink, the cigarette dangling from the side of his mouth, left eye closed against rising smoke, Henry said:

"So, are we finished?"

Bagwan burst, "She has insulted me very gravely, *sahib*. She insulted my family back to creation. Bagwan believes that it is a reasonable request that whore be taken to marketplace and flogged."

"I'm not a whore, Harry. He cannot call me that. Give him the sack. He is

9

a thief, and gives you double finger salute when your back is turned. Sack him this instant."

"I don't have time to adjudicate your petty squabbles or whatever causes the bad blood between you. You're the only people left in Bombay that like me, so please don't kill each other. Now, if you don't mind, I have to go and let a common little office-*wallah* take a set from me. But look here, Bagwan, Jamila's a permanent fixture here now, just like you. We must accept that times have changed."

"Nothing changed much, *sahib*. Look, Bagwan still houseboy, you still *burra-sahib*, she still whore. Independence has. . . "

"My brothers will kill you, Bagwan," shouted the girl.

"Oh stop it. Do something constructive, Jamila, like getting dressed or ironing some of my shirts or something."

"That is my duty, *sahib*. I am shirt ironer."

"You hate ironing, Bagwan. Christ, I had to do it myself last week."

"Bagwan loves ironing, *sahib*—simply adorable."

Jamila was raving: "They will kill him—cut his stupid throat and let him bleed like a pig in the street."

Bagwan turned his back to her, went over to Iona's dresser and adjusted the angle of the old photograph. He blew a speck of dust from the glass.

"There'll be no throat-cutting, no whipping, and no more name-calling around here. Now Bagwan, do you think you can get that new cook to get some *cha* going? I might even be able to keep down some rumble-tumble."

"Bobajee impossible to locate, *sahib*. Vanished from household. Bagwan begs to remind that he advised against hiring a Mohammedan. As demonstrated, very very unreliable."

Jamila's arms flew up again, but Henry held them down.

"Oh dear. Perhaps he didn't like us. Would you be a good chap and make some tea for poor sick *sahib?* You can have some, too—we'll have a cigarette together."

"Jolly good, *sahib*, righto."

"That's the ticket."

The girl turned away and sulked for several minutes, but soon turned back again, the funk all cleared out of her. She said:

"Harry, why is everyone angry at you?"

"Because they think I'm a swine."

"You are not a swine."

"I'm afraid I probably am."

"You must marry me, you see. My family will protect you."

Henry chuckled and said, "You silly thing, it's probably them that put the scorpion in my jacket."

"But not them that shot at you?"

"No, probably not. I don't know who that is yet, but I will. I'm in direct competition with someone but don't know who — yet." Speaking now to himself, he continued: "And when I find out who they are, they'll find me a little more efficient in the assassination business." He poured another drink, added plenty of water. "And what about you, my dear? What are your plans for the day?"

"At the moment I would very much like a wee-wee," she said.

Henry laughed, pleasantly drunk now, saying, "There's a potty under the bed, use that, I'll watch."

"Only if there is nothing foul in it. I do so hate to wee-wee in a foul pot."

He laughed again, pushed aside the *teapoy* and swung his legs off the bed. He wiggled his toes on the bedside *dhurri*. When he stood, his feet were full of fluid and felt spongey against the rough cotton fabric. "Sod it," he said, "doesn't bode well for this ridiculous tennis match. Absurd bloody fiasco, the whole thing. Better spring about a bit. Have a spot of breakfast, plenty of vitamins in breakfast, more than other meals."

The bungalow, big and airy as it was, no longer had running water. He had to wash at a basin on his dresser to the right of the window. He could have Bagwan heat water, of course, but it would be better to wait until after the match, then he would have a bath. In the mirror he caught sight of his whites draped over the high-backed wicker chair. He wore the same pair of shorts eleven years ago, a year before the war, in the semi-finals of the all-India championship, and they still fitted him. "Lost in the fifth set," he muttered, "due to a sprained ankle. Soldiered valiantly on, despite severe pain."

"That's another of your bloody lies," he said to himself. "You lost because you were blind drunk when you came on court. You don't even remember how many sets it went to, although by Iona's account you put up a decent show. Of course, hers was an account witnessed under extreme inebriation — no doubt, worthless. She was way up in the stand, wasn't she, sitting with some sporty New Delhi types. That Higgins bastard. You spotted her, and served a ball up to her, to the delight of the crowd. Your father was disgusted, and your mother never again showed her face at the *gymkhana*. You were a bloody fool and you still are."

"What?" laughed Jamila, still sitting in the bed.

"I'll forego shaving. I shaved for you last night so's not to rough-up your cheeks with these prickly whiskers."

He could see her in the mirror, watching him. She lay behind the net, the sheet wrapped around her, fingering his cigarette packet. As he vigorously splashed his face and neck, he said, "Do you want to smoke one?"

"No," she said. He watched her set her head, getting ready to mimic, to show off. He smiled. She was a young romantic Englishwoman this time, a deliberately fine elocutionist, probably with orchestral background music playing in her head:

"I just like touching this raised emblem on the box, darling. I like the sailor's face — his red beard. You would have a red beard, too, Harry, if you let it grow.

You'd look like one of those Sikh warriors from the north, so fierce and terrible. I'm glad you're not fierce and terrible, darling. Isn't life wonderful?"

He laughed at her as she elevated her little pointed chin and pouted her lips. How good she is at being English, he thought. What a comedienne. She telephoned him once from the hills: she was lonely and bored, and being so good at accents almost passed herself off as a distant relative of his from Surrey — "Just simply dying to meet you for a spot of luncheon, Harry dear." He had honestly not known it was she until a servant gave her away by giggling in the background.

He went around the side of the bed where his tennis clothes were. He put on the shirt, pulled on the jock-strap and shorts. Jamila parted the netting so he could sit on the edge of the bed to put his socks and plimsolls on. As he sat, slipping a sock over the toes of his left foot, she snapped the jock against his thigh and leaned on his back, lightly holding his shoulders and laughing. She held his ear between her teeth and brushed her breasts against his shoulder blades.

"Stingy old Harry," she whispered, "not even one little love for poor Jamila?"

"Bitch," he said, "No tempting the athlete."

"I am your bitch," she laughed. He could feel her heart beating on his spine.

The left plimsoll was suspended in his right hand. She was moving her fingertips down the middle of his torso. He was about to drop the shoe, forget the match, and take her in his arms, but Jamila shrieked and fanned wildly with her right hand. Madly, she launched herself across him and pulled the shoe from his grasp.

He saw, only for an instant, the small darkly patterned snake dart from the shoe and strike at her wrist, attaching itself to her. He leaped up, sending the girl head-over-heels against the wall. The shoe and the snake landed together next to his old sea trunk. The snake rolled out of the shoe and slithered under the trunk.

"Bagwan!"

The girl leaned against the wall, staring at her wrist.

"Bagwan!"

There were two small red holes in the underside of her wrist, directly in the vein.

Bagwan was behind him.

"A snake, Bagwan. Under the trunk."

Bagwan went and looked.

"It was very dark, Bagwan — almost black, coiled in my shoe. What kind is it? It's bitten her on the wrist. Kill it, then go and find Doctor Pal. No — where's that damned cook? Send him."

"No cook, *sahib*. I send the *mali*."

"*Juldi*, Bagwan, *juldi!*"

Bagwan was almost out of the door when he stopped and looked back. He returned gingerly and looked at the girl.

"*Sahib?*"

"What? Bagwan, what?"

"Describe snake again, *sahib.*"

"I don't know, black or dark red — and markings — I don't know."

Bagwan shook his head and walked slowly from the room. The girl continued to stare at her wrist, holding it in her other hand. Henry picked her up and put her in the bed. Vaguely, he was aware of Bagwan coming back into the room with something in his hands, moving the sea trunk and thumping and crashing and cursing.

"It was a krait," Bagwan said, holding something up that Henry saw only in his peripheral vision, "its tail was stapled, and very poorly I might add, inside toe of your plimsoll, *sahib.* This is once again very deliberate murder attempt, fortunately unsuccessful."

"Get out, Bagwan."

The servant wrapped the snake in a cloth and took it out of the room.

The girl began to shiver and sweat. The whites of her eyes went yellow, the pupils dilated. She tried to focus, like someone very drunk.

"Jamila," he said, "my little bird."

One of her hands, the uninjured one, gripped his bicep. She squeezed slightly, then let go. Her limbs were spread-eagled and his hand was pushed into the bedding between her legs. Her eyes crossed. There was a smell of urine, and an instant later he felt the sheets dampening. The brown gleam drained from her face; he tried to prevent it escaping by holding her tightly and breathing his own breath into her mouth, but it was happening too fast, taking seconds instead of years. He squeezed her until her eyes lost connection and she became, quite suddenly and without a sound, a limp grayish sack, a thing like all the hundreds of other abandoned things he had witnessed all his life, lying in the dust of India with flies on their eyelids.

Henry lifted up his head and looked for Bagwan. Above the disturbed sea chest snake blood fanned in a arc across the white wall like a peacock's tail. Fallen over the edge of the bed, held only by the mosquito net, was the cigarette pack Jamila had played with minutes before. The brand emblem on the pack was the face of a blue uniformed mariner with a red beard.

"Bagwan," the *burra-sahib* shouted, "Bagwan, I need you!"

The girl lay in a tangle of limbs, hers and his, dead and alive, eight jointed appendages in the soiled bed linen.

PIGGYBANK

Calum, a large, slightly overweight boy, sat in the back of the Hillman Minx with Dora, the ex-maid, and Flops, the black labrador. It was a hot morning and his bottom stuck to the red upholstery. In his lap was the piggybank won by his father on the rifle range when the fair came to Richmond. The pig contained Calum's savings, pocket money unspent for two years; it was plaster of Paris, molded into a smiling sit-up-and-beg style, more like a poodle than a pig. It had lost one of its red cut-glass eyes and the pink paint was chipped off in several places.

Until an hour before, the Hillman had had a vinyl roof that matched its seats, but it blew off on the A13. Henry Leith, Calum's father, was furious. He had stopped, reversed back to find it, but it lay on the other side of a waterlogged ditch among a herd of munching cows. The red roof in the green field, folded across itself like a crashed kite, seemed to make the edges of the cows' lips turn up. They observed the object that had landed among them with the amused grace of ladies at a tea party. When Calum laughed at this he got a cuff on the ear from his father who had not had his morning drink. Now Leith, red faced and scowling, one hand on the wheel, the other on the gear stick, watched for street names.

In just over a month Calum would be ten. Ten years was a long time to live. His father told him that as he grew older he would see life differently than before. It was already true; the magic of his life was leaking away with every new aspect of it that he understood. He understood why they were moving from London: the word bankrupt made a sinister but vague impression on his mind, something dark and dangerous, a great spreading black fog with something evil and squidlike lurking within it. He didn't worry so much about the atom bomb anymore, he was more concerned about whether or not he would have his parents when he woke up in the morning. Terrible things had happened, and his family, once well-to-do, was now poor, but this seemed impossible because it was 1960, a bright new age, one of spaceships, sputniks and guitars.

Henry Leith sat like a volcano because he needed a drink. Every so often his hand banged the steering wheel when he thought about the roof; or was it one of the many other things that made him angry when he thought of them? Calum never knew. Leith's nose was so big and hooked that it nearly touched the steering wheel as he bent forward, trying to find Manor Road. It wasn't really that hooked, it just looked that way when trouble was brewing. To tease him, Mrs. Leith would say Henry was the last Viking: the type that would plunder monasteries, skewer obese monks, anything to get the price of a drink. But she was very careful what she said at this time of the morning.

Judith Leith's suntanned arm lay over the door and strands of her long light brown hair blew occasionally into Calum's eyes. She pretended to look for Manor Road but her eyes were closed most of the time against the wind and sun. Calum had her straight nose and round chin, but he had the broad Leith cheekbones and blond hair, and everyone said that he'd go bald just like all Leith men, so he really shouldn't dance around his father's chair on lazy cricket afternoons when his father was passed-out, chanting:

> Baldy oh Baldy, Oh bald bald eagle,
> You are the hunter,
> And I am the beagle,
> Baldy oh Baldy, Oh bald bald eagle...

It was a rhyme he'd made up himself; he didn't know what it meant. Sometimes he felt sorry for his father. He felt sorry for him now because he was the only one searching for Manor Road.

Calum's mother was usually jolly and chirpy like a film star; she used to hold squares of chocolate with the tips of her long red fingernails and drop them into his mouth as she told bedtime stories. But after he saw his father crying in her arms at the house in Richmond, he noticed that she became sad, and now, when she told him stories of being lost in the forest as a young girl and being rescued by the elves and being taken away to the castle where the kind prince lived, she could no longer send him into that forest on the magic carpet of her voice — he remained in his bed watching her red lips move while her troubled eyes hid a grown-up mystery more dreadful and threatening than fairy tales.

Southend-on-sea was to be his new town. His father told him that before the Romans came, this was the land of the Icinii. Queen Boudiccea had lived here, perhaps fought battles with the Romans on the river flats. His father had taken him to a museum where, in glass cases, he saw the corroded helmets, shields, amulets and swords of the ancient Britons. Some of these things had been found in the river mud.

In two weeks the Leiths would move into a maisonette over a chemist in a district called Leigh-on-sea. They would be on holiday until then at the hotel in Manor Road and his mother said he could practice his swimming when the tide was in. He loved swimming in the sea. He loved holidays when they stayed in hotels with nice fat Irish waitresses, and maids in black and white uniforms who brought milky tea and egg and bacon in the morning. When he excitedly confided this to his mother she laughed harshly and said, "It's the last hotel we're going to be staying at for a while, buster."

For some time now Calum had been looking at things rather closely, and life became increasingly mysterious. Real pigs looked nothing like the piggybank he held, yet it was a kind of pig, and since he was very young cartoons had bothered him: cartoon people got slammed about without much damage but when your father threw your mother down the stairs she stayed in hospital for weeks. And when, two years ago, mother went a bit looney and poisoned the household pets, they stayed dead. When she left the first time she didn't take Calum with her, but the second time she did. He had no reason to think she wouldn't leave again. Recently, he began to suspect that he was part of a comic strip life, that there was some drunken fool with a pen making one thing happen after another. People just seemed to do things, it was amazing.

He rattled the piggybank up and down to listen to the jingle of coins and the rustle of notes. Dora, who used to be the maid but was now his mother's helper, looked over the dog's head at him with her hairy black eyes, enlarged by the thick lenses of her glasses, and said, "What are you doing, you miser?"

Calum frowned, put his left arm around the dog.

She pointed her cracked fingernail at the pig, "How much you got in there now, eh?"

Calum's hands sweated around its neck.

"Come on, tell us."

In a rush he whispered,

"Twelve pounds nineteen shillings and fivepence threefarthing."

Turning away, Dora muttered, "Bloody little miser."

Dora's age was a mystery. She spent all her money on chocolate which was why she was fat and pimply with smelly armpits. She had a deep sickening mole on her chin, half an inch across, with coarse black hair curling from it. It looked to him as if there were a spider trying to climb out of her face. Calum's mother kept Dora with them because she had nowhere else to go. She was supposed to be in charge of Calum but he was already as tall as she and hated the way she wore her glasses on the end of her nose like some squinting, smart aleck dwarf; it infuriated him when she tried to make her thick lips thinner by sucking them in. He wished himself free of her.

"Hell's bells, here it is," Leith said, abruptly swinging the car left, and down a hill toward the sea. "We've passed it twice – you weren't looking, you fatheads."

Calum's chest thrilled at the sight of blue water ahead. He started singing:

> Oh I do like to live beside the seaside,
> Oh I will like to live beside the sea...

"You've got the words wrong, miser," said Dora.

"I know, you dimwit," he replied.

"The Rose House Hotel!" pointed Mrs. Leith, "See it, Henry, on the right?"

The long red fingernails of her right hand absently spread in the gold hair at the back of Leith's head. He said, "I hope they have a bar, I'm in dire need of a noggin."

She took her hand away.

Sycamores lined the road and Leith found a shaded parking place outside the hotel. The engine clunked after being turned off. There was a smell of cut grass, seaweed, flowers, hot tarmac, all blending in the breeze. Most of the buildings were white and glared in the sun. A man was soaping down a car. When Calum kissed Flops's head he smelled the hot plastic of the seat. Leaping over the door, the dog ran up and down the pavement stiff-tailed, sniffing, leg-cocking.

At the top of the road, a train shunted into Westcliff-on-sea station, sending up plumes of white steam; at the same time, two buses crossed the opening at the top of the slight hill that led into Station Road; one was cream and blue, the other green. Calum was struck by how odd a non-red double decker looked. The houses were just like London though, but there were fewer people around. When he told his father this, Leith said, "You wait till the weekend, lad. The place'll be packed with Cockneys."

Calum got told off for talking Cockney. His parents said it was common, but his mother did it when she was being funny; sometimes Dora tried to talk properly, like Mrs. Leith, but the Cockney was always underneath. The accent Calum did when he was being funny was Indian. He mimicked the smiling Sikh bus conductors, and because his father had taught him some Hindustani insults, they let him ride free to Brentford football ground on Saturdays. He didn't know what the phrases meant but he could always make an Indian laugh. When he was being taught, his mother would look on, smiling, smoking, drinking, saying: "You shouldn't, Henry. You are awful. Suppose he remembers it and repeats it to some bus conductor." Calum did just that, to his friend, Sid Singh, who laughed so hard the first time he heard it that he nearly fell down the stairs of his bus. Sid always grinned, he was a Queens Park Rangers supporter, he always smelled of curry, and Calum would never see him again now that he had to live in this new place. He would never see any of his friends again.

As Henry Leith pulled cases from the boot, a man with hands in pockets sidled up behind him. "Hoy, mate," the man said, "can you stop your dog pissing on me fence?" He was a broad man with black hair and red cheeks, not as tall as Leith, but tough, like a workman.

"I beg your pardon?"

"Your dog, he's pissing on me fence."

Leith put a case down and stood with arms folded:

"Dogs do that, squire. All fences get their attention, wouldn't you say?"

The man stood still, then bent forward suddenly and said, "Get your fucking mongrel under control, you stuck up streak of piss."

Leith slammed the boot and Mrs. Leith held Calum's hand tightly. The dome of Leith's head turned purple, and a vein stood out on his right temple. An unfocused look that Calum and his mother knew well had entered Leith's eyes.

"Henry. . . " warned Mrs. Leith.

"It's all right, Judy. This man's finished bothering me."

The man folded his arms while Mrs. Leith tried, unsuccessfully, to pull Calum into the hotel. Leith turned slowly on the man:

"I must say, the language you use in front of women and children reminds me of a farm yard. You were born in a pigsty, weren't you? Was your father a pig and your mother a whore? And are you married to your sister? I'd imagine that would be the case."

Calum laughed.

"Oh Christ," said Mrs. Leith.

The man unfolded his arms and took a step forward.

Flops came and growled between the legs of Calum and Mrs. Leith. The man said, "You lardy-da bugger. I'll ram your toffee-nosed fancy talk down your bastard's throat."

Calum saw Leith's left fist hit the man in the middle of the chest and his right fist made a dull chug on the man's chin. The man flapped backwards into a light green hedge. Leith's forehead was purple, he looked puzzled when Flops ran and grabbed his trouser cuff, trying to pull him away. Dora screamed. Leith shouted, "For Christ's sake get this bloody fool of a dog under control and shut that bitch of a maid up." Mrs. Leith said "Oh Christ, Henry" several times, while the man struggled out of the hedge. With his guard up, he came forward – then he was lying on the pavement with blood flowing from his mouth. Flops ran up and bit his leg. The man yelled, "Hey!" Leith shouted, "Flops! Here!"

Another man walked over the road. His shirt sleeves were rolled up from washing a maroon and gray car and a long quiff of dark brown hair fell down over one ear; he said, "You'd better give up, Paddy – looks like you're outclassed, old chap."

An old lady with white hair watched from a window; her curtains had blown outside in the breeze and were stuck to the wall. Sparrows chirped in the trees, the roof gutters, the hedges; a huge gray and white seagull squawked as it glided overhead. The train started pulling out of the station; Calum saw the carriages moving, heard the engine shunting, hissing hoarsely: home to London, home to London, home to London. . .

The man in shirt sleeves stood next to Leith as the other man struggled up from the pavement. Pulling an oily rag from his pocket and mopping his face, the man said, "I'll 'ave you for this, you ain't seen the last of this."

"Paddy, just go inside and forget it," said the newcomer, "You're tough enough to take a licking."

The man called Paddy spat and sauntered into his own front yard — right next door to the hotel — wiping his mouth with the rag.

"The name's Urquart," said the man in shirt sleeves, holding out his hand, "Indian Army, Lahore. Couldn't help overhearing such splendid phraseology. You must have been in India."

Leith shook hands, his face losing some of its high color: "How do you do. Henry Leith, Royal Indian Navy, Bombay."

"I knew it," said Urquart. There was a silence, then he continued, "Paddy's always a problem, I'm afraid."

"A problem dealt with, I hope."

"Oh, I expect so. I think he held his own rather well with the insults, don't you?"

"Very crudely perhaps."

"He didn't have your finesse, but it was colorful."

Urquart was clean shaven, thin faced, with dark wispy hair that he rearranged with his fingers to flow over a bald patch; he had close-set, slightly crossed blue eyes. His hands were pale and strong and there were brown freckles on his forearms. He gazed at Mrs. Leith. Calum saw that his father's hands shook slightly as he said:

"This is my wife, Judith."

"How do you do, Judith."

"How do you do."

What a silly phrase, Calum thought. So stiff, when a moment ago everything was loose and mad with the fight. And the fight was over and everything was becoming normal, cartoonlike.

"And this is my son, Calum Andrew," announced Leith.

"Well I'll be blowed," said Urquart, "I've never met another Callum in these parts." He had a slight Scots accent all of a sudden.

"His grandmother was from the Islands," said Leith.

Urquart took Calum's hand in his, crushed the bones together, "You've got the sacred names of Scotland, laddie," and the accent got stronger, and the eyes went all watery.

Calum tried to sound like his father:

"How do you do."

There was another uncomfortable pause before Leith said:

"Like to have a couple of pegs this afternoon?"

"That would be lovely," said Urquart, inclining his head. "The Overcliff at the bottom of the road here has a nice lounge. Pal of mine runs it, ex-Welsh Guards, rugby type. Spent time in Calcutta — good for a few after hours."

"After lunch, then?" said Leith, "We can have a proper chat."

"Yes, a good chin-wag."

"Meet you in there, then?"

"Righto. Perfect."

Calum's father seemed to completely forget the man called Paddy and whistled as he carried the cases into the hotel. Calum was terrified they would be turned away and his father would be embarrassed and cause another roughhouse, but the proprietor, a little brown man with thin brown hair spread over a pink pate, whom Leith later referred to as a laconic little yid, seemed to have missed the incident. There was relief in Mrs. Leith's face when the little man said they didn't have a bar.

The Rose House Hotel was really a boarding house for permanent residents, many of them Jewish which made Mrs. Leith uncomfortable because Marcus Michaels was a Jew. When Leith came down to Torquay two years ago to bring Mrs. Leith back to London, Calum watched from an upstairs window of Michaels's house as Leith smashed Michaels's face repeatedly on the bonnet of a white Mercedes, shouting, "Filthy fucking Jewboy, filthy fucking Jewboy, keep your dirty claws off my wife!" He kept saying, "Do you understand?" And when Michaels groaned Leith would wham his face into the white metal again: it seemed that he wanted to draw blood, but none came. Calum had quite liked Michaels while he lived with him. But mention of anything Jewish made Leith go red in the face, and sometimes he would cry unexpectedly. Mrs. Leith would say, "I'm sorry, I'm sorry, please don't think of it, darling, I beg you. Can't you forgive me?"

They would either have a big row or a long sad silence after that. Calum did not like to think of Michaels now. But when Leith noticed all the Jewish names on the mail boxes he merely tutted and said, "Only for two weeks down among the Jew-men, Judy."

Feeling safe, Mrs. Leith began to nag about the fight, how it was an ugly example for Calum, that he had seen too much violence and that we could not afford to make enemies in our new home. She talked on and on up the stairs to the big airy room overlooking the road, while Calum followed, holding the dog by the collar and the piggybank around the neck. His parents left him on the landing. Dora was in the toilet, avoiding work, so he banged on the door, "Hurry up, spiderchops, or I'll pee myself."

She replied, "Go away, I'm doing something."

Calum explored the bedroom he was to share with Dora. Opposite his mother and father's room, it was tiny with two little beds and a bare floor. After a while, he heard his mother's voice rising across the hall; the familiar atmosphere he so hated flooded over him as if it was going to pop like a bubble.

"You're a bloody fool," Judith said. Calum could hear her walking around the room. "What's the matter with you? Are you going to start that ridiculous Bombay behavior again? Well I won't have it. I won't. You're mad, you're too old to brawl in the street like a hooligan. I'm so ashamed, no sooner do we get out of one mess than we're back in another."

"Look, just skip it, won't you? I've said sorry."

"Sorry! You'd better be sorry, old boy, if that man calls the police on you we'll be right back where we started. You bloody fool!"

"All right. It was you who got me into the first mess, if you recall . . . darling."

"How dare you? You're the violent one, you're the puncher, the kicker, the breaker of bones."

"Perhaps. But you're the Delilah, aren't you, you're the bloody fucking whore who cut the bottom out of my life." Calum heard him stand and move in the room like a vast weight.

They were startled when he appeared in the doorway holding his pig. His mother was seated in a wicker chair by the blocked up fireplace with his father standing over her. She glanced at Calum. Leith moved to the window and looked out. She said, "And why on earth did you invite that bloody little captain for a drink when you know perfectly well we don't have two farthings to rub together?"

Lighting a cigarette, Leith replied in a hot, dry voice, "Urquart? I'll have him eating out of my hand. And besides, we have the checkbook."

"No, Henry," she looked at Calum out of the corner of her eye, "we're turning over a new leaf — we agreed, no rubber money here."

Leith didn't respond, he stood in the bay of the window with one hand in his pocket and the other holding his cigarette.

"I'm hungry," said Calum.

Judith looked into Calum's face for a long time, until her eyes began to water. Then she said:

"Perhaps we have enough for a little lunch — he hasn't had any breakfast, Henry." Leith nodded, turned away. His mother took Calum in her arms, kissed his cheeks. "You're such a good little chap. You never complain."

He knew she was crying because he could smell her wet make-up.

The Leiths sat drinking in the lounge of the Overcliff Hotel with Callum Urquart, his wife Catherine, and her two younger brothers, Charles and James. Lunch had been a disaster and Calum was in disgrace. He sat between his parents at a round, polished table, loaded with empty glasses, holding the piggybank in his lap: now it contained only eleven pounds nineteen shillings and fivepence threefarthing. Earlier, before meeting the Urquarts, they had eaten at a sidewalk cafe on Western Esplanade, and the bill came to more than Mrs. Leith had in her purse. She said someone had stolen the pound she'd been saving. His father insisted Calum give up a pound; he said, "We're a family — it's your duty." Calum wouldn't let them break the plaster pig, so, with two fish knives, Leith had to ease a note out of the slot between the pig's ears; "Like a blasted brain surgeon, what?" he joked, but no one laughed.

Mrs. Leith and Dora had been served their meals first. They had ordered plaice and chips and beans on toast respectively. Calum filched a chip from his mother's plate. Dora scooped up beans as though she hadn't eaten for a week. Calum was bored and hungry. He started up, snorting like a starved dog. They ignored him. He giggled louder. They kept ignoring him. He took two baked beans off Dora's plate and pushed them up his nose.

Mr. Leith frowned and said, "Ugh."

Dora's eyes narrowed with hatred at losing two beans.

Mrs. Leith said, in a quiet but deep voice, "Get those out at once, you disgusting little beast."

Calum's gush of laughter shot the beans out in a stream of mucus; one bean flew down the front of Dora's frock. She stood up and screamed. Leith smacked Calum twice on the side of the head so that his ear rang. He was about to cry but saw the smirk on Dora's face, so pushed his bottom lip out and put his head down instead.

After that they took the pound.

He held the pig tightly now, glaring at anyone who looked at it. It was 2:00 P.M. and the hotel lounge was packed with women dressed in summer frocks and men wearing cravats; their voices would suddenly burst into laughter, then fade back down to a murmur. The room was full of smoke, the sound of clinking glass, the smell of beer and roasting beef.

The open windows overlooked the Thames estuary and Calum was puzzled by the vast wasteland of mud that seemed to stretch all the way to the Kent coast. Leith was getting on well with Urquart: they were flushed with drink and were telling Jewish jokes, saying nasally, "Yes, it's werry nice to live in Vestcliff." When he asked his father where the sea went his father replied, "Moses moved it," and the glasses on the table rattled with the laughter of Leith, Urquart, Catherine, and James; Charles and Judith didn't laugh.

Calum was disappointed that the sea was only in half the time: Southend was only half seaside. Urquart explained that the Thames was out there and the ships could still get up to the Port of London even when the tide was out; it was eight miles across to Kent, he said, and the river was a deep trough in the middle going out to the English channel. Calum was getting to like Urquart because he didn't smoke; he asked him, "If you could, could you swim up the river to Richmond?"

"Yes, you could," he said, "it's the same river all the way to Oxford."

Calum was about to ask how long it would take to swim such a distance, but his father, referring to Oxford, cut him off:

"The womb of our nation," he said. Urquart and Charles lifted their glasses and drank soberly. Calum noticed tears in Urquart's eyes.

Leith got up and said, "Who's for another?"

"Right you are," said Urquart.

Standing behind Catherine with his hands on her shoulders, Leith asked, "Catherine, James, Charlie? Same again? Darling?"

"Not for me," said Catherine, "I've hardly touched this."

"Maybe a half," said James.

"Same here – half," said Charlie.

"No thank you," said Mrs. Leith, without looking at him.

"Let me get them, Harry," said Urquart, "you're the newcomers."

"No no no no no," said Leith, "gin and squirt, old boy?"

"Aye," said Urquart.

Leith omitted to ask Calum and Dora.

Mrs. Leith excused herself, taking her handbag.

When she had gone, James said, "A strategically bought round."

Charles grinned. Catherine fussed in her handbag, pulled out a mirror, looked at her gray eyes, applied lipstick.

Answering James, Urquart said, "He has to go careful I expect. Poor bugger's bankrupt, you know. I hate that: a man serves his country – a bloody hero, I tell you – and he ends up with fuck-all to show for it."

"I think he's full of hot air, myself. I know the type. You want to watch him, Cal," said James.

"Ruddy hard lines – a man like that. . . " said Charles to Catherine.

"And what type's that, Jimmy?" said Urquart.

"The type that was in the Indian Ocean during the sinking of the Ark Royal and on the Murmansk runs in the Arctic. Oh and I forgot Normandy, he was in that one, too. When he comes back ask him if he was at Agincourt and the Little Big Horn."

"Sometimes you're a very silly fellow, Jimmy," said Urquart, "I know a man who's been in battle – you can see it in his eyes."

"Oh, you can tell he's a hero," said Catherine, then blushed as the three men looked at her.

"Drinks like a bloody fish, though," said Charles.

"Don't we all, Charles, don't we all," said Catherine.

"If you're like poor old Jimmy," said Charles, "you drink like a goldfish."

James went red, "I can hold my booze, you sods. . . "

Urquart openly suppressed laughter.

Calum giggled. He liked the idea of James as a goldfish.

"What are you laughing at, little man?" said Catherine, leaning over and ruffling his hair. Her hand smelled faintly of lavender and her eyes were kind but raw as if she didn't sleep enough. She wore a white frock that showed her long brown neck with gold curls resting against her lightly freckled skin. She wore pearls the same color as her teeth. Her fingers felt cool as she cupped Calum's cheek in her hand. Her face grew serious: "What a nice boy you are," she set her jaw and squeezed his cheeks hard, "Ooh, I could just squeeze him."

"You are squeezing him, Cathy. For goodness sake don't rip the poor kid's face off," said Charles.

"Ever wonder what you'd look like without a face, boy?" laughed James.

"Do you think he'd get on with Hugh, Cal?" Catherine said to Urquart, who, pursing his lips and staring for a second, said, "Would you like someone to play with tonight, old son?"

"Don't mind," said Calum.

"Okay, then. We'll bring our Hugh along to the Peterboat tonight. We've already arranged to go there with your mum and dad, you know that don't you?"

Calum shrugged.

Catherine said, "We usually leave Hugh at home because he can be a bit of a bugger in public, but you're the type he might get on with." Sitting back in her chair, sipping gin, Catherine smiled at everyone and said, "That's settled then."

Judith came back and gave Calum a kiss. She whispered in his ear: "I think your dad took that pound out of my bag." Calum shook his head and nodded accusingly towards Dora who was looking out of the window. Judith frowned, "Where did he get the money for that round, then?"

"Urquart," said Calum.

Judith shook her head.

It was well after 3:00 P.M. when they stood outside with Brian, the manager of the hotel. He'd been plying the group with drinks since closing time. Urquart swayed slightly with an arm around Brian who moved his head fast like a sparrow when he talked. Catherine held Leith's arm; her brothers rivaled for Judith's attention. Calum leaned on his mother and scowled at the two men. He stabbed his toe at a tuft of weed growing from the cracked pavement. It reminded him of Dora's chin.

"Come to the Peterboat in Leigh with us tonight, Brian. Take a night off from this creaking monstrosity," said Urquart, gesturing at the mass of wooden additions and flagpoles encrusted upon the Overcliff.

"I'll try," said the Welshman, "but I doubt if you'll make it, Captain. You're as pissed as a parrot, sir, if you'll forgive my saying so."

Leith laughed loudly, so did Catherine, but all the while she gazed up at Leith as though she were laughing at him. Earlier, Calum overheard her say to her brother, Charlie, "Look what a fine specimen Harry Leith is – and look at his son." She slurred her words. Charlie warned her to watch herself. She laughed, gave him a big kiss.

"Until tonight then, you bloody taffy, you bloody Welsh nanny-goat," said Urquart. Brian waved him away with a smile.

They walked up Manor Road, Catherine holding the arms of Leith and Urquart, Charlie and James with their arms around Mrs. Leith, while Calum followed with the dog and Dora.

Dora said, keeping her eyes on the pavement, "I'm sick of all this sitting in pubs. I want to do something on me own. They never give me any money and I want to go to the pictures tonight. Lend us ten bob to go out with?"

"You must be joking!"

"Go on," she pleaded.

"Not bloody likely," he said.

"You stingy little bleeder, you're like an old Jew."

"And you're like a maid, an ugly maid," he replied.

"I'm not a maid."

"Maid maid maid!"

"You're the rudest little rat-bag I've ever set eyes on. You're fat, mean, and foul mouthed."

"And you're the ugliest maid I've ever known and you have a squint like a pig and you're fatter than I am."

"No I'm not. You're like a barrel of lard and you're a backward child. God, you can't even dress yourself, never could, I have to fasten your clothes in the mornings. You can hardly bleddy read yet, neither."

"Well, what about you? Dad says you're partly mongoloid which explains why you never wash. And you never get any boyfriends because you're so ugly with that swarm of spiders crawling out your chin."

She sucked in her lips and tears rose into the corners of her eyes. He was sorry as they walked silently under the shade of a sycamore with the dog panting at his heels.

He blurted, "Dora, you can have ten bob."

She told him to stick it up his miser's arse.

Outside the Rose House Hotel, Urquart said to the Leiths, "I was just thinking, you know, if Calum and Dora wanted, they could spend the rest of the afternoon walking along the seafront to Leigh. They could meet us at six-thirty at the Peterboat – get to know the place a bit. I'll draw them a map, it's a lovely walk – beaches, boats and seaweed – they can watch the tide come in."

Mr. Leith's bleary eyes focused slowly, "What do you say, smiler?" Calum's stomach fluttered; he hated being too far from his mother. He heard Dora's faint groan; she loathed walking. "What about my piggybank?" he said.

"We'll put him on our mantelpiece. He'll be safe there," his mother said.

"All three of them could do with a little exercise," said James as he patted the dog excessively hard on the rump.

"I don't mind," shrugged Calum glaring at James.

"Oh, no," hissed Dora under her breath.

Calum helped Dora tidy the room while Flops slept on one of the beds. He was relieved that Dora didn't want to bother unpacking the cases straightaway.

When he first tried to take his piggybank into his parents' room, the door was locked and soft sounds and bumps came from within.

Mr. and Mrs. Leith had argued fiercely after the Urquart party left. They were both jealous, Dora explained, and now they were having a little fuck to make up. Fuck was a nasty word and Calum didn't believe Dora when she told him people did it for fun. He hoped his mother would survive it because sometimes he had heard her moan and cry out. Dora told him not to worry, his mother had had a lot of practice.

Now that he was used to the idea he got excited about walking to the Peterboat – he was impatient to leave. He took the piggybank to the toilet with him and had a think for ten minutes. The thick carpeting seemed to make the guest house very quiet, and there was a distinct odor which made him think of old people. The toilet had pink tiles and smelled of pine disinfectant. He closed the door gently when he had finished so as not to disturb the quiet landing, then padded along to his parents' door and knocked. There was no answer. Dora watched from across the hall, she whispered, "Try the handle, they've probably unlocked it." He did and the door clicked open, allowing him to tip-toe into the close, quiet atmosphere of their room. He found them asleep, curled together with an eiderdown over them, their clothes scattered over two chairs.

Calum placed the pig in the middle of the mantelpiece so that the back of its head and pointed ears were reflected in the mirror that hung there. Dora was also in the mirror, eyeing him from the doorway; in reverse, she was different, one of her eyesockets was lower down her face than the other. And there were his parents, lying peacefully with soft breath puffing through their lips. A warm breeze sucked the net curtains in and out of the window. He tip-toed out and clicked the door to.

When it was time to go, Flops leapt off the bed and scrambled on the linoleum, going nowhere. Calum caught his collar and calmed him down. The dog choked against Calum's grip all the way down the stairs and out the front door, then, with a bark, he bolted down the road with Calum and Dora running behind. At the bottom by the railings, Dora said, "Hang about a mo, I've forgotten something," and ran back up the road. Flops pricked up his ears. Calum leaned on the railings and gazed at the wide vista of the Thames estuary, spread before him.

On his left Southend Pier stretched southward like the skeleton of a centipede – the longest pier in the world, his father told him. He could see strips of blue and turquoise water in the distance and guessed the tide must soon be coming back in. Big silent ships were moving east and west against the green background of the Kent coast, and nearer to shore, several men mysteriously stabbed at the mud. The esplanade was dotted with groups of strolling people and slow moving cars. A cream, open top bus growled by. It struck him that a day was a queer thing, a series of episodes, some connected, some not, one thing after another until the night came, and your life was the same, only bigger, a series of days until the night came. It suddenly felt very strange to be alive, to be standing there in so much open space.

He got fed up waiting for Dora and walked back to buck her up. Flops meandered ahead, sniffing – and cocked his leg on Paddy's fence. Calum was relieved when Dora finally appeared having changed into jeans and a dirty yellow sweater. Paddy's curtains moved and Calum said, "Let's get out of here!"

Calum walked in the wet, sloppy river sludge twenty feet from where the beach ended, holding his plimsolls and socks, and singing:

> Mud, mud, glorious mud,
> Nothing quite like it for cooling the blood...

Dora walked thoughtfully further up the beach. There were more and more people on the beaches as they approached Chalkwell. Urquart's map was rough but easy to follow. Flops splashed up and down near Calum, the mud plastered on his legs already dried to a light green powder.

There had been a tiff with Dora the moment they got to the beach: she wanted to take an open air bus to Leigh but he insisted upon walking. She stayed quiet as they plodded along slowly in the sand and pebbles. As he skimmed flat stones across the mud she said, "You know, I'm sick of this family. I get nothing but grief. You're a lot of bleddy mad people." She said it calmly enough so Calum didn't get angry at her; he couldn't say anything, so he just shrugged.

"You're not such a bad little sport though," she said suddenly, putting an arm around him. He felt compelled to say, "Neither are you."

She drifted off into thought, so he left her alone.

Walking in the mud fascinated him as it oozed through his toes; it felt warm like the skin of some soft creature, and made a clicking, dripping noise all around him. One of the men he had seen from high up was nearby. Calum asked him what he was digging for and the man showed him the ancient-looking ragworms he dug up to sell to fishermen. The sharp little creatures reminded him of what his father told him about how life started in river estuaries, just like this, millions of years ago. He imagined all life starting here at Southend-on-sea but in his mind's eye the pier was still there and so was the esplanade. Then he imagined invading Romans trying to land, getting bogged down with their heavy armor in the mud, and the tattooed Icinii, fighting naked, hacking them to pieces. After the battle, the tide would come in and float the bodies away, leaving their helmets and weapons to gradually sink in the mud. What if he were digging for those ragworms one day and discovered the sword of a British chieftain? He would hold it up and it would flash with the power of the sun. He would take it home and touch his father's head with it and his father would turn over a new leaf.

Discovering a deep pool beside a groyne, Calum watched a small water beetle crawl agonizingly from the water. The pool was clear, little streams of water purled into it from the beach, he bent down and looked in. A starfish slowly moved the tips of its limbs, small fish flashed in the sun, a snail bumped across the bottom, organisms drifted and squirted, seaweed waved like green hair in the minute currents within the pool. A crab shifted position in the silt, revealing its outline for a moment and stirring up a cloud.

It reminded him of London. The pool of London, the pool of London, he kept thinking. He went to Dockland once to see the Cutty Sark, after the Millwall-Brentford match, then they went to the Isle of Dogs to do a deal with a man. He expected to encounter packs of gray, fleabitten hounds but there were only men in cloth caps and derelict warehouses with windows like blind eyes and a constant smell of rotted vegetables. And all the time you could smell the river and the river ran home to Richmond.

With his index finger, he pushed the struggling little beetle back into the water. Richmond: the word produced yellow in his mind; he thought of the great piles of autumn leaves in the park, and the hot coal fire in the living room of his house. The faces of the family looked back at him from the pool: old Peg-leg and Grandpa, who died only weeks apart; the Scottish uncles and pretty Flora Mac-Donald who all drowned in the Clyde while sailing; his older half-sister and brothers, married, living abroad – all dead, dispersed or forgotten.

A big stone landed in the pool, splashing his face and T-shirt.

Dora was beside him, grinning, and several people laughed on the other side of the barnacled tide-breaker. "They're chucking stones at you, Calum," Dora said.

"Who are?" he asked.

"Them Southenders," she pointed over the groyne. The pool was cloudy with mud. We wondered if the crab's shell had been shattered by the stone, whether other creatures were pinned beneath it or killed by the shock. "Who did that?" he shouted. Four faces peered over the black boards of the tide-breaker and each had pale gray eyes, brown hair and gaunt cheekbones. One was a girl with long wavy hair. A fifth head appeared, older, with coarse black hair and short stubble on his face. "Tell him, Pete," said the older one in a high, almost effeminate voice.

"I did!" said the one called Pete.

"Well, don't," said Calum.

"And who's gonna stop me?"

"Me," Calum answered.

"Yeah? You and whose army?" They all laughed, including Dora. Calum was just regretting being nasty to her when she said, "He don't need no army to do you in, you puny little pratt." She was talking to Pete but Calum was somehow aware that she was against him, too. A peculiar sinking feeling ran through him and his legs shivered. The gang jumped over the breakwater boards, sinking up to their ankles in the shingle as they landed. All three of the younger boys wore short trousers, the older boy and the girl wore tight jeans. The older boy said, "So you want trouble, do you, porky? Well, my brother'll give it you all right." He was about seventeen, the type who couldn't pronounce an *r*.

"You started it," said Calum – he was really only afraid of the big boy.

"You shut your mouth," said Pete.

"Shut yours," said Calum calmly.

"You gonna make me, eh?"

"Yes," said Calum, crossing his arms and thrusting out his lower lip. As he did so, he noticed again how they all had the same lovely clear gray eyes.

"Yeah?" said Pete.

"Yeah." said Calum.

"Yeah?"

"Yeah."

"Yeah?"

"Yeah."

"Yeah? You and whose army?" Pete pushed his hands deep into the pockets of his shorts and his eyes darted this way and that. "I notice you need an army," said Calum, nodding at the rest of Pete's friends. He couldn't stop swallowing. "Eh?" Pete said. "What's he say?" he asked the girl.

"He says you're the one what has the army," she answered.

"You've got half of Southend to back you up," said Calum. Pete seemed confused: "These are me brothers — and me sister."

"We ain't gonna interfere none," said the older boy, "we like a fair fight."

"So you wanna bundle, do you?" said Pete, barging at Calum with arms folded over his chest.

"I don't want to fight, it's you . . . "

"He's chicken. Porky's a coward," said one of the brothers.

Pete said, "I can do you any time, fatty."

Dora said, "Gawd, Calum'll flatten you like a pancake, you dopey little git." Pete barged him harder, making him slip down the pebbles into a tide trough, saying, "Bleedin' daytrippers, fink you can push us around, do you?"

"We live here," said Dora.

"Coming down here . . . " Pete's eyes were large and glassy. A wet patch appeared in the crotch of his trousers. Calum leapt at him suddenly, swinging and lashing and prodding the smaller boy's face. As Calum pushed him backwards, Pete threw out a hand and scratched the skin above Calum's eyebrow. Blood suddenly leaked from Pete's nose and he lost his balance, and dropped to one knee.

There was redness around Calum's vision; he thought he could feel a vein pulsing in his forehead; he saw blood and aimed a kick at Pete's head — it missed; one of the brothers caught Calum by the shoulder: "Hey, that ain't fair."

Calum grabbed the brother's hair and tried to fling him down the beach. The other brother and the sister both jumped in, and the four of them fell struggling in the pebbles. Flops charged, growling, and scattered them like bowling pins, but they came together again, pulling, holding tight, attempting headlocks. Flops tugged Calum's collar. The older boy came between them, gently plucked them apart, and laughing, said, "All right, you lot, all right, that's enough. Come on Iris — remember you're a girl."

"No Charlie," said Iris, "he's made us bleed — I want him to bleed!"

Oh, get stripped," said Charlie and pushed her away, "You've all had enough."
He looked at Calum, pulled him to his feet but kept his arms stiff in case Calum
swung at him:

"You're in a right old paddywhack, you are."

While Calum tried to struggle out of Charlie's stiff-armed grip, he said, "I'm
not scared of you, either: I'll hit first, hit hard and ask questions afterwards."

It was a stupid thing to say, an embarrassing statement.

"Calm down nipper, I'm not gonna hurt you. You put up a good fight. Come
on, shake. You all right, Pete, Ted, Joey, Iris?"

Dora's eyes were heavy-lidded. Pete reluctantly shook Calum's hand, then
Ted and Joey did the same but Iris turned her back and folded her arms. Her
brown hair was long and straight and shiny down her back. When Charlie shook
his hand, Calum expected his fingers to break, but the boy's grip was surpris-
ingly limp and damp.

"If I weren't going back to the army I'd let you join our gang."

"I don't like gangs," said Calum.

"Don't they have gangs up the Smoke?" said Pete.

"Yes, they beat people up," said Calum.

"Everyone's in a gang hereabouts," said Charlie. His voice sounded friendly
and harmless with its impotent *r*'s, but Calum had the feeling that he was still
being bullied.

"We're the Lightfoots," said Pete, "We're famous for trouble in this town –
you'd better watch out for us."

"How did you know we were from London?" asked Calum.

"You talk snobby," sneered Iris.

"We just moved down here. My dad got bankrupt, so we have to live in
Southend. It was the government's fault."

"Oh yes, the government does that to everyone," said Iris, as if she didn't care.
Suddenly, in an inexplicably kind tone, she asked, "Where you gonna be living?"

He had to think for a moment. "Over a chemist in Leigh-on-sea."

"That's right near us," laughed Pete.

"He'll go to North Street, he will," said Iris, her nose turning up.

They all began talking at once as if there never was a fight. It turned out
that Iris and Pete were twins and were the same age as Calum. Joey was eight
and Ted was eleven. Flops was making friends with Iris. Pete's nose still oozed
blood and the scratch over Calum's eye itched.

The boys dabbed their wounds with crusty handkerchiefs.

"Maybe we'll be mates," said Pete suddenly.

"My best friend back home is named Peter," said Calum, "but he cries when
you belt him."

"We never cry," said Iris.

As they threaded their way through the sunbathers and old ladies, Ted kept asking people for cigarettes; finally an old man with a few brown teeth, wearing a greasy tartan cap, gave him a Woodbine and lit it for him. Calum found it disgusting the way the boy imitated adults by blowing smoke down his nostrils. They walked on and on, climbing over each groyne. The old man in the cap was following a long way off on the promenade.

Ted smoked his Woodbine down to nothing. When he'd finished, he coughed and spat green phlegm up on a broken chunk of concrete. Woodbine smoke rose from the phlegm, and Calum's stomach contracted, he felt everything coming up: it came out in a orange fountain, sour and putrid, retaining the odor of eggs and chips and lemonade.

The Lightfoots were astonished.

"He's always doing that," said Dora, from behind him, "he hates smoke. He'll never be a man."

People moved their deckchairs away from the sick. Ted walked off on his own with his hands in his pockets. Pete said: "It made me wanna honk, too."

"You're another wanker, then," said Charlie.

Joey said: "Come on Calum – there's a Punch and Judy show on about now by Chalkwell Station."

Calum was staring down at the debris of his vomit in the sandy pebbles. He held his hands on his hips and heaved again. There was a painful pressure on his temples as a stream of bitter bile came into his mouth. His vision was red.

Dora bobbed down quickly, touched her hand to the pavement, and said, "Blimey, look what I've found – a fiver!" She held up the blue banknote. A man passing, laughed, "Oh thank God you found my wages," but kept walking. A horrible depression stabbed Calum at Dora's sudden fortune: she always found money.

"Ice cream all round," she said, but Calum declined.

"My God, miser, you must be ill to turn down ice cream. Come on, it'll soothe your stomach."

"I'd rather have a buttered roll," he said. So that's what he got, but it was stale.

The tide was coming in, spreading wider and deeper across the miles of mud. Calum sat in the sand with the others, waiting for the Punch and Judy show to start and avoiding the eyes of an old white-haired man who walked among the crowd collecting money in a hat. The pressure from vomiting was still in his temples; it changed the way things looked, everything was outside him, he was not a part of it.

The puppet theater was a rectangular cream and red tent with Victorian Punch and Judy scenes painted on the side. The colors were faded and the canvas tattered. Children of all ages, a few of them accompanied by adults, knelt in the sand before it.

Pete said, "It's like church."

After a while the old man stopped collecting money. He went into the tent. Children started to shout, "Hello, Mister Punch!"

A voice screamed from inside the tent:

"Hoy, oy, oy, oy! How about it then, 'ow about it!"

There was laughter.

"Naaaaaaaaaa . . . " louder and louder " . . .aaaaaaaaaagh!" And the small curtains sprang open to reveal the scarlet Mister Punch, sweeping back and forth on the stage, holding his massive truncheon. It was the most horrifying Punch Calum ever saw. His face was livid, the end of the enormous nose was red, and his mouth was pulled down at the corners in a fiendish grimace of gritted teeth. Punch pounded the stage with the brown truncheon as he swept up and down.

"Now then, who's for a bashing?" he shouted, "Who's been naughty? Come on, girls and boys, own up!" and he clouted the stage such a crack that it echoed against the station wall. "Come on, playmates, who'll volunteer for a bash on the bonce?"

A little foreign girl with white hair screamed, but most of the kids laughed. Then:

" 'Lo boys 'n' girls," yelled Punch, waving, his personality changing with such suddenness that the audience laughed.

"Hello, Mister Punch," everyone shouted back.

It was too hard to witness Punch prance and bellow upon the stage. Calum looked away, watched the tide's progress, and the ships in the distance. He felt Dora look at him. The word *charlatan* kept repeating itself in his mind, he'd heard it somewhere, someone said it a long time ago in an argument, "Liar!" and "Imposter!" they had shouted. "You're a fucking bastard, Leith. You charlatan!"

The dingy colors and faded doll faces of the tent theater impressed upon him the word *Victorian* and he felt sad. Under his breath, he said, "Charlatan, liar, imposter: Victorian." These words all meant the same thing to him. Something with sharp claws was scratching to escape from his stomach.

A London-bound train had pulled into Chalkwell Station.

The sinister word, *charlatan*, made him think that everything that happened was some kind of test for him, and that all the other people that surrounded him at any time were all actors in a special contest designed to support his existence in the world. They're all imposters, he thought. He wanted to ask Pete, "Come on, level with me, who's behind all this — what do they want from me, what do I have to do? How much do I have to learn before I get let in on this?"

Or should Calum grab the little foreign girl, bend her fingers back until she admitted to the conspiracy? Sometimes he caught eyes looking at him before they glanced away; they were the failures who gave the game away – they would be punished somehow by the Charlatan, sent to the dark place where the Bankrupt lurked. The Charlatan was watching him: the dirty old man who gave Ted the fag? The white-haired old puppet master hidden by the canvas? Who or what

32

was the Charlatan, and where was he? He thought about this until the show was nearly finished.

When he paid attention, it made him want to cry, it made him want to run home to London. Mister Punch had pulled the baby away from Judy and was slamming it again and again into the stage.

Behind him, the train was starting to leave the station. The tide would soon be high enough for him to swim out like a dolphin, out to the river channel, up past the Isle of Dogs, through the pool of London, up to Richmond Bridge, back to the place where it all began, to start again, safe.

"I'll stop the baby crying, honest I will," begged Judy, "don't hurt it anymore." "Kill the bloody baby, kill the bloody baby!" Punch ranted. The Lightfoots laughed because Punch swore, but some of the adults were looking alarmed, giving each other quizzical looks, removing children from the show.

To swim home, you dive through the waves like a smiling dolphin. No charlatan thing can catch you, you swim faster and faster up the river until you spring from the whirlpools under Richmond Bridge and turn into yourself on the stone steps. They are all there to meet you, the dead and dispersed relatives and friends, and they are sad because you're so worn out with swimming, but you hear the lovely fairy music that you heard the night of your grandfather's death, and you know that you'll see him very soon in the great hall where the family live.

"Don't kill the baby," yelled the little foreign girl in her funny accent. She was a bit slow — the baby was already dead; its neck hung over the edge of the stage. Punch beat Judy to death, then he killed a policeman who tried to arrest him, and then, disarmed by the law, he got free and bashed the judge over the head with his own gavel, but the judge survived and sentenced Punch to be hanged by the neck. All the children cheered when Punch swung from the gallows with all the dead bodies laid out before him.

Just to make sure Punch was dead, the judge, who was all wig and robe with hardly any face showing save for a bit of nose that poked through the wig, gave Punch a smack on the head with the confiscated truncheon. Calum felt sorry for Punch because he was so stupid, and even though the law was right, the judge was even more sinister than Punch; he judged you and killed you — his face was hidden.

The curtains closed, the children stood up and Calum was surprised to find that he'd been drawn into the drama; now that it was over, everything seemed dull and he could no longer conjure the vague mental image of charlatan, the charlatan feeling had disappeared behind the curtains of the puppet theater.

When Dora offered him ice cream, he accepted, but as he ate it he continued to think about the scarlet Punch and his big red nose.

They walked along the sea wall path by the railway line. A locomotive was hissing at a standstill behind the railings. A man in a T-shirt leaned from his cabin and stared out to sea. The man looked friendly and Calum wondered if he could ask to be taken back to London. The tide was almost touching the rocks below the sea wall. Between the railings and the downward sloping sea wall the pathway was narrow; tall weeds grew under the railings and in the cracks of the steep embankment.

The dirty old man who had been shadowing them suddenly sprang in between them and starting lashing at Ted with his greasy cap, yelling, "Don't smoke, you little beggar, you poxy little whoreson."

The man whirled among the knot of children like a mad cartoon character. His eyes were wild and there was a discolored film around the brown iris. He had two overly long eye teeth that were yellow and scaly like the fangs of an old zoo animal – the teeth between them were missing – as he burbled and snorted incoherent phrases, the pink ridge of gum made Calum's stomach quake. The man held Ted by the ear, and slapped him. Ted's face was grim and angry, but he didn't cry out, just tried to cover himself from the blows and looked at his brother Charlie for help, but Charlie stood watching, trying to look as if everything was normal and interesting. The tramp pulled Ted to the railings and pushed his head down between his knees. It looked as if he had a stick in his pocket that swung slightly as he moved. As they struggled, the heel of Ted's shoe spread an old dog turd wider and wider into the tarmacadam.

Then a pair of muscular arms, with a tattoo of a curvy girl on the bicep, came through the railings and grabbed the tramp around the neck so the back of his head and shoulders slammed against the metal bars. He choked quietly: his mouth gaped and his eyes were slits; wrinkles spread over his face as if it would fall to pieces. A forearm was jammed under his chin, and a hand dragged the long springy carrot-colored hair back from his forehead with thick, coal-encrusted fingers. Ted sprinted away.

"You fuckin' pervert, I ought to pop your eyes out. How do you like being grabbed, eh? How do you like it?"

The train driver had greasy blond hair and dark eyes, and his muscles rippled over his shoulders as he squeezed the tramp's neck.

"You kids better scarper, 'cos I can't stand here all day holding this rubbish – gotta drive the choo choo, ain't I?" The driver laughed with big, crooked teeth. His mate, a sprightly older man, walked briskly across the tracks, saying "Let him go, Malc, you'll kill him – then we'll never get these punters back to Barking." Malc let go of the tramp's neck but held his hair through the bars: "Go on you nippers, piss off out of it."

"Thanks Mister," shouted Iris as she ran off. Charlie and Dora were already walking on. Pete, Joey, Calum and Flops eased carefully by the wild-eyed tramp. Calum smiled, Malc winked. And the boys ran and ran, laughing, with the black dog bounding, its ears flopping.

They passed Iris and Charlie and Dora and caught up with Ted. They ran laughing and punching all the way to Bell Wharf in Leigh Old Town.

Mrs. Leith waved as the Hillman pulled into the car park of the Peterboat Inn. Behind the Hillman was a maroon and gray Daimler with Callum Urquart at the wheel and Catherine leaning out of the window, smiling at Calum with her lovely teeth. Her brothers sat in the back with a boy between them. The man called Brian and a small dark woman with sharp features were smiling in the back of the Hillman. Brian's face was flushed – they'd been drinking already. Flops bounded up to the car.

Calum sat on the sea wall among the Lightfoots with his back to the water. He was starting to talk like them and said, " 'Oy, Flops, get over 'ere!"

Dora had bought a shandy and was staring at the boats because Charlie had lost interest in her already and gone home. The four boys ignored Iris, but she stayed with them, butting into their conversation, and scraping her heels on the whitewashed wall. There were tables and benches arranged along a concrete platform, raised above the car park, so customers could sit out and drink in the sea breeze. Sunk in the mud, half way to a flat swamp which Pete called Two Tree Island, was the skeleton of a wooden ship; its ribs and keel stuck out of the water like black bones. The last of the cockle boats and fishing brigs were chugging out with the incoming tide, leaving a smell of diesel in the salt air. Two Tree Island had a corporation dump on it and when the wind turned, it brought in a stench like rotten cheese.

But from the pub came pleasant smells of buffet food and beer. Like all the buildings of the Old Town, it appeared cozy and a little crooked. Onto a small brick pub had been built a glass and wood addition that was now the saloon bar. Most pubs had misted glass but this bar was all clearly visible and Calum watched the bartenders moving around.

He was happy and wanted to run and hug his mother but he knew the Lightfoots wouldn't understand. Dora ignored the Leiths' arrival by turning away and swigging down the rest of her shandy.

Mr. Leith came over and said, "What would you like to drink, smiler?" Calum asked for lemonade. "Are these your friends?" said Leith, eyeing the Lightfoots. Calum nodded. Leith raised his eyebrows and huffed, "I suppose they all want lemonade?"

The eight adults went into the saloon and could be seen at one end of the bar smoking and laughing.

After a while, Mrs. Leith came to the entrance and beckoned Calum to come and get the tray of drinks which she placed on a bench by the door. On his way across the car park, Calum noticed the boy sitting in the Daimler; he'd forgotten what Urquart called him, so didn't say hello. He went into the shaded entrance and picked up the big tin tray, loaded with glasses of lemonade and packets of crisps. Just inside the double glass doors, which were thrown open, stood his father, Urquart, and Brian with drinks in their hands. Conducting with his finger, Leith counted to three and a song, familiar to Calum, burst from the group.

Arseholes are cheap today, cheaper than yesterday;
Big boys are half a crown, standing up or sitting down;
Little boys are three and six, because they know more tricks;
Oh, what a joy, is the fat bottomed boy. . .

Urquart's eyes looked seriously to heaven and something moved up and down in his throat as he sang. So it was to be high cockalorums again. This made Calum nervous for when his father got together with old colonials there was usually trouble.

Calum took the tray of drinks over to the sea wall. It took him several minutes to thread through the parked cars. When he got there, Dora came over and took a glass before everyone else, and by the time Iris, Pete, Joey and Ted took theirs, there was none left. "That's mine," Calum said to Dora, "Dad forgot you."

"Looks more like he forgot you," she scoffed, shoulder up, nervous, glasses sliding down her nose. "No," he said, keeping a reasonable tone in his voice, "I remember – you were over there, he didn't count you, he asked me if I wanted it, he called me smiler – you heard him."

"That's right," said Pete.

"Bollocks!" Dora said. Ted tittered but Joey and Iris frowned. For a moment Calum didn't know what to say. The boy who had been in the Daimler was coming slowly across the car park to them. There was something odd about the way he walked and the way he held his head; his eyes were just slits and his hair stood up like a wire brush. Iris said, "Look, it's a blind kid!" He cocked his head, said from a way off, "Yes, I'm blind, but I'm a good listener," and he laughed up high like a seagull.

"I'm Hugh. They've forgotten me as usual," said the blind boy, waving a hand behind him, smiling. "My dad was going to bring me out a Coke and some crisps. . . "

Calum grabbed the shandy glass out of Dora's hand while she gawked at the newcomer. "Gimme that back," she shouted. She tried to grab the glass but Calum spun away and took several gulps from it. She slapped his face so that his teeth crunched on the rim of the glass and the lemonade spilled over his T-shirt and jeans. Flops barked once, the Lightfoots shifted out of the way and Hugh screamed.

Pete said, "Give her one back."

For some seconds they flailed at each other until she slapped him over the eye where his scratch from earlier was, and it stung badly. Seeing red, he punched her face, making her glasses fall on the concrete. He stamped on them twice, then picked them up so that they hung like the bones of a dead bird and flung them into the sea. "There," he yelled, "There! Bitch. Bitch bitch bitch bitch!"

"That's it!" Dora shouted and ran, dodging through the cars.

He saw her yellow sweater disappear around the corner.

Callum Urquart touched his shoulder. In his other hand he was holding a

Coke and a bag of crisps. He caught Calum by the head and looked at his eye. "Nasty graze you've got there. Having a scrap with your sister, were you?"

"She's not a sister, she's a maid and a bitch."

"Oh shush now," said Urquart, "I'll bring you out a beverage."

"No!" said Calum.

Urquart shrugged, said, "Suit yourself, young Leith."

Hugh's ears were big and flexible. The Lightfoots sat off a little way, sipping their drinks and whispering. The car park was filling up with sunburned people from the beaches. The masts of the moored boats pinged as the taut rigging beat in the wind. The engine of the last cockle boat going out went put-put-put and the tide lapped against the sea wall. Hugh said, "You must be Calum. My mum told me about you. She said you'd play with me. She said you looked kind but you don't sound all that kind. You won't beat me up will you?"

"That was only Dora. She's deserved a bashing for a long time. She hit me first. I wouldn't fight a blind kid or anyone who didn't hurt me first. I hate fighting but I do it . . . "

"If you'd let yourself cry," said Hugh, "you wouldn't feel sick or upset after. That's what my child psychologist told me – go on, bawl your guts up, you'll feel better."

The strange boy's words nearly made Calum burst, but he kept his hands over the sides of his face until the sobs that threatened to spring forth diminished. "You cry too quietly," said Hugh. "Me, I sound like an express train coming, so my dad says. The child psychologist says it's some kind of compensation and I have to be allowed to get it out. That must mean you aren't letting anything out, you should cry like a thunderstorm . . . "

"What are you talking about?" laughed Calum through his hands.

"Oh shut up, mole-face, and stop upsetting him," said Iris, "he'll be bawlin' all bleedin' night if he listens to you. Cryin's daft – it don't get you nowhere, just into more trouble with your old man for makin' a row."

"Sorry," said Hugh.

"He's all right," said Calum to Iris. She sniffed, bent down suddenly and petted the dog: "Flops, nice old Flops-dog, old black fleabag." She pulled his ears and kissed his velvet head.

"Have some Coke," said Hugh to Calum, handing the bottle almost into his hands. Calum took a long swig at it and burped. "Is this your dog?" asked Hugh, touching the labrador's thick ruff, then running his fingers through it.

"Yes. His name's Flops – because when he gets tired on a walk he'll flop down and go no further and you have to bring him home on a bus." Iris burst out laughing at that and Hugh bent down and took the dog's face in his hands, stroking and fondling: "Flops, dear old Flops," he whispered, "what a lovely, lovely dog."

The dog licked Hugh in the eye.

"He likes you," said Calum.

"Does he, oh does he?" said Hugh, "I like him. Old Flopsy-whopsy!" The dog's heavy tail beat on Iris's leg and she giggled.

"My dad calls him a black bastard when he barks at the postman," said Calum. Grinning, Iris crooned, "Oh poor old Flopsy-whopsy."

"Don't take the piss," laughed Hugh.

Iris looked at Calum as if to say with her big wide eyes: Blimey, he's sharp.

Hugh said, "I like you lot, you're all right. Can I feel your faces so I know how you look? I used to see once, you see, so I can work it out – you don't have to be shy. Calum goes first."

Blushing a little, Calum stayed very still as Hugh's fingers crept over his eyebrows, eyesockets, nose, lips and cheeks. The fingers smelled like old toilet carpets. But there was also a faint smell of soap and his nails were clean, even though the cuticles were shredded and bloody. He was very tall, and he stooped all the time as if in fear of hitting his head. He wore beige trousers and a gray flannel shirt with the collar button fastened and the sleeves rolled up to reveal skinny, freckled arms. His neck was long and there was a pointed Adam's apple in his throat. "You should lose some weight, Calum," he said.

"You should put some on," replied Calum.

"Touché," grinned Hugh, sounding like his father. Iris asked him how old he was and he answered, "Twelve and a half in my bare feet," as he plied his fingers over her face and hair.

"Calum and me are nine," Iris said.

"That makes us about equal then," said Hugh, "I'm smart and you can see."

Ted came over, Pete and Joey tagging behind, and said, "Let's play a game – we're bored with all this mumbo bloody jumbo."

"Can I play?" asked Hugh.

"No," said Ted.

"Of course he can!" said Iris.

They looked at each other and shrugged. Finally Calum said, "Let's play Treasure Island."

"That's an idea!" said Iris.

"I'm Long John Silver," said Pete.

"No you're not," said Calum, "We're gonna pick up sides and do it fair."

"I refuse to be Blind Pew," said Hugh.

"You can be Jim Hawkins," said Calum.

"A blind Jim Hawkins," chirped Iris.

They picked up sides; Calum was Long John, Hugh was Blind Jim Hawkins and Pete was Squire Trelawney. Joey, Iris and Ted were to be pirates but would have a turn at being the goodies later. They decided they needed to build a stockade out of a pile of fish boxes that were dumped by the wall at the other end of the car park. The wall sloped down slightly to a slipway that broke the continuity of the raised sea wall. They decided to fill the slipway opening with boxes to make believe it was the gate to their stockade on Treasure Island. Hugh said it didn't make much sense because the pirates couldn't attack from the sea, but he was shouted down.

Despite his thin arms Hugh was very strong and carried eight boxes at a time. Within minutes the boxes were piled across the slipway, some stacked so high that they leaned out over the water's edge. Calum liked how excited Hugh was to be the workhorse – once he had the steps worked out he went faster and faster. The game had already begun – they had to finish the gate before the pirates came; they went back and forth, playing in their heads, imagining.

They could hardly believe it when Hugh barged right through the boxes and fell over the edge into the sea. The remaining boxes slid in after him. They stared at where he had disappeared as though it were still part of the game. Several people on the sea wall exchanged shocked glances. An old man shouted "help!"

Calum found himself at the edge looking into the muddy water, wondering whether or not to dive. Boxes bobbed in the waves, then Hugh's arm appeared a few yards out.

Calum jumped, and the water was shallower and warmer than he expected when his feet hit the slimy bottom. As he came to the surface he simultaneously wished he'd taken off his shoes and that Hugh's dad was doing this instead of him. But he was a good swimmer and splashed to where Hugh struggled and gasped. The current was taking Hugh in the direction of the saloon, but his feet were on the surface more than his head and his struggles were getting weaker. Calum shouted, "Put your feet down, it's shallow, you can wade out," but Hugh's face, when it surfaced, was white.

Finally, Calum caught up with him, gasped, "Put your feet down, you fathead – you're tall, you can walk ashore." Hugh grabbed him by the hair and both of them were dragged under. Calum swallowed water and choked, he struggled for freedom but Hugh was amazingly strong and Calum realized he too was panicking and that he could no longer tell which way was up and which down through the bubbles.

It was calm and quiet under water.

When he burst to the surface, the noise of life was unexpected and strange. He breathed, tried to stabilize himself, and was alarmed at how far down the sea wall he'd drifted. He tried to pull Hugh to the surface as they drifted closer to the saloon where the water was deeper and colder. There was a black ladder affixed vertically to the pebbledash side of the sea wall and a man in shirt sleeves hung by one arm to it and beckoned to him with the other.

Suddenly, he was grabbed from behind, pulled and lifted away from Hugh by a man with a red beard – another man with no hair anywhere on him pulled Hugh the right way up as if he were no more than a rag doll. The man with the beard said, "Come on nipper, you've done your bit. Can you make it to the ladder under your own steam?" Calum nodded, spitting water, and swam wearily to the ladder where the man hanging there heaved him up and pushed him through a little gate that led into an enclosed patio attached to the saloon.

There were crowds of people cheering him. His mother and Catherine Urquart grabbed at him, crying like seagulls. People kept patting him, touching him, saying "Jolly good show, plucky little blighter, stout fellow, need more like that." His father was there, red-faced, cigarette in left hand, right hand extended, "That's right my boy, that's the ticket."

Charles and James and Urquart gazed over the sea wall as Hugh was pulled and pushed up the ladder by the two fishermen. The Lightfoots stood in a knot and stared with their beautiful gray eyes and Calum smiled at Iris and she smiled back and he winked at Pete and Pete winked back.

And Calum saw blind Hugh fall coughing into his mother's arms, then his father's, then his uncles', but didn't say a word because he was embarrassed at being saved and being blind and being nothing but trouble and by being looked at by people he couldn't see.

Callum Urquart stood beside Calum, held his hand out with a serious expression on his face, squeezed Calum's fingers; there was something in Urquart's hand pressing into Calum's palm. When Calum looked, he was shocked to see a neatly folded five pound note.

Urquart said,

"Heroes should be well rewarded. No Harry Leith — I'll not hear any objections — I want him to have it. It's a principle, or should be: reward honesty, reward bravery."

Everyone was drunk and emotional, anxious to make speeches, but Urquart continued, "If I was about to make a present of it I could understand objections, but this is a principle — we should reward our heroes. Not another word now."

Urquart raised his finger at Leith who was beaming and hadn't actually said anything. Mrs. Leith walked over to the wall and hugged Catherine and Hugh. Her eyes didn't focus very well and her voice was slurred. Calum had never seen her have too much to drink before — enough to get merry perhaps, but never drunk. She looked over the sea wall and roared with affected laughter.

"Oh no!" said Iris and pointed.

Below the ladder, paddling in frantic circles, with nowhere to land himself, and the tide pulling him out to sea, was Flops.

Already wet, the two fishermen jumped into the water and dragged the heavy dog up the ladder. The patrons of the Peterboat formed a ring around the dog as he plodded, dripping, onto the patio. When Flops shook himself, several of the women screamed and ducked behind their husbands.

Because Calum got the shivers from sitting around too long in wet clothes, the Leiths were obliged to go home earlier than expected. Henry Leith borrowed blankets from the proprietor of the Peterboat and wrapped them around Calum and the dog. It was a warm night with the smell of flowers and sea in the air. Calum sat in the back seat, nestled in the blankets with Flops, as the open-roofed

Hillman cruised along the seafront toward the colored amusement park lights of Southend.

Calum shivered, partly from being damp and partly from being happy. He kept thinking of how much money there would be in the piggybank when he added his new fivepound note to it – nearly seventeen pounds. It was enough to look after himself if they left him or killed each other. It was enough for a good bike. Enough for all sorts of things.

The sea was lovely; an almost full moon spread a pathway of light from one coast to the other, and the moon's face looked down with its ambiguous smile, behind which, quite suddenly Calum realized, was the darkness of outer space. The moon was a big flat white mask, and when he thought of it this way the atmosphere and feelings of the charlatan thing returned. To get it out of his mind, he imagined smacking the charlatan thing on the head with Punchinello's truncheon. He shifted his thoughts to being a hero: heroes should get paid lots, he knew that now; and he knew that, at least today, he had been a hero.

Calum was so tired when they got home that he almost didn't notice that Dora's luggage was gone. He stood amazed for a moment before running into his parents' room to tell them. They stood together by the window and stared at him. The chills came back and tingled all through him. The back side of the pig was reflected in the mirror and there was a neat black hole punched into its fat, plaster buttocks. Calum ran and pulled it down. All the banknotes were gone; the change had been left. He stared at his parents. His skin burned and prickled.

His father turned and gazed out of the window toward the sea, took a pull on his cigarette and blew smoke into the net curtains so that it curled and coiled to the ceiling and spread out.

GREENACRES POND

The oak Calum leaned against was on a rising salient that jutted five feet into the north end of Greenacres Pond. It was the last of several old trees that a year ago had shaded the water. There was no trace of the trees now save for some furrows where they had been pulled out of the ground; the bulldozers had not filled in the holes properly. The trees were used as filler for the road that was being cut through the swamp. Thin steel poles with red flags marked where concrete would soon be poured. Where the trees had been, dark green weeds grew tall and thick, barely concealing the empty paint tins, oily auto parts and old perambulators that people had dumped in the furrows during the winter. But what disturbed Calum most were the new townhouses that, in various states of completion, advanced closer and closer from the eastern end of Greenacres Common. There were several new *Welcome to Green Acre Estates* signs.

Calum looked at what only the previous spring had been wild. You could see nothing but blackberry bushes and trees then; there had been no rooves in sight and you had to listen hard to hear traffic on the nearby road. He was more than disturbed, he was frustrated, no, furious, at the workmen with their broken teeth and cigarettes who blindly drove bulldozers and poured concrete.

And, his father had forbidden him to see Iris.

But here she was, Iris, on the other side of the pond.

On Thursday they had been separated forever by their angry fathers, and now it was Saturday and there she was, close to him again, fifty yards across the pond.

It was Pete's idea to come here, not Calum's. Pete wanted to watch the frogs

42

spawn, or at least that was the excuse. Pete had quietly fixed it so Calum might have a chance to be alone with Iris. "Come up to Greenacres," Pete had told her, "Calum'll be there." He told Calum that he wanted his sister and his best mate to be together and never mind all the mess that was going on, it would all blow over sooner or later. It was nice of him. But now Calum's glum reaction to what the workmen had done to the pond had Pete thinking he was a stupid sap. He told Pete how he hated the way all the nature was disappearing. "Here we go again," Pete had said, "getting all high and bleeding mighty over stuff that don't concern you. I'm gonna go and muck around with Iris and her mates 'til you come back to earth."

Calum had laughed and said he wanted to sit quietly under the tree for a while. "Oh, yeah?" Pete said, "You're gonna have a quiet little wank, more like!" And he bounded away as Calum picked up a handful of gravel to throw at him.

A frog broke the surface and swam to the reeds on Calum's left where it clambered over what he at first thought was a long thin prophylactic, spread beside a broken brick. Then he thought the brick was a huge turd because there were flies buzzing around it. Then he realized it was a toad, a big rust colored one, and that which he had thought was a prophylactic was in fact its tongue. The frog sat on the dead toad's tongue and ate flies as they landed.

Across the water came a laugh. It was Iris's. She looked strange even though it was only a few days since Calum last saw her. She wore her faded blue frock that was a little too big and her navy blue plimsolls with white socks, and she was fooling around with some tough looking kids who shouted and punched each other. Pete was with them, standing to one side a little, absently sharpening one end of a long stick with his penknife.

Calum did not want to join the others yet. Sitting under the oak, he was putting Greenacres Common back the way he liked it, populating it with its past generations: long-haired naked men stalking stags as they drank from the clear water; a host of ancient Britons stooping to drink on their way to fight the Romans; then he saw Saxon children laughing and splashing in the warm shallow water while their parents gathered flowers – Iris would be on the bank, watching the children, and he, a Norman warlord, strayed from the boar hunt, would ride up to her and gaze down. She would touch his stirrup and he would suddenly clasp her wrist and yank her up over his saddle and go thundering away across the Common while her father, the wicked black-toothed pagan rogue, gave chase.

He was just wondering if an old tree like this he leaned against had any sort of memory of what had happened during its life, and was imagining – for he was sure the bulldozers would soon come to tear it out of the earth – what it would be like to ingest the tree's soul into his own and see through its ancient eyes, when Iris, who had not spoken to him since he arrived, called from the other side of the pond:

"Hey, Calum, stop moping and come over here!"

43

He looked across the pond at her and a warm, kneading sensation came into his chest. He did not much like the look of her companions, but he got up, brushed off the seat of his jeans and hitched them up. He tucked in his shirt, then pulled it out again so the layer of fat around his middle would not show as much, and then wandered, hands in pockets, around the edge of the pond, careful to avoid the tiny toads that leaped away as he trampled through the weeds.

Pete had wanted to watch the frogs spawn, but the spawn was already hatching and the mating frenzy was dying down. It seemed childish now to care about pond life, but Calum liked the delicate splashes and rustlings that went on in the reed beds and profuse weeds – the confused amphibians, late arrivals, shit-out-of-luck lovers, amused him. "Poor little sods," he thought, "they haven't got a clue."

He lingered to look at the wriggling tadpoles, swarming among the gelatinous wads of frog and toad spawn that clogged the brown water like bilious clouds.

Faintly, he heard Iris say to Pete, "Here he comes. Looks like he's still got the 'ump."

"Too right," said Pete, "he's mooning again."

Iris sang a few bars of "Mister Moonlight" and did a little dance around Pete, touching him with her back. Calum loved her voice – when he heard it he could smell her breath and the scent of her skin. As he came closer Iris lifted her lovely eyes to him and then looked away. Her eyes were the color of rain clouds. She had washed her hair, it was the color of shining chestnuts and he could smell the fragrance of the shampoo. He thought, "I kissed her last Tuesday after school in the library gardens."

He had kissed her under the old tree, the one in the lower garden with the green, circular bench around it. She sat on her hands with her eyes closed while he held her jaw gently with his right hand, the left, just the fingertips, touching the bottom of her rib cage, and now he recalled the warm silk taste of her mouth, her long shiny dark eyelashes, a tiny blackhead in the crease between the bridge of her nose and forehead, and, breathlessly drawing away from her, avoiding her eyes, he saw again the hint of a smile in the corners of her lips. Then she pulled his head down and kissed him her way, her fingers lightly moving through the fine hair on the back of his head, her rich brown hair against his face, the slight touching of her tongue against his. . . .Then somebody shouted. Iris pulled away and looked over his shoulder. He felt as if their lips had been glued together, nearly set, and the sudden separation dazed him. His eye was an inch from hers, it seemed hardly human, frightening – like gazing into a storm cloud.

He turned and saw two short troll-like creatures shuffling along the path; they were flushed and their jowls quivered with anger. The old woman waved her walking stick while the old man helped her along, huffing and blowing with pursed lips and owlish eyes. The old man shouted:

"Hey! That's enough of that. Disgusting! That's enough of that. Hey!"

The woman shook her walking stick in the air. "They're kids, nothing but children," she croaked, "It's criminal. That boy ought to be flogged."

The old woman wore a brown coat and black beret; her spindly legs were encased in rumpled stockings. As she got closer Calum saw that her wide-set, brown eyes were bloodshot and had a white crescent around the outside of the iris.

Calum stood. "Shut up, you disgusting old faggot," he said, "You're bloody half dead, you are, bloody half dead."

The woman staggered, her mouth dropping open. The old man, whose face had become very flushed, said, "You say that to her? How dare you, how dare you?"

"Get away from us. Mind your own business."

"I'll thrash you."

"Touch me, you old git, and my father'll come and flay you alive."

"Your father? Your father?"

The incident seemed unreal.

Iris had pulled him away, and said: "Oh, bugger off Captain Dobson. We weren't doing no harm. Come on Cal, let's go."

"You're one of the Lightfoot girls, aren't you, yes?" the old man said, turning on her, "I'll tell your dad, I will. I know your dad. Yes."

Taking Calum by the hand and pulling him up the hill, Iris said, "Oh, piss off, you silly old rat-bags."

As they passed the library, she told him that the Dobsons were in the Salvation Army and Captain Dobson had got her dad out of trouble with the police a few times. Her dad did odd jobs, cash in hand, at their meeting hall. Elsie and Norman Dobson were influential among the Old Town non-conformists and were capable of bringing plenty of trouble. They were, as Iris put it, pillocks of the community.

And trouble came. On Wednesday, while Calum was at choir practice, Mr. Lightfoot went to Calum's house, all in a rage over the kissing, and banged on the door and swore in the street. Calum's father listened to one hysterical abuse-filled sentence then stepped forward and knocked him over the bonnet of a parked car.

As Calum approached Iris and Pete he saw that five or six youths were wrestling in a furrow, making a lot of noise. Several of the smaller boys and a tall freckled girl with hair the color of dried blood held jam jars full of tadpoles. To one kid Calum said, "There's too many in there, they'll suffocate." The red haired girl smiled at him and he was about to talk to her but Iris nudged him and pointed to a rock in the middle of the pond: "Look, Cal, on that there stone – the biggest bloody frog I've seen in me born days."

Calum looked and smiled. The creature resembled an old brown boot. It was of the same species as the one dead in the reeds. "It's a bit like Captain Dobson," he said.

"Or Elsie from Chelsea," laughed Iris.

Pete said, "It's more like Winston Churchill."

"He's the king of the pond," said Iris.

A big youth, whom Calum did not know, with skin so freckled across his nose and cheeks that he could almost be wearing war paint, looked at Iris and frowned. "Nah," he said, "looks like Floyd Patterson after Sonny Liston done him in." He wore a tight white T-shirt and was lying in the weeds, sucking a stiff stem of grass with his hands behind his head. "And I'll tell you another thing, that ain't no bleeding frog – it's a bulltoad. Horrible things, bulltoads."

As he spoke the youth's Adam's apple moved up and down in his muscular throat. Calum, in as conciliatory voice as he could use, said, "he's not horrible. We like him."

"Speak for yourself," said Iris, but Calum only half heard this because the youth had roused himself and was meeting Calum's eyes. Calum looked away. The youth said, "A toad is an 'orrible filthy fucking thing what witches put on their clits."

The wrestling boys stopped, looked up.

"You're nuts," said Calum.

"And you're a fat fuck-arse," said the youth, jutting his face forward. He spat out the grass stem and supported himself on his elbows. Veins stood out on his forearms, and his fringe fell over his small eyes so that they shone through the hair.

The others watched.

Calum's legs shook. He had been in many fights. In a high school like his you had to stick up for yourself, and because he had always been big and a bit overweight, he had to do it a lot, so he was good at it and there was not much that scared him, but there were danger signs on this fellow. He was not quite as big as Calum, an inch shorter perhaps, and not as heavy, but he had small sharp teeth, and his bony hands with nicotine-covered fingers were the hands of a fighter; a scar under the left eye had needed stitches, and there was that thick neck and those small fearless eyes. Calum calculated these things as the wobbles moved into his stomach. He thought of just wading in, a tactic he had often used – a non-stop battery of punches; but what if he were to muff it and get humiliated – in front of Iris?

Calum said:

"There's no need to get stroppy. I'm just saying that I can't see anything wrong with a big frog or toad or whatever it is. I'm not after any trouble over pond specimens."

Pete laughed, and then the others laughed, too.

The youth grunted, then yawned and looked away, trying to suppress a grin. He lowered his shoulder blades back onto the flattened weeds and coughed. Calum smiled, then walked to where Iris stood, looking across the pond. Her dress was wrinkled and grass stained, and her ankle socks were muddy. From the corner of her mouth she said, "Watch your big gob, Calum Leith, that's Mickey Wheeler you're back-chatting."

Calum knew of the Wheelers, a Gypsy clan with a bad reputation. So this was the Mickey he had heard of, the youngest of a swarm of hot-blooded brothers and cousins. Mickey was the type that would be after distinguishing himself in the eyes of his relatives. "Great," said Calum quietly. Iris shrugged, shook her head, "You're ever a one for trouble, you."

"Oy, Iris?" called Mickey Wheeler, "Is old Porky here the geeser your old man wants me to look out for?"

"No," said Iris, "just a mate of Pete's. Eh, Pete?"

"Yeah, Mick, he's just a mate from school," said Pete, and turning to Calum, said, "Come over here and see the newts."

Calum followed Pete.

"Go on Porky," shouted Mickey Wheeler, "go and have a look at them newts."

The sky was deep blue with tall clouds that intermittently blocked the sun and cast cool shadows that brought goosepimples to the skin.

Calum huddled with Pete in what they supposed was a disused duck blind. The road was two hundred yards away, hidden by a row of poplars whose branches curved upwards like elegant green wine goblets. Through a break in the line of poplars, beside the road, Calum could see three idle bulldozers, yellow ones with rust stains and muddy tracks, one of them with its bucket dangerously raised in a way that made him think of the neck and head of some prehistoric reptile. He remembered the first time he had seen a bulldozer here. It was the previous autumn and he and Pete were gathering berries for their mums. They were on their track bikes, and burst into a clearing in the blackberry bushes to be startled by the presence of the huge machine. It seemed to have a face and its bucket was laid flat on the ground as though it had been shot by trophy hunters. They climbed all over it for half an hour and came away stinking of diesel oil.

Without speaking, Calum and Pete watched the small newts wriggling in two inches of warm water near some reeds. Calum concentrated on their tails. The air was warm and heavy when the sun shone, and the surface of the pond was still. Save for a few murmurs from the other side of a green wall of weed there was a kind of thick silence.

Pete, never able to stay quiet long, became cheerful, and said, "What are them trees that line the road called?"

"Poplars, I think."

"They're supposed to be like that because King Arthur hid the Holy Grail in this tree and the branches all came up like that to protect it and then all the trees that descended from it had their branches like that instead of like normal trees."

Pushing a red pebble around at the water's edge, Calum said, "That's from school. Baxter taught you that, I expect?"

"I dunno. Fuck school. I just remembered it."

A bright green frog swam gently through a swarm of tadpoles, its eyes staring vacantly. Calum muttered, "Look at this brainless little bugger."

Pete laughed. Then they stayed quiet and watched the pond life. After a while, Calum said:

"Maybe I should climb up in one of those poplar trees."

Pete looked at him, gave his arm a push, said, "Don't worry about it, Cal. You're no match for a Wheeler."

"But Iris saw me back down. I feel cowardly."

"Well, you know what you always tell me — something about it's better to take a beating than to spend a week feeling like a wanker."

"I know. I've just had enough trouble lately. I'm sick of it."

"It's all my old man's fault. He's out of his head."

"They all are," said Calum, "all dads are out of their heads."

"No, but he's worse, he's incon . . . inconsomething or other . . . "

"Inconsistent?"

"Yeah, that. He ain't bothered about you and me knocking about together, but he won't let Iris see you because your old man decked him. So what does that make me, a spunk bubble?"

Calum laughed, "He thinks there's no danger of you and me snogging in the library gardens."

Nodding his head quickly, Pete said, "Too right."

A batch of tadpoles seethed beneath Calum's grinning reflection on the surface of the water and the moving reflection of the clouds ran counter to the tadpoles. He looked up to see a daddy longlegs fly out of the reeds and move over the surface of the water, its legs dragging; it landed, and its spread limbs indented the surface ever so slightly as though it stood on cellophane.

Someone laughed over beyond the weeds.

Calum said:

"So, Pete, why's this Mickey Wheeler bloke hanging around your sister?"

"What do you think? He's going to fuck her if he ain't already."

"What?"

"You heard."

"She's only thirteen."

"That don't matter to no Wheeler. Gypsies do what they like."

Calum hurled a red pebble over the pond. It plopped in the water under the overhanging roots of the oak. He looked around for another but there was nothing but dry mud.

Pete went on:

"I don't know what they have on me dad, but me two other sisters married into the Wheelers as soon as they were sixteen — Madeline to George, Irene to Geoff — they lived with them before they got spliced, too, but me old man never done nothing. And then when Charlie — you remember old Charlie — wanted to go out with Sylvie Wheeler, George and his cousins, the Sweeney twins, beat the shit out him. I reckon that's why he went in the army – to get the bleeding hell out of all this. And now me dad's asked old Swanny Wheeler, he's sort of their family chief, to have someone keep an eye on Iris. So Swanny tells his son, Jackie Wheeler, and Jackie puts his youngest son Mickey on her tail. I fucking hate this."

"Your dad's scared of them."

"Well, they're wild, see. They'll come round your house, all of them. Do you in on your doorstep with broken bottles." Pete was quiet for a moment, then chuckled and said, "I know one thing though, me dad never told nobody about what your old man done to him. Serves him bloody right."

"What would happen if he did tell the Wheelers?"

"Gawd knows. Probably they'd laugh at him. And your old man's a bit of an upper class type and sort of out of things so they might not think of bothering him, but if he'd hurt one of theirn, he'd be one sorry chavvy, I can tell you that for nothing. I hate them Wheelers, it gives me a pain in the prick just thinking of them."

"What about this Mickey, then? Is he any good?"

"Forget it, Cal."

"Is he?"

"He's a tasty old mush, as it happens – and dirty, a right old nutter."

"What year's he in?"

"Fourth. He'll be leaving school soon. But don't even think what you're thinking. Even if you did take him, which I don't think you could at all, first there'd be Geoff and then there'd be George, and you'd have to fight them all, one after another, 'til there was nothing left of you but scabs."

"I told you, I'm not up for any trouble," said Calum.

Pete shrugged, looked up at the sky. Calum looked at him, and then said; "You're trying to goad me, aren't you? You're always doing that."

"Leave off, 'course I'm not. Anyway, Wheeler'd murder you."

They watched the tadpoles circle back around again. There were more of them now and they made the water so black that the newts became invisible. Pete nudged Calum's arm suddenly and said, "Hey, look at that!"

"Blimey," said Calum, "It's coming right at us."

"What is it?"

"It must be that bulltoad from the rock."

"The king," laughed Pete.

"Churchill," said Calum.

Six yards away the toad swam languidly toward the reeds, its eyes just above the water, leaving only the faintest wake. From further along the bank came another shrill burst of laughter, and, for a moment, over the tall weeds, Calum saw the grinning head of Mickey Wheeler, jerking at something.

Pete was saying, "You remember when we made that frog corral in the old bathtub in my back yard?"

The sight of Wheeler brought a weightlessness and hollowness over Calum, but he said, "It was to be our terrarium. Where is it now, that old bathtub?"

"Still there, behind me dad's pigeon shed. It was full of his scrap metal for a while, but now I keep me pet ferret in there. That was last spring, weren't it, when we done that? Remember how they tried to squeeze through the chicken wire and sliced half their skin off rather than miss the mating season?"

"Poor sods. We should've brought them back here and set them free."

Pete shrugged, looked at the sky, said, "You're not gonna start mooning again, are you?"

Calum looked away and watched the toad rise from the water and crawl onto the damp mud at the edge of the reed bed. It turned itself around and backed in, gradually burying itself by wiggling its rear. It was the same color as the mud, a reddish brown. "It's looking right at me," Calum said.

"We know its hiding place," said Pete.

Calum's throat was dry. "It's because we stayed still," he said, but his mind was on Mickey Wheeler. Mickey Wheeler Mickey Wheeler Mickey Wheeler, he thought as he pushed Mickey Wheeler's strong throat out of his mind's eye, replacing that image with one of his fists beating blood out of Mickey Wheeler's face. He lay back and watched the sky, trying to calm himself by sucking on a firm grass stem. He could hear his heartbeats. He turned his face and looked for the toad again, but it was too well camouflaged to see. It struck him suddenly that the hidden toad might have been responsible for the death of that other toad that looked just like it over in the reeds by the oak tree — he had an absurd vision of two bulltoads locking horns.

Relax now, he told himself, just relax.

He watched the silent clouds pass over, casting their cold shadows. They were clean and white and stacked high, and seemed to Calum like the powdered wigs of long dead landowners.

Iris broke through the weeds, startling him. She sat on a tuft of grass between him and Pete, and it was plain that she held back tears. Pete asked her what was up.

"They won't stop him," Iris said.

"Who?" said Pete, "What you on about, you silly cow?"

Gritting her teeth, she looked from Pete to Calum and said, "Mickey. He's killing frogs."

Iris never cried, it was her pride not to cry. She held it back by closing her eyes and putting her hand across her mouth, but the water leaked through her eyelashes and ran off her face into the dust. But she controlled herself, and looking away, said, "That sod. He's a dirty sod."

Calum felt the shakes and wobbles return to his legs, and the hollowness

50

inside him deepened for a while until a sort of prickly calmness took over and a pink haze inhabited the periphery of his vision. His mouth was dry, metallic, everything became deliberate and furious and he heard himself think: All right then, do it, do it now. His voice said:

"I'm going to do him."

"Cal?" said Iris.

"Oh yes, here we go, oh yes," said Pete.

"Calum, please don't, oh bloody hell, please. . . "

"You may as well get out of his way, Iris. He's going to play kamikazi third-year."

Spitting out the chewed stem, Calum was up and already kicking through the weeds. Other things were said behind him but he stopped hearing because his eyes were on Mickey Wheeler who held a long straight stick, the one Pete had been sharpening earlier, and with it aimed, stabbed, then pulled it from the water and pointed again, stabbed again.

The others, Gypsy boys mostly, and the red-headed girl with the tadpole jar, looked at Calum as he came forward, but Mickey Wheeler continued to stab, the side of his mouth turned upward, the nose, in profile, unexpectedly blunt. The girl with the jam jar full of tadpoles held it against her mouth as if she was about to drink; her eyes were red.

Calum's feet thudded on the dry mud. Frogs and toads were skewered, still living, on the sharp stick, some small and green, others fat and brown, moving their limbs slowly, clutching at each other with their fingers.

Calum stood beside Mickey Wheeler. The stick was poised above a mating pair whose united skin and bulging eyes made them oblivious to danger. "Two in one," Wheeler said in a high, happy voice like a child fascinated with what it was about to do. "Two horny little bastards in one stroke. Hold still, you fuckers."

Looking at Wheeler's jaw, Calum said, "Hey."

"What's on your mind, Porky?"

The jaw had dark stubble on it. Wheeler lifted the stick a fraction. Calum had not thought about clenching his fist but there it was, swinging upward. He felt nothing of the impact as Wheeler fell sideways and dropped the stick into the water, holding a hand to his face. Calum thought about kicking him, but did not want to fight dirty.

Wheeler straightened up and started swinging his fists and kicking. Calum heard the zing of knuckles knocking against his face and head. His own hands, and after a while his feet, too, flew furiously. There was bleeding from somewhere.

It went on a long time and Calum was tired, and breathing hard. Wheeler slowed the pace and began circling with his guard up, jabbing lefts. Zing zing zing, was the sound and feel as the punches connected. Soon both his fists had

Calum's blood on them. Calum touched the inside of his lip with the tip of his tongue and found it deeply split – his mouth was full of blood.

Winding up a big right, Wheeler edged closer. "You're going to sleep now, Porky. Oink, oink, oink – knock out time."

Calum spat blood in his eyes.

Someone said: "Nice one, Leith."

Calum kicked Wheeler's legs and stomach, hammered the top of his head, while Wheeler tried to wipe blood from his eyes. Calum's hands seemed to hit gristle, the blows just bounced off. Wheeler launched himself blindly and they rolled in the dust and weeds, scratching, biting, and butting. The others were yelling, their cartwheeling faces wild with excitement – most were for Wheeler, but not all.

Wheeler jammed his knee in Calum's groin and pushed as hard as he could, Calum's thighs holding it off. Calum got his fingers up Wheeler's nose and tried to tear it. They rolled around like that, maiming.

Nobody, Calum realized, was going to break this up. He kept thinking: you're in the right you're in the right you're in the right.

Pete shouted, "Come on Calum!" and kicked Wheeler in the side of the head.

Wheeler went berserk. "Two of you now, is it, two onto one?" And he got his hands around Calum's throat, squeezing and shaking.

Calum wriggled frantically, his vision reddening.

He thought: think now, now it's time to think now now now pull your hands under him and join them and try to pry him off. Your ears are clogging. Fight fight fight join hands, join them. There's Wheeler in the dock of a juvenile court, standing trial for murder, he's killed you. Your hands are together now, cup your hands and bash his fucking nose in bash his nose in bash it in.

Half blind, Calum hit Wheeler repeatedly on the upper lip and at the point of the nose until blood dripped into his mouth. Wheeler kept shaking his head, trying to hang on, but he finally let go and his hands went up to his face.

"Look!" Wheeler screamed, "Christ, what have you done to me? Look at me!" And he picked a big stone out of the dust with his bloody hands and smashed Calum in the eye with it.

Calum rolled on his side, a splitting sensation running through a mass of flashing colors in his vision. My eye's gone, was his thought, but there was no pain, no pain yet. And he saw the clouds overhead and the poplars and the pond's surface and a lot of legs, all spinning. He got up on his knees, shaking his head, expecting a kick in the face.

Someone yelled, "Dirty! Dirty! You dirty fucking bastard, Wheeler!"

Wheeler cried, "Give up now, kid, you're finished. And it's your turn next, Lightfoot, I'm gonna drown you, you little. . . "

He turned back to Calum who was standing now. "You're finished, if you give up now I'll shake your hand."

He should have given up, it would have been right, but it did not hurt anymore, and there was nothing but the word "Never" that slid out of his mouth. Calum was up now and the spins were gone and he saw that Wheeler stooped a little – it was he who had had enough, his eyes gave it away. It did not matter anymore how long the fight continued, it could go on forever for all Calum cared. It was a moment he knew from previous fights, though none had been like this. It was a moment before something very vicious set in, a moment when you felt close to the one you were going to hurt as though you were dancing with him.

He half boxed half chased Wheeler around the pond, amazed at the other's sudden lack of fight, landing nothing painful, just leading with his left and lunging upper cuts, while all the time that viciousness strengthened in him with the intention of getting Wheeler to the old tree with the exposed roots and finishing him there.

When Wheeler stumbled backwards on the first of the roots, a fury overcame Calum and he battered Wheeler's face until Wheeler held his hands out, shouting, "All right, all right, enough." Calum kicked his balls, and got on top of him, and, holding his ears, repeatedly banged the back of his head against a root until the others pulled him off and sat on him so it was impossible to tear out Mickey Wheeler's heart.

They got off him and he crawled to the tree and sat with his back against it, trying not to vomit. Everything whirled and he could smell his own blood. His head felt shattered and the scuffed shoes at the end of his body belonged to an oaflike creature other than himself.

The Gypsy kids, laughing and patting Wheeler's cheeks to bring him around, had him sitting up, groaning and spitting.

The red haired girl came with a soaked handkerchief, and held it to Calum's face. He asked her where she had put her tadpoles but she did not answer. She had lightly freckled cheeks and white eyebrows, and wore a green pullover and faded jeans. The handkerchief felt cold against his swollen eye – it smelled faintly of frogs. His shirt was gone and the scratches that covered his chest and back began to sting.

Shadows stood above him.

"You all right? You've gone really pale."

"Is he all right?"

"Yeah, he's all right."

"Calum? You all right, mate?"

"I feel sick."

"Oh, he can talk, then."

"Christ, Leith, that was a bloody good fight."

"I'm gonna be sick."

"Don't be sick," said Pete, "They'll claim it."

Rough oak bark dug into Calum's spine, but he couldn't move himself. Holding the red headed girl's handkerchief to his face, he said:

"Where's Iris? Is Iris all right?"

"Christ knows. Scarpered, ain't she? All upset about them frogs, the silly cow. You went one way and she went the other."

Someone brought the torn rag of his shirt, threw it in his lap and said, "You ain't seen the last of this, Leith."

As if in a dream, Calum waved whoever spoke away with a hand movement, and mimed "bollocks" with the side of his face. The red haired girl took his shirt to the water to rinse it, leaving him the handkerchief. Calum sat up a bit, and being careful not to move his split lip, said to Pete:

"I'm glad old Iris didn't see that. She hates fights."

Pete gave him a sideways glance and laughed, "Pull the other one, Cal, it's got bells on."

"What?"

"You done it for her."

"I didn't. Not really, anyway."

"Get away."

"Honest, it was. . . "

Pete walked away and began cleaning his fingernails with his penknife. Calum shrugged. Some kids were hanging around: hero worshippers. He wanted to chase them off but he was too tired, his eye throbbed and itched terribly.

He saw Wheeler being helped away through the weeds by his mates.

The red headed girl's handkerchief felt tepid now against Calum's face. He watched her, crouching beside the water, scrubbing blood from his shirt. "Why're you doing that?" he called, but she did not answer, and the silently passing clouds, casting cold shadows, seemed to him like the powdered wigs of high court judges. He was in a packed courtroom – it was the unfinished interior of a new town-house. "Now," he was telling the court, "this land belongs to Southend-on-sea Corporation, and by ancient charter it can't be parceled out to builders. This, friends, is progress." There were three frowning magistrates; his father was one, and Captain Dobson and his wife, Elsie, were the others. The jury was made up only of women. There was something odd about the women of the jury, they all had bulging red eyes and big smiles on their green faces.

Pete shook him out of the nice scene.

He had the shivers. Pete said, "I don't think you should fall asleep, Cal. Shall I go and get your mum?"

The cool, wet shirt was rolled up behind Calum's neck. The handkerchief was gone.

"Where's that red headed bird?" Calum said.

"What red headed bird?"

"She was just here, she gave me that handkerchief and washed my shirt – that red headed bird."

"I dunno, but I reckon you've got a bit of concussion, mate. She's one of

Wheeler's old bunk-ups, I expect. You wanna come with me, or should I go and get your old lady?"

Calum looked at him and shook his head, "You don't understand anything, Lightfoot. You're an ignorant fuck."

"I'll go and get your old lady," said Pete, and took off through the high yellow-topped weeds toward the part of the road where the bulldozers were parked.

Calum could only see out of one eye, but he thought he caught a glimpse of the girl with red hair disappearing into the trees at the Thundersley end of Greenacres Common. He was calm now. He had done something right and he had done something wrong, and there was nothing to be done about it now because it was all tangled up together like a complicated headache that would take a long time to go away.

THE
ANOBIID

Awareness rises from an abyss and you're stimulated by pink light piercing your eyelids. As yet there's no inner sight; no self. Slowly, you cross the boundary between inside and outside.

Then there is the sound of bells.

Then there is the sound of birds.

A fading dream flickers, its severed tail vanishing; but without halting it, fixing it with memory, you let it unthread itself and hurtle into darkness and deformity.

You feel and see.

You recognize your parents' bedroom. This is a slight shock because you're on the floor in the corner, opposite their double bed, in a makeshift nest of eiderdowns and musty smelling winter curtains. You're sweating. You want to shut out all sound. You're sorry that you can't sink back into oblivion and escape the gruesome pink light cast by the thin red summer curtains in the window facing due east.

It's around nine o'clock on a bright morning in early autumn.

This is like selecting the peripheral pieces of a jigsaw puzzle – this haphazard registering of details with straight edges. You're learning to be selective, to not choose terrible pieces from the center of the picture. But the room is full of smells and impressions that cause a prickling sensation to creep along the layers of your skin. You know what you've done but you hold the hardness of it behind the vision of your mind's eye.

These pealing bells of St. Clement's mean it's Sunday.

Sunday.

You used to sing in the choir. For a second you smell thick incense, and a small part of you is soothed by the ringing bells. And the sparrows, it sounds like a mighty flock of them, are squabbling in the gutter that overhangs the window.

Downstairs and along the passage in the kitchen, the kettle begins to wail, low at first, then louder like a train coming out of the night. Your mother is there, clattering things. Soon you must face her.

The number twenty-five grinds by in The Broadway, its weight shuddering up the building to the floorboards under you. You put your hands over your ears and shut your eyes so that colored patterns swirl around in the red blackness. You can feel your own heartbeat through the palms of your hands: nine beats every ten seconds: "Fighting fit" your father would say. You want to shut out all sound of him but your memory booms with night movements, crashes and shouts. You sit up so quickly that your back muscles hurt. Inside your head you plead: Be quiet, be quiet, be quiet.

Somehow Mother made the double bed without waking you, but she left clothing strewn over the furniture in the room. The pink light coming through the blood red curtains is similar to what comes through eyelids, only back where the brain should be is a dried up shrunken pith in a hollow skull. It's painful being so condensed. Coming from the void, like the afterbirth of your waking, you experience the sudden knowledge of death. It's there in front of you, a familiar but uncontrollable pall dropping across your vision, invisible yet black. When you die you leave the world and enter oblivion and the world carries on without you for ever and ever. . .amen. You try to stave this off with a sweet song:

> All things bright and beautiful,
> All creatures great and small;
> All things wise and wonderful,
> The Lord God made them all. . .

but there's no softening the stiff knowledge of non-being and annihilation. Your face sweats. You're committing the big sin, despair.

You suffer in this state until the bells stop. When the sparrows fly away it sounds like the single flap of a giant prehistoric wing. And now you can hear your mother again, down at the far end of the maisonette, clanking kitchen utensils. Your dog, the old black labrador who always sleeps beside you, is gone. You touch your face and feel the swollen cheekbone; your jaw is stiff and painful to open, and you're sweating, sweating.

Memories out of the walls, out of the snowy ceiling that absorbs shadows, out of the mirror, the wardrobe, the drawers, the smells of bedding, attack you. The last crisis, a year before perhaps: Your mother flew across the room like a rag doll and landed in your long tin toy box, her legs in the air, one slipper flying off. Her nightie went up around her waist and you saw her cunt. You stood in the doorway, shouting. Your father came toward you, his face expressionless, lips tight; his left fist hit your stomach and the right went bang in your mouth, splitting the upper left side of your lip. You spun away, stepped into your windowless room and fell gasping on the bed, acting a little. He returned to her. . .ʾshe screamed your name. . .you heard punching and kicking . . . .Trembling, you went and stood on the landing by the stairs and yelled, "Leave her alone, you fucking bastard."

The house shuddered as he left her and ran across the room in a fury. He pulled the door aside and flew at you, but you ducked, and with all your weight, barged him under the left ribs, so that he tumbled down the stairs.

He lay half-way down, puffing, floundering on his back, you'd hurt his war injury, his delicate spine. "You've buggered up my back," he said, "You'd better come and help." He didn't feel beaten because you'd cheated, fouled him like the hooligan you'll always be. You helped him up the stairs; he was suddenly an ancient man with fragile bones. "You're bleeding like a pig," he wheezed, "It isn't manly to bleed like that. Stop it." And when you helped him into bed, your blood dripping on his tea-stained singlet which is all he ever sleeps in, he tried to hit you again from his prostrate position. You can still feel the wind of his fist — it could've knocked you senseless. You went to your room and slept until noon the next day, missing school again.

From that night on he got sicker and sicker. Doctor Lenox said it was alcoholic poisoning, but you knew that pushing him down the stairs had set it all off. There are things beyond a doctor's knowledge.

Your father was dying. You carried the television upstairs and put it on the chest of drawers close to him. You and your mother would sit in the double bed with the dying man and watch "News at Ten" and "Danger Man" and "The Saint" and "The Avengers." One night there was a news flash: President Kennedy had been shot. You thought the world would soon be at war. The room smelled sickly sweet, a smell you couldn't get used to; it clung to you, you took it to school with you, you could smell it on your fingers.

You came home one night from a dance and found the place filled with a queer atmosphere. All the lights were dark yellow and your mother sat by the coal fire wrapped in an eiderdown. She told you things that made you shiver and keep an eye out over your shoulder:

Your father was in his crisis. His soul was trying to pull away from his body like a fly from glue paper, but it was stuck fast in him, corroded into place by an abominable life. He was trapped between life and death, locked in the temporal, the corporeal, like a vampire, a zombie, an artificial human. When she'd gone to check on him, she'd seen a black cloud hovering over the bed. The room, as always, was lit by one heavily shaded bedside lamp. The cloud, she said, had tried to descend onto him, but kept bouncing back up, sometimes as far as the ceiling. In his delirium he repeatedly said there was a Highlander waiting for him in the corner. She was afraid and came downstairs, shut all the doors except the one to the living room so that she would hear him if he cried out, and sat by the fire with the dog, hoping you would come home early, but you didn't. At midnight, she heard someone walking around in the bedroom. She said the dog began to whimper and moan. Everything was quiet for a while until a heavy man came clumping down the stairs in hard walking shoes; he was a giant man with red hair and a kilt. He walked down the hall into the kitchen, and she knew that the crisis was over and that your father had cheated death.

"And this all happened tonight while I was at a dance?" you asked. "Just now," she said, "It all happened just now."

Terrified, you went up to see for yourself. He was lying comfortably, with the eiderdown pulled up to his chin, looking around the room with his wild blue eyes.

"You all right, Dad?"

"Yes, lad. How was the dance? Were there lots of pretty girls?"

"There were, but they're all taken. And the ones left are giggly and plastered in make-up."

"Och well, you're all bairns yet. There's plenty of time to grow up, isn't there?"

"I suppose."

"Will you do me a wee favor and get me a glass of milk and a chunk of white bread?"

"Okay."

"Thank you. And ask your mother to come up."

"Dad?"

"Yes, lad."

You sat beside him on the bed and put your arm across his chest:

"Why can't you always be like this?"

So that he couldn't see your eyes, you laid your head on the quilt. He put his fingers through your hair. His heart was beating rapidly under your ear. He said: "You need a haircut. You look like a yobo. Go on, bugger off and get me some supper." He ruffled your hair and gave your head a gentle push.

Keeping your face turned from his, you went to the door.

"Dad?"

"Yes, boy."

"Was there a man up here earlier? Mum said there was a man, a Scotsman."

"Hell's bells," he laughed, "What on earth . . .?"

"I don't know. She said she saw him come down the stairs and then she knew you'd be okay."

He laughed:

"That's my Guardian Ancestor yarn by the sounds of it. Mum's always been quite bonkers over that sort of nonsense. It's that touch of blarney running through her, I'm afraid. Now, what about my milk?"

Once, much later, you dreamed that the Highlander was leaning over your bed, looking into your face. You screamed and Mother came into your room and sat beside you. It was three in the morning. You shouldn't be frightened of him, she told you, he's here to protect you. He protects your destiny against the forces that would, if they could, break up the pattern of life. He'll always be there to back you up.

Another time, you were frightened in the night and cried out; there was something invisible in the room. Mother came in and said there was no such things as ghosts, that a great big thirteen stone prop forward like you had no need to be afraid of shadows. What you wanted was to crawl into bed between your parents and sleep safely one last time, but you were bigger than both of them by then and it would've looked ridiculous.

This room terrifies you. Vaguely you know that it is your mother that has dislodged something in your mind with her Celtic propensity for spinning ordinary life into nightmares. You're sick of lies, they always end in battles; you're sick of battles, you want peace. There's no future for you — what will you be when you're thirty, fifty, seventy? A failure with an unusual name, and then you and your unusual name will die and be oblivious as the world goes on without you for millions of years until the whole thing has nucleated into a system of cold pebbles circling a chunk of coke.

You hear your mother come to the bottom of the stairs and listen. She will want you to rest, she won't give you a wake up call. She walks quietly back to the kitchen.

Last night was the culmination. Your analytical powers are too primitive to identify what it is, but there's something that you can never go back to, something that will remain forever inchoate; you've got the smell of your father's blood awash in your nostrils.

You leap, naked, from the floor and look for your dressing gown. It is in a blue pile on the gray carpet next to your father's side of the bed.

Behind the door is your father's old brown dressing gown. You make do with that, ramming your arms down the sleeves. You stamp into your slippers, trying to control the hairs which are beginning to stand up on the back of your neck.

Attempting composure you begin to descend, counting each step, resisting a look back up in case you catch a glimpse of the kilted legs on the landing behind the banisters. It's a predominantly white stairwell, with a skylight in the sloping ceiling that floods the stairs with light from the western side of the roof. The walls are white, the banisters and wainscoting are cream, but the struts supporting the rail have been maintained in their original varnished state. The stair carpet is a floral pattern, predominantly red. But none of this matters because you notice that two of the struts have been punched out, and pale splintered wood shows where the square heads have broken away from under the cream railing. Above this the railing is smeared with dried snot and blood.

Half way down you stand still: look, there's nothing there. It's all a lie, a dream.

No dream, your mother has said, I've seen him. He's your ancestor. He's always here.

Last night your father consumed two bottles of Black and White scotch whisky, and around one o'clock something came loose in his mind and he wanted to kill everyone: your mother, you, the dog. He put a carving knife down his sock for protection against the ancestor he saw staring at him wherever he looked. "It's my dirk," he said, "get out from under my roof, you traitors. You've brought this mercenary into the house, this devil. It wants my blood . . . blood will have blood. Get out of my sight!"

You look up and the emptiness of the landing scares you. You bound down into the hall.

The hall is different. You associate it with anger, and anger is safer than fear. The long walls of the hall are painted pink, but it's very dark because there's no light coming from the lounge, and so the pink is distorted into yellows and grays. Mother hasn't opened the curtains or started the fire in the lounge. You feel cold.

The kitchen is thirty yards away at the end of the hall but there are three closed doors to pass before you get there. With your left hand you touch the railing of the stairway that descends to the street beside the shop window of the chemist. You could go down the stairs, open the front door and look into the street; it might be full of sunlight, or it might be a white blur — there might be nothing beyond the conspiracy of the door, just a sanitary white void the opposite of sleep.

Underfoot are sharp particles from the grandfather clock. You switch on a light to inspect it. The clock is stopped at 1:35. Quick, avoid being sucked back into the electricity of last night: switch off the light.

The clock's silence is weird — its first silence. It has internal damage. You heard its inner workings fall through the trunk when you helped Mother lift it upright after the police and ambulance men left. The carpet is covered in spilled faece from the serried flight holes of wood-boring beetles that have infested the clock for generations: "*Xestobium refuvillosum*," your father taught you, "the Death Watch beetle." Once he told you that they're impossible to eradicate and that their tapping in the old oak clock had accompanied many a solemn family death. Some panels of the clock casing, especially at the plinth and feet, had long ago been replaced with pine which was now riddled with common woodworm, the *Anobium punctatum* whose yellow powder leaks like dried blood from a pharaoh's sarcophagus. You bend and touch the faece with your fingers, sniff it into your nose, finding no smell. You imagine how it must feel to live so long in the wood as a soft, hungry grub and to suddenly emerge, hard shelled and brittle, for no purpose other than to breed and die. The antique's hood will soon snap off from its own weight.

You're standing between the two bedroom doors. The first door, which you managed to pass without thought, leads into a room where the deaths of

Mr. Lloyd, Mrs. Turk and Mr. Robinson occurred. The bedroom door that you have yet to pass used to be called the lucky room because no one had died in it. But the Reverend K. C. Jones changed that.

The rooms are empty because Father has driven away Mother's convalescence business. The old people won't come now because it's known that your father sits, steaming in his lounge chair all day, drinking whisky and smoking pack after pack of Players. There have been no referrals since Reverend Jones passed away six weeks ago. If his family hadn't all been so old there would've been a lawsuit.

You stand in front of the stopped clock, listening to your mother finishing yesterday's washing up. When she seems to be done, you walk to the half-decorated kitchen and look in as she picks up a cup of tea and sips, staring out of the window.

Paint cans are stacked in the corner by the back door and two brushes have gone hard in a large Maxwell House jar of evaporated turpentine. The kitchen smells of turps and earthy potatoes. Mother blows on her tea, sips it, staring ahead fixedly. You want to shake her, wake her up; but her light red hair tumbles over her shoulders, the hem of her white nightie is showing beneath her green dressing gown and her sleeves are rolled half way up her forearms.

Outside, indirect sunlight reflects off the whitewashed brick wall of the building across the alley. It's not going to be a sunny day, but overcast and gray as usual. You stay in the doorway and murmur: "Mum."

Your mother spills some tea in her saucer as she turns around. Her right eye bulges like a ripe compressed plum. The deep purple mass threatens to burst off her face. The cheekbone back as far as her ear is blue and puffy. Sensing your suffering, she quickly turns her face away from you.

"Oh, Darling, you scared me. I thought you were Dad in that old dressing gown."

"Sorry."

"It's all right, my darling. Funny you should be wearing that. I bought it for him at the bazaar in Bombay the year before you were born. I was just dreaming about India. . .how I loved it. I expect you'd like a nice cup of tea."

"All right."

You feel as though you fill the doorway. For the first time there is a scent of your father — his shaving cream on the collar of the dressing gown. You go and squeeze into the chair between the table and the refrigerator, the dressing gown pulling tightly across your shoulders.

Visible through the window, perched on an orange chimney pot above the gray slates of next door's roof, is an almost motionless seagull. It puffs out its chest, the yellow bill thick and hooked at the end, made for digging deep in the guts of dead fish.

"I wonder what time it is?"

"God knows. He buggered the clock good and proper, you know." Facing the window again, she picks up a pint of milk, shakes it above the draining board and selects a mug from the rack of drying china.

"Not that one," you say. "Any but that."

She reselects, pours in milk, then a teaspoon of sugar, and holding the pot above the mug with both hands, pours the tea. Its steam smells like hot flowers. She lowers the pot, snaps off the flow and plonks it back on the hob. Stirring the tea with a spoon in the mug, she turns and brings it to you at the table.

Watching her monstrous eye, you absently stir your tea. She goes back over to her place by the sink and picks up her own cup.

"How's the tea?"

"The best."

"You've not tasted it yet, boy."

"Good smell."

"Are you hungry? Want an omelette?"

"Don't mind."

She puts her tea down, comes over and holds your face in her cold hands, and asks, "Did he hurt you, love? I saw him catch you one before he staggered upstairs to try and find his bottle."

"Hurt me? Christ, Mum, it doesn't matter if he hurt me. What about you — look at you. And look at him. What about him?"

"But are you hurt?"

"Nothing worse than I get from rugby."

Touching your swollen jaw, she says, "If he's harmed those lovely teeth of yours, I'll kill him." She places her forehead on yours so that the tips of both noses touch and you can see window light penetrating deep into her hazel iris; it makes you think of the sea. She has made up her good eye with fresh mascara and her skin smells of Ponds Cold Cream. Her smashed eye is demonic: If the lid should open you might shriek in terror.

"You mustn't think about it, darling. Keep it outside you, separate."

"But I keep playing it back."

"What?"

"That last hit."

"It's a bad dream. Let it go out of your head, my son."

"But I did it. I can feel every second of it. The impact is still in my knuckles, all up my arm and into my neck."

"Some things are fated to happen."

"Rubbish! That's bloody rubbish, Mum. Like all the family stories, all the ghosts and weirdos. . . . It's bullshit and I'm sick of it."

"Well." She turns her back to you, probably thinking you're hysterical, and of course, you are.

The dog whines and scratches to come in at the back door. Another gull lands on the roof opposite, and a flock of sparrows flashes across the window. Mother

63

turns and gets a carton of eggs out of the larder — a peppery smell of spices, cheese, earth, damp plaster, comes into the kitchen.

She says:

"Have you got rugger today, son?"

"It's Sunday. I played yesterday."

"Oh yes. Who did you play? Did you win? Did you score a try?"

"Mum. Will he be all right?"

She opens a drawer, hunts noisily for something among the cutlery: "I expect so."

The dog scratches louder at the back door.

At the other end of the table, at Father's place, there's a folded copy of last night's *Evening News* with the crossword half done in your father's immaculate lettering. Its incompleteness is infuriating. You would finish it yourself but you know you're stupid and won't be able to get the clues: Good for nothing but rugby and being a dustman when you leave school. You are a brainstem, laddie, perfect cannon fodder for the Americans to use in their next war. It is hard for me to believe that I have brought a being into the world with the form of a god and the content of a reptile.

Mother says:

"It was like having Titans in the house with you two going at it. The whole place shook. He's had it his own way long enough. He'll think twice before throwing his weight around in future." Then she starts her routine:

"The booze has done it to him, of course. Rots the brain, rivets the soul to the rib cage. And he's drunk up any heritage you might've expected. The bills from the off license still aren't paid and probably won't be — you never recover from liquor debt — if they make me bankrupt too, we're finished. But he'll be okay: that bugger's tougher than old boots."

Mother opens the back door, letting in the black labrador who parades around the kitchen, grinning and fanning his tail. Your eyes are on the matte red hues that spoil the gloss of his coat. You ask:

"What'll they do with him?"

"Stitch him up, dry him out, and send him home, most likely. He'll charm them, just like he's charmed everyone who ever confronted him over his behavior. They'll be thinking it's all my fault by now. He'll have them eating out of his hand with those big blue eyes of his. You can't help admiring it. There's something irresistible about him, you see. I'd swear he's a reincarnation of that Rasputin chap."

"But all the blood . . . "

She interrupts you:

"I'll deal with that. Don't think about it."

"It's in the gray carpet. Last night it was as black as tar. I threw my dressing gown over it."

"He's got black blood. Black blood from a black heart."

You shake your head:

"No. It was red. Light red. I could smell whisky in it. It pumped out of his eye and onto the carpet. I tried to stop it but it kept coming, pint after pint, and he just sat on the edge of the bed insulting me, letting the blood flow onto the carpet and turn black."

"Oh, for heaven's sake stop being so morbid, it's unmanly. Enough about blood."

"No, Mum, no. It made a black pool in the carpet. It'll never come out, it'll be in there forever, it'll be in the floorboards forever, it'll come through and stain the living room ceiling."

"You're getting on my nerves, boy."

You slug back your tea and push the mug across the table. You both watch the dog lap water from his bowl. After a minute, Mother says:

"I always call you and I shouldn't. I shouldn't involve you . . . the things you've seen in your young life."

"I'm not a child anymore."

"No. You're a big strong lad, but it is wicked of me to call you when he starts."

"He'd have killed you."

"I doubt it. I can handle him."

"If you can handle him, why do you always whip him into a rage? He's all right until you start needling him."

"I see. I'm to blame then?"

"No, of course not. But you do egg him on. You twist the knife in him and you both start saying terrible things. You think I don't understand it all but I do."

"What an imagination. What have you heard? Nothing! And what about the things he's said to me? Christ almighty!"

"I know."

"You don't know. You think you do, but you don't. I've spent my last penny on that bastard. He's wasted everything since we came back from India. I buy him his booze and fags and he sits on his arse all day, complaining of his bad back, his so-called war injury."

"His back was hurt in the war."

"Is that so? Why can't I get a pension out of the Admiralty for him then? They're very hush-hush and frightfully polite, oh God yes, but there'll never be a pension. I bet he ruined his career with some heinous outrage. He was an incorrigible piss artist even back then."

"Well Mum, it's you that buys the booze. Then you hide it when he's had a few too many. Buy it for him, and then take it away? That's brilliant, that is. It turns him into a whirling dervish, a human cyclone."

"You're a stinker to blame me. How can you suddenly take his side when you've seen all that's happened over the years?"

"Nothing's changed. I'm just trying to think more clearly."

Her face is pale; she's gritting her teeth. "Huh, it'll be a miracle the day you get a clear thought. You'll never have the mind of your father you know, and . . . "

In a low calm voice, you interrupt:

"I didn't believe him, but he told me once that you manipulate me against him. You don't do you?"

She stares at you. Her swollen eye seems to throb: you're more frightened of her than anything alive. She turns around and pours another tea, her nostrils flaring as if what you said brought a filthy smell into the room. She mutters:

"He's jealous. He hates us to confide. But believe what you like."

"I'm sorry, Mum. I'm just confused. Stuff isn't the way I've been told. I used to believe everything but now it's all such bullshit. All of it. Do you know what I mean?"

"I know damn well what you mean, my lad. Life's not easy, as you'll learn all too soon."

"Wouldn't you say I am learning?"

"You'll learn. I've tried to protect you from the worst of it, but soon you'll find what a lonely thing life is. It's time for you to grow up . . . "

You roll your eyes, there's a throbbing in your ears again. You can't communicate now; she's talking from deep inside herself where the actual meaning of words doesn't matter, only the emotion that sends forth the sound. She's disconnecting from you, sounding instead of speaking, and the only things you can rely on are hard, real things like chairs and table tops and animals who can't think deeply enough to create mysteries.

Your mother has her damaged eye pointed at you, she says:

"Anyway. Why did you hit your father so hard?"

She cracks eggs into a blue bowl as you stare at her.

"I was protecting you."

"You followed him upstairs, and you punched him. I was down here . . . "

"You were in the bathroom with an ice pack on your eye . . . "

"I was beyond help. You followed him upstairs and beat him up."

"Mum, I'm not going to let you do this, you know it wasn't like that. You should argue fairly. Why are people unfair in arguments? Why do they say what they and the other person know to be wrong? Why is it like a game?"

"Life is not a game of rugby. There are no rules for arguments. You've got to just get on with it." And she raps on the top of your head with her knuckle, speaking through clenched teeth: "Why" rap "don't" rap "you" rap "wake" rap "up?" rap.

"That hurt."

She begins vigorously beating the eggs in the blue bowl:

"Go and tidy the bedrooms and light the fire in the lounge. I'll call you when the omelette's ready. Go." Her red hair has come down across her cheek and the taut muscles of her forearm stand out as do the distinct veins in her large sculptured hands.

You go into the hall. The grandfather clock is leaking dry yellow powder. You go past it, stand at the top of the stairs that lead down to the white street. The rooms of the dead have their doors closed, and upstairs, a ghost that you know doesn't exist awaits you. If you can get rid of him, disperse him in the sleep void, you will know there is no such thing as a soul, and if there's no such thing as a soul, you are lost, doomed to the black eternity that yawns below the thin net of dreams that your life swings in.

Behind, you hear your mother mutter something. It takes a while to understand the words, for them to become English. She'd said:

"Bloody vicious little swine."

Her words make you hollow and silent as you stand still in the dark hall. You wish, oh how you wish, that circumstances were such that you could be new again, and that it would be possible to love such a thing as a father.

BOTTLES AND BRICKS AND WALKING STICKS

Hiho hiho, it's off to work we go
With a bottle and a brick
And a walking stick
Hiho hiho hiho hiho . . .
— old London football song.

We're in Mavis's caff having a bit of breakfast, waiting for the drizzle to clear so we can get cracking on the fascia wall of this factory we're almost done with. Ken Cooper, he's our governor, pays by the day, so we don't exactly mind sitting around. It's not like skiving or anything. He's not the kind of bloke to take liberties with our old bones. He trusts us and we trust him, so we'll work 'til the light gives out — once the rain stops. We never work in no rain.

Ken's not here yet, he's probably lost again, picking up this new laborer over Thundersley way. Poor old Ken's always getting lost. Distracted, you see, too many worries. He needs an extra bloke to help get this contract finished by Friday so we can start the Wiggins job on Canvey Island — and this weather's a right bastard, buggering up everything. Spike, Ken's son, didn't help neither when he laid in bed all Wednesday with an hangover. When he doesn't come in neither does the other hod carrier, Hammer, because Spike's got the motor and Hammer's banned – hit the jackpot with speeding tickets. So we didn't get very far Wednesday – bricklayers make lousy laborers, specially our lot – and Ken was going spare, too worried to get any speed up with the old trowel. Yes, Wednesday was a right cock-up.

It's not often Ken gets a new bloke. He relies a lot on Hammer, who's about the best laborer you ever saw – a bloody great ox of a boy he is, about six-two, the brick shit-house type. Though I'll tell you, he's brighter than all of us put together. Reads all the time, see. God knows why he hangs about with Spike, who's about the laziest, most irresponsible, redheaded little git you ever saw. You have to blame Ken, of course – he pampers that boy. But it has to be said: the kid's a nutter and that's all there is to it. He ought to be locked up and the key flushed down the karsi.

The trouble with Hammer is he's always got a book with him – economics, politics, sociology, philosophy – all that bumf. But you have to admire the lad for trying to better himself. He'll go to college one of these days if he can get past all this socialist stuff he's into, but right now he's the best hoddy and ditch digger you ever saw, and you never seen him skiving unless that little sod, Spike, put him up to it.

Anyhow, Ken wants a big push today – get this fascia wall finished. Then Friday we'll take down the scaffold and do all the clean-up so we can yomp our clobber over to Canvey Island Saturday morning.

In spite of the rain outside and the misted-up glass inside, you can just about see the factory wall through the window. From here you wouldn't know it's not finished. It looks like the side of a bleeding great river monster, a blue one, lying in the mist. Blue because it's built with high-grade engineering bricks what're four times as heavy as your ordinary house brick. The boys hate hodding them and we hate laying them, but they're beautiful once they're up. Some Kraut company's building this whole industrial estate, so the quality's there. Ordinary bricks would do just as well. Still, it's their money.

There's something that gets to you about a building site in the rain, the heavy equipment just lying about. You can look across the road from Mavis's here and see the nearest part of the wall, looming above the gouged-up ground, two and a half stories high, studded with rusty scaffolding, rising to meet the steel framework that's the bones of the factory. When you're out there working there's the smell of cement and diesel and wet air. But go back a few months later: the building you sweated your balls off on, even bled on, will be bright and new. The muddy pits and potholes you trudged through will be landscaped over – grass and shrubs and trees and car park – nothing to do with you. It's as if the whole thing appeared by magic off some bloody great set of plans. You see those little ponces on the evening news, architects and civil engineers, standing beside some porky princess as she cuts the blue ribbon. That's why we sometimes leave a little memento, something that'll outlast us: a new coin laid into the masonry, names and insults scratched into the bricks. The blokes are always pissing in the mortar, and sometimes we find a nice long turd to cement into the brickwork.

I never used to think much about any of this until Hammer started talking about it. He calls it proletarian alienation. That's a bit of a mouthful for most of us. Gut-wrenching's more my way of putting it.

Talk about alienation, here's a gut-wrencher for you:

We've never been keen on new blokes. We know who we like and stick to them, so new blokes are hard on everybody. The last one was a big curly-headed mick called Corrigan. He was a bit of a plonker in some ways, but to give him his due he could lay bricks with the best of us. He'd work steadily all day, puffing fags, rabbiting on to no one in particular, getting more and more out of line, until someone gave him a mouthful. Then he'd laugh his head off and say us English are a grim race of god-forsaken miseries. He'd sing them silly IRA songs — he wasn't really political, he just liked to get your goat — so it wasn't surprising when young Spike starts to get a bit quiet and give him the evil eye.

From the first, though, Corrigan and Hammer got on well. Corrigan had a quick mouth on him and Hammer liked that. They'd crack back and forth all day, joking, taking the piss, singing dirty words to popular songs. After a while they'd have made a good team.

Once, we were rained out and sitting in the tea hut of some site and Corrigan started talking about Ireland. He said he came from the far west where people didn't speak English and on a clear day you could see across the Atlantic to Boston if you were that way inclined. One day a Dublin firm wanted to build a plant in a field that once belonged to his grandfather. Corrigan got the contract to do the brickwork, hired his relatives and finished the job, which made the publicans of his town rich men. Some years later, he said, when there was no work and Christmas was close and his kids needed shoes, he had to go along and ask for a job at the plant.

They weren't going to start him, but someone reminded the boss that Corrigan had done the brickwork, and very fine brickwork it was, and what a strange thing it would be if there was no place to work inside a shelter you'd built with your own hands. The boss didn't see the logic in this, but the word got around and there would've been a strike if they hadn't started Corrigan as a janitor. He spent eight hours a day, he said, sweeping the concrete floor with a wide broom — sweeping up specks — all the time thinking of the walls he'd built with his own hands.

The tea hut was very quiet that day and you could hear rain falling soft but steady on the tarpaper roof. Us brickies sat real still, looking down into our tea. Corrigan's teeth were clenched, and it's hard to be sure, but there may have been tears in his eyes — they're like that, the Irish, emotional. After several minutes a chair scraped: Hammer's got up and taken Corrigan's mug over to the tea urn for a refill. He comes back and plonks the mug down in front of Corrigan. Corrigan nodded at it, picked it up and drank. Hammer says to us:

"You know something? Only you blokes could understand this shit. When you think about it it's a right bastard, isn't it?"

And then Spike burst into the hut, full of jokes, and the moment ended. We don't often get deep like that in the building trade but when the odd moment hits you can rely on some pillock like Spike to bugger it up.

Oh, Gawd, here we go now, Spike's Capri roaring up with his radio blaring. The doors slam. In walks Hammer, yawning and scratching his blond crewcut, his eyes looking tired and small from reading. He nods, winks, and here it comes:

"Here we all are then, the seven dwarfs."

Every day he says this.

Us, all together: "Fuck you, Snow White!"

Laughing and shoving our shoulders, Hammer says, "Morning Dave, you old dosser. Win anything yesterday in the three o'clock? No? Well, you will take tips from that Reg bloke. Oh, hello, Reg, me old darling, all right, are you? All right, Jack?"

"Wotcha Pete, you wrinkly old bleeder," he says to me, "How's the iron lung, how's the pacemaker, how's the club foot?" I swing one at his goolies but he dodges it. "You'll have to move faster than that if you're gonna feel me up, Pete."

"Oh, and fuck me," he says, "if it isn't little old Albert the fascist, sitting among the workers. . . "

A volley of insults makes him put his hands in front of his face as if to protect it from flying turds.

Spike saunters in, hands in pockets, says, "Morning all," and goes to the counter. He has this high piping voice for when he's taking the piss.

"Hello Mavis," he says, "My, you do look tasty this morning. All dressed up for me old man when he gets here, are you? What's the special today, then? Fried foreskins?"

Mavis doesn't even look at him. "The Works," she says, "You know perfectly well that Thursdays is always The Works."

"You're right, love, I should know perfectly well. Silly old me," he pipes, looking around at us, winking. "So come on then, Mavis. Run through it."

"Piss off."

"Oh come on, old love! I've been looking forward to you running off the works menu all night. I could hardly sleep."

Mavis, knowing he'll keep on, gives in and sighs:

"Egg, fried slice, bacon, sausage, tomato, mushrooms, black pudding, bread and butter. Tea."

"Oh Mavis. Are you trying to cheat me? You forgot the choice of baked beans or bubble 'n' squeak."

"I said beans or bubble."

"You never."

"I bloody well did."

Laughing like a machine gun and looking around at the rest of us, Spike says, "All right, Mavis. Have it your way. Give us a special, but hold the beans or bubble. I hate that navvy food."

"Little ponce," says Mavis. She smiles at Hammer: "And what would you like, Ham?"

"Ham!" interrupts Spike, mimicking Mavis's voice, "I expect you could use a big sausage this morning," and fires off his stupid laugh.

Hammer, ignoring Spike, leans across the counter, winks and says, "I want your body, Mavis."

Mavis cocks her eyebrow at him, "Yeah well, you might get it if you're not careful," and angling her eyes back toward the kitchen where her old man heats up food, she says, "The chance'ud be a fine thing."

Hammer looks down, smiling, calming down the silliness, says:

"Right you are, Mavis. Give us a couple of fried egg rolls and a cup of tea, all right, love?"

"Righto, darling," she laughs, then frowns at Spike:

"And you, you little bleeder, get out of it!"

The boys sit down by the window. They don't talk. Hammer pulls out a red paperback and starts reading. Spike doodles with his finger in the condensation on the plate glass. He writes *North Bank Rules OK*. That's him and Hammer's football gang, named after where the hooligans stand during the matches. Then he draws a big pair of tits hanging down from a very lifelike horizontal torso. He goes on to do the rest of her body and then the balls and cock of some geezer going up her from behind. Where he did her nipples, the condensation's gathered and two streams of water suddenly run down the glass.

No restraint, you see. The kid's got no restraint. You daren't say anything — get your head kicked in. That's how it ended with that Corrigan. What a shambles that turned into. Corrigan didn't know what he was dealing with, of course, coming from the west of Ireland and all. It's Ken you feel sorry for, though. It's him'll have to foot the bill to keep that hooligan offspring of his out of borstal and he'll pay Corrigan's workman's comp for the rest of his life.

We were working down Benfleet way one Monday and Corrigan had been mouthing it off all morning and afternoon as usual. We'd been down the pub dinner time because it was a real scorcher, and he'd had a bellyful of cold Guinness. Spike and Hammer had been on the strong ale, which is stupid at that time of day and stupider still in hot weather, and they were trying to sweat it out, getting some steam up with the bricks and muck. We were all joking about Spike working so hard — his dad was flabbergasted. Old Ken loves it when the lads get a rivalry going, it's money in his pocket.

But Corrigan was purposely staying ahead, straining himself just to needle them, and every time he ran out of materials he'd wail like a banshee and start saying what lazy, useless hoddies they were, and that we'd be better off hiring nig-nogs at half the wage. It got a bit beyond a joke, and even Hammer, who'd been bantering back at him, warned him to leave it out. So Spike's walking along the scaffold with a hodful of muck and Corrigan makes some crack which prompts Spike to dump the whole thing over his head. We laughed at first, but a scuffle started and the whole scaffold wobbled. Holding Spike by the throat, Corrigan lifted him off his feet and was about to throw him over the side.

It just blew up: Hammer got between them and freed Spike, but Corrigan went berserk and started throwing punches. It was awesome watching Hammer fending off the blows with his forearms, and then, like a pro, delivering a kick, a headbutt, a left, a right, another left; and Corrigan's on his arse wondering what week he's in.

That should've been the end of it – when you got young blokes working hard in the heat that sort of thing'll happen now and again – but as Corrigan's getting up, rubbing his jaw, saying, "Good roight hand you've got dere, Hammer, me son. Oi'll concede to you, by God," Spike comes running up and smacks Corrigan on the back of the head with a spade.

The flat side of a spade hitting the back of a man's head is a sound you never forget. If Hammer hadn't grabbed him, Spike was that furious he would've used the sharp edge to cut that paddy's head clean off. Pretty soon there's an ambulance and the site's swarming with old bill. Ken's looking in the window of the squad car, crying, "For fuck's sake, son, for fuck's sake!"

Hammer, all covered in blood and shouting orders, showed the ambulance men how to get the stretcher off the scaffold. Spike sat in the squad car, staring down at the handcuffs, while the cops stood around, having a smoke. Hammer had to go along to the cop-shop too, but he didn't get charged. He didn't talk for a week after that – moped around like a big woman.

Spike was out on bail the same night. Ken's a freemason, you see, and it's odds-on the chief of Benfleet Police is too. The case keeps getting delayed because they can't get Corrigan back from Ireland; apparently, the poor bugger's having trouble walking. Spike could easily pull some time; he's already got grievous bodily harm and actual bodily harm on his record – from the football matches, of course. But is he bothered? He's already got his convictions tattooed on his bicep, ABH, GBH – Gawd knows what he'll have next.

Mavis puts Spike's and Hammer's steaming plates up on the counter. Spike goes and pays her and brings the food back while Hammer reads his book. The book's in German and Hammer's been reading it for several weeks. Spike sets the fried egg rolls in front of Hammer, his own plate opposite. Hammer never looks up. Spike goes back to the counter for the teas, puts his bread and butter plate on top of his cup, and walking slowly, brings it all over and sets it out. He goes back a third time for the cutlery which he lays out carefully around the plates. Hammer looks up suddenly and, as if he just came out of a trance, says, "Oh, cheers, mate. My shout tomorrow."

Spike stuffs his mouth with a slice of bread, and flicking Hammer's book with a spoon, grunts, "You understand that bumf, do you, Rod?"

"Starting to."

"What you wasting your time for?"

"I told you, I'm gonna get my GCE's and go to the college. I'm not gonna do this shit all my life."

Black Jack, the Geordie, sitting close by, has been listening to this. "This *shit* as you call it," he says to himself, but so's Hammer can hear, "is what us lot will always do." He takes a packet of fags from the top pocket of the brown boiler suit he always wears, takes one out and taps it on the table. Pushing his thick glasses up his nose with his thumb, he says:

"Still want to go into labor relations, do you, Hammer?"

"Yeah. What of it?"

"Do you have to read Marx and Lenin to work in labor relations, son? Does it help to know the Chairman's thoughts?"

Hammer puts down the book. "It helps to understand things. I read all kinds of things. Everything you need to know is in books. It wouldn't do you any harm, Jack, to read a few books, or don't you have any up there in Geordieland?"

"Ah," said Jack in his heavy accent, "Books! There's nowt in 'em, man. Gimme the reddies and the lasses and me daily ale. That's all of it, that's all there is, man."

"Bollocks. You're ignorant, and ignorance is a neat little tool for the Tories. You should know what's going on, and you won't read about it in the *Sun* or the *Daily* bloody *Mirror*. It's all in books."

"Ahhhhhh," laughs Black Jack. He fans Hammer's words away as if they're flies, and lights his fag.

Spike shakes his head, "That's not my scene at all, Rodney. Not my scene at all, mate."

Hammer, with eyebrows raised, shrugs, picks up one of his fried egg rolls and squeezes the crust a little too strongly so that yoke squirts out of it and plops into his tea. Plop it goes, just like that. Plop! A big yellow dollop right in his tea.

With Spike's cackle leading us, we laugh until our guts ache. Hammer'll keep quiet about books for a while.

Rain pelts against the glass as we see Ken pull his clapped out Land Rover onto the pavement just behind Spike's Capri. Him and the new bloke run to the door with newspapers over their heads and come inside, stamping and shaking off the water. Ken takes off his anorak and says:

"You monkeys all right this morning, are you?"

Hammer turns around smiling, all attention, always pleased to see old Ken.

"They're moaning again, boss," Hammer says, playing the lackey, "talking of industrial action, the proletariat scum."

"Well," says Bert, "If you pay peanuts, you get monkeys."

Ken puts on a good smile but we all know this rain's worrying him, you can see it in the rings around his eyes. His hair's got white streaks in it, and he's smoking sixty a day. He nods at Spike. Spike ignores him. It's obvious what the boy thinks of his dad – calls Ken a wally behind his back.

The new bloke puts his soaked *Guardian* on the table and looks up at the chalkboard menu on the wall above Mavis's head. Ken announces, "Well, as promised, here's a new dogsbody. This is Mason. Mason, meet the other two laborers: my son, Michael, and our gentle giant, Rodney Thorson."

Spike nods and looks out of the window. Hammer gets up and shakes the geezer's hand, "All right, Mason? They call me Hammer, and him they call Spike."

While he's facing Hammer, we get our first good look at Mason's face. We all look at each other because it's the saddest bastard of a face you ever saw. As Ken introduces him to each one of us, Mason looks for a second into the center of your eye and then away. He's obviously scared and shy; you get the feeling he's about to blubber. He's even taller than Hammer, clean shaven, too, with neatly cut hair. His work clothes are good quality cast-offs: a pair of paint-dotted suit trousers, a green button-down Oxford and, on his big flat plates, a fairly decent pair of Puma trainers. There's a thin black briefcase under his arm, and, stooped over slightly, he clasps his long white hands in front of him like a priest. Hammer's standing beside him, staring at him and frowning slightly. Everyone's speechless. Ken nudges Mason, "It's all right, they never say a word unless it's a complaint – miserable pack of fuck-pigs."

We grin.

From the back of the caff comes, "Oh fuck me, Ken. Nice one!" All eyes go to old Bert, sitting by the fag machine, wearing his cap cocked over one eye. He's only got about one tooth in his head and it sticks down from his upper jaw like a brown clothes peg. Now he's got our attention. "Brought in a little amusement for the yobos, have you, mate?"

Ken ignores him, says, looking at no one, "Everybody ready for another tea?" and gives the nod to Mavis who starts pouring. In a lower voice, but still loud enough for Mason and the two boys to hear, Bert says to Black Jack, "They'll tear him to pieces, skin him alive, poor sod. Look at him. It's not on, it's not on at all." And Black Jack, the coal dust of his beard already showing through his face, grins and agrees, "You're reeght, man. Ah'll wager a tenner he'll no last the day."

"You're on, mate. A tenner it is."

And Mason's off to a very bad start.

It gets worse when we all troop up to the counter to get our teas and smell his soapy clean pong and notice how thin and stringy his limbs are. But he has one thing in common with Black Jack: he's already got four o'clock shadow at nine-thirty. Up nearer the counter you could also feel Spike's dander rising; instant dislike as usual, but this time egged-on by Bert and Jack, the gormless twats.

Mason's the type who's practiced at dodging certain kinds of trouble: he looks away when a joke is about to be made on him. He turns, has a quiet word with

75

Ken, or stares at some spot on his briefcase. But once we're all seated again, the rain pounding down outside, tea steaming in front of us, Mason and Ken sitting well away from Spike, the trouble starts to show itself. Loudly, Spike says:

"Well, Mason old son, it don't look like you done much of our kinda work, eh? Eh?"

Hammer whines under his breath, "Give over, you pillock," but Spike ignores him.

Mason looks across at them and his very dark eyes remind you of a dog that's about to be strangled. "No," he says, "I can't say I have." His accent's well educated, not what you'd call posh, but different from ours, a touch of northern in it. Spike and Hammer speak simultaneously:

"What'd you do before this then, Mason?" says Hammer, while Spike looks around at Black Jack, and with a straight face pronounces, "How-now-brown-cow?"

Mason looks out at the rain, waits, then says, "I was in university. For a very long time. In the Midlands, then in the States."

"I wish I could do that," says Hammer. "What colleges did you go to?"

"West Point, the Sorbonne, Roedean," says Mason.

With a slight frown, Hammer, says, "There's no need to take the piss. I'm not stupid, you know." And he tries again:

"I expect you're just filling in here? Between post-docs, or something?"

Mason looks at him as if he's a moron:

"No," he says, blinking rapidly, "not at all. I'm finished. Some time ago actually."

Bert pipes up, "Waiting for a good job offer, eh?"

Still staring at the rain, Mason shakes his head:

"This is the best offer I've had so far."

Hammer susses something and goes real quiet. Ken's stirring his tea. Spike's mouthing something at Jack. Bert says, "Blimey. You're shitting me."

Hitting his stride, Mason shakes his head and slowly says, "No, no kidding. There are no places for young historians in Britain, not in academia, not in industry. But a number of peripheral factors have contributed to my failure."

Well, that does it: Spike lets out a guffaw and announces, "Oh my Gawd, peripheral factors! I had one of them once but its universal joint got AIDS."

There's a crack of laughter; even Mason's mouth widens ever so slightly, showing straight white teeth.

Ken says, "Sorry Mason, but you're better off using *Sun* and *Mirror* language with us."

"Yeah, bog wall lingo," says Bert, wiping water from his eyes.

"I'll remember that," says Mason.

After a while the rain stops, the sun comes out, and Ken says what he always says: "I suppose we'd better go and have a shufti at the work." With an all-round groan, we haul arses and tool bags out of Mavis's caff and plod across the muddy road, through the gate made of two dented oil drums and a four-by-two, and up the dripping ladders to our soaked blue wall.

There's a sputtering row and a stink of diesel as the boys start up the mixer. We hang coats on the scaffolding, pull out trowels and start banging yesterday's mortar off the boards.

It's good to get started. It's best up high where you can see across the slate roofs to the Britrail shunting yards, and to the Thames – big tankers going so slow you can barely see them move – and the clouds all lifted and the air very clear, which means more rain, and the smell of ozone and tobacco smoke and cement and wet brick and armpits. We get stuck in.

About noon we have some steam up. There's even the odd song. Spike and Hammer really went at it and are well ahead of us, enough so that they're both hanging around a bit, having cleaned up and done the odd jobs already – trying to show up the new bloke, the pair of sods.

Mason got the job of filling the footings at the base of the wall. He's a steady worker, a plodder, but getting the job done. His trousers are covered in dirty yellow clay.

Black Jack starts bellowing "Edelweiss" to a chorus of ridicule. When he stops someone starts "Please Release Me" and we all join in. We do a fairly good "You've Lost That Loving Feeling," but then we murder "What's New Pussycat," because everyone's wiggling his arse, faking the parts he don't know, and the scaffold's rocking and rattling. The boys jeer at us the whole time, doing cat calls and trying to get an oar in with some tuneless Dire Straits number, but we like the old hits and we can always out-sing them, in spite of all the practice they get at the football matches. We look down to check on Mason and he's happy enough, even caught him whistling something. When Spike's out of earshot, Hammer'll join in and sing anything with anyone. But he's quiet now, cleaning out the mixer with some half bricks while Spike finishes a bit of pointing for his dad. We're having a right old grin and we're threatening to knock this thing on the head by nightfall.

About half twelve, Spike takes a 'baccy break. He leans on an upright scaffold pipe, directly above where Mason's struggling in the clay. He stares down between the wall and the scaffold planks for a while, then sings:

"Look at him working. . .that's the way to do it. . .play the guitar on the MTV. . . " He sticks his fag in the side of his mouth and starts unbuttoning the flies of his army greens. He shouts, "Happy as a pig in shit, ain't you, Mason?"

Black Jack, without interrupting the motion of his trowel, glances up at him and says, "Aye, happy as a nigger with new red shoes."

Spike turns around laughing, "Nice one, Jack. I wish I'd said that."

"You will, Michael," says his dad.

"Leave it out!" Hammer says to Jack from the top of the ladder, "That's racist, that is . . . "

"Oh, Mister Liberal!" interrupts Bert, "Mister Kick-their-heads-open-then-mourn-for-a-week! Fuck me, Hammer, get off your white horse, will you, boy!"

Bert and Hammer are about to get into one of their rows that'll cover just about everything arguable on the planet. This always buggers up our work because we take sides, and bricklaying gets lost in the big muddle of highfalutin ideas being flung around by blokes who usually keep their opinions to themselves. It gets a bit dangerous sometimes, up there in the wind, with everybody's blood boiling. But Spike saves the day by yelling real loud:

"Hoy, Mason! Put your back into it, you great pansy!"

Ken, trying to make a joke of it, calls down, "Doing all right are you, Mason?"

"Yes," calls Mason, "but it's getting a bit tiring because the clay's so wet."

There are three replies, all coming at once:

"Clay's always heavy, son," says Bert.

"We'll stop for some tea soon," says Ken.

Spike yells, "Oh no, poor old Mason's knackered. Having your period, are you, love?"

Black Jack lets out a whoop and doubles up. Everyone's grinning. Mason's face is red. Jack, sitting on the planks, chokes breathlessly, "Och, that just caught me funny. Wouldn't ha' been funny yesterday. Having your period, love? Och, fuck me, that's ace — having his period — Jesus, I wish I'd said that."

All together, we shout:

"YOU WILL!"

Hammer's sitting atop the ladder trying not to laugh.

And about now it's time to knock off for a bit of tea. After a good laugh you might see brickies sliding down the ladders, their hands and feet tight to the runners like young hoddies. A laugh's one of the things about the building trade — we do have a laugh and a joke now and again. It don't do no harm — new blokes always get it in the neck. You have to have a giggle, don't you? Trouble is, these days, a laugh tends to go too far.

Mavis saw us knock off. As we walk in, she's standing with the teas steaming on the counter in front of her, and has her pencil and pad ready for our orders. The specials are chalked up above her head: meat pie and chips, savaloy and chips, shepherd's pie with two veg, toad-in-the-hole with gravy and two veg — not what you'd call special really, although if you butter her up she'll have her old man slop gravy over everything so you don't taste the grease. You got to watch her old man when the place gets busy; he'll deep-fry everything.

We pick up our teas, give our orders, and sit down. While Mavis licks the lead of her pencil stub and writes frantically, Spike nicks a KitKat from behind the display cabinet. He sits at his place by the window, sucking the chocolate off the biscuit, and looks around at everyone with one eyebrow arched, cockier than shit. Hammer's got his book out, and the rest of us sprawl in our shirt sleeves, stretching in our chairs. Black Jack lets out a fart – a luscious raspberry, squashed tight to the seat.

"Bloody hell," says Mavis, "Put a cork in it, you Geordie pig."

"Newcastle United!" says Spike.

"Hey, watch thy mouth, tha' cockney wazzock," says Black Jack.

"Coreblimey," says Bert, changing seats, "the air's going yellow. He's been on the vindaloo again."

Hammer looks up, laughing, "Poor old Mason," he says, "Look what company you've fallen into."

Delicately making a sign in the air in front of him, Mason chants, "Amor fati, amor fati, amor fati."

In the corner, the quieter ones, Dave and Reg, interrupt their study of tomorrow's racing form to have a rare verbal interchange:

"What the fuck's a wazzock?"

"I'm buggered if I know."

"What about an amoor farty?"

"An encore – you know – give us a few more of them farts."

"Ah."

Then there's a zipping sound.

We all look up to see Mason taking a brown paper bag out of his briefcase. We stare as he takes out a red and green pear, a banana, a dense square of tinfoil, a Mars bar, and a white paper serviette. He unfolds the serviette and finds four colored vitamin pills and two sachets, one of salt, one of pepper. Around the pills is a piece of yellow paper which he holds up and reads. With the first smile we've seen out of him, he folds the paper and puts it in his shirt pocket. Black Jack sighs and holds his heart. Bert shakes his head and says to Reg, "It's hard to believe a skinny party like that could scoff all that nosh."

Mason unfolds the tinfoil real careful, straightening out the edges with his forefinger in the serviette. Inside, there's a brown bread sandwich, double layered and quartered, that looks a lot more wholesome than anything Mavis ever served.

"Gawd," says Spike, "What you got there, then?"

As if he just woke up, Mason turns, frowns at us. He's surprised to find us staring at his grub and to no one in particular, replies, "Sandwich." He bites into one of the quarters.

Spike screws up one side of his face, says, "I know that, silly-bollocks. What is it that pongs like a Jew's kitchen?"

Black Jack says, "Fried foreskins," but no one laughs.

Looking at him and chewing, Mason says:

"It's smoked cheddar, marinated bacon, fresh spinach and tomato, raw onion, with a mayonnaise and mustard spread on wholewheat. Would you like one?"

"What in the name of Christ is marinated bacon? Bacon's for frying, for fuck's sake."

"You fry it and then marinate it. It enhances the flavor and cuts the cholesterol. It's a lot cheaper than ham." Mason takes a second piece and bites.

"Bloodynora," says Bert, "we are not a brown bag crew, mate."

"Gordonbennet," says Ken, smiling, "You'll be pulling out the plonk next."

Still chewing, Mason raises his eyebrows, holds up his forefinger, and searches deep in the folds of his briefcase. You have to feel for the boy, he's trying hard to fit in. And damn it all if he don't pull out a sample bottle of Blue Nun. Everyone starts cheering as he holds up the little bottle. In an eyeblink he's turned it all around, it's like scoring the first goal in the eighty-ninth minute of a tense nil-niller. He'd've got a nick-name out of that, the poor plonker.

We're just starting with stuff like: "Give us a sip, Professor," "Order one up for me from Mason's basin," "Boozing on the job, Ken!" and off the cuff stuff like that, when that nasty look on old Spike's mug becomes impossible not to see.

"Oh, Christ," mutters Bert, "here we go."

"Well, Mason, old chap," says Spike, trying to catch Black Jack's eye, "did Mother make you a hearty workman's lunch?"

Jack forces a smile.

"Actually, my wife."

"Christ, it's actually married. And eating marinated bacon – very healthy – that'll keep your strength up for digging ditches and laying pipe, won't it, me old darling?"

"Leave him alone, Michael," says Ken.

"You can shut your little head and all, dad. I'm getting to know me new mate. Is your wife health-conscious, Mason? Give you a lot of roughage, does she? Does she like you to have a good shit? I bet you two leave some bleeding great piles in the porcelain, eh? Hammer, what's that posh word you taught me about shit, I forgot it."

Hammer replies: "Scatology."

"That's it, scatological. Are you and the missus kinda scatological, do turds on each other and . . . "

"Leave it out, Spike!" yells Hammer.

"Michael, don't say things like that, boy," says Ken.

"Shut your trap!" says Bert.

"You're out of line, man," says Black Jack, and moves away from him.

Mason says:

"I'm not sure what the problem is, but I wish you'd leave me alone. I can't help who I am."

"Just asking questions, old son. Getting to know you like."

"It's verbal intimidation. I hate it. Leave me alone."

Spike's face flushes, and he points stiffly across the table:

"How about a little physical intimidation then, you sodding great fairy."

Hammer snaps his book shut and says, "Come on Spike, drop this shit. Let's go and get some muck going for these old farts."

"Don't be silly, Rod, dinner ain't been served yet. Now, how about it, Mason? Would you prefer a bit of the old physical, boot-up-the-arse-type aggro?"

Mason's whole body's shaking as he says:

"Frankly, I doubt if you could manage that."

"Oh yeah. Why's that, then?"

Mason answers:

"Because I'm bigger than you."

Someone laughs, and then the caff goes quiet. Everyone looks at Spike as he sits, stiff in his seat, his eyebrows knitting together, his nostrils flaring, his mouth drawing down at the corners. Mavis had come around the counter with a plate of pie and chips in each hand; now she stands still. Ken looks at Hammer; Hammer pulls a face. Dishes clank in the kitchen.

The chair legs scrape the floor as Spike springs up and lunges across the table. He's got a fork in his left hand and tries to jab it into Mason's eye. Mason lurches backwards, and over goes the chair so that he ends up on his back with his legs in the air. Hammer's up and over his table and lands on Spike with such force that the table they fall against collapses. Hammer pins him to the floor: "Cool it, all right! Cool it now!"

Helping Mason get untangled, Ken says, "I can't understand him. I pay him a fortune."

"He's banned!" screams Mavis, "banned for life. Banned, I tell you, banned for life." She's thrown the pie and chips in the air and is having a fit between the tables. Her old man rushes out, drying his hands on a tea towel. Spike's wrestling and cursing uselessly under Hammer's weight. Everyone's standing, treading pie and chips into the linoleum.

Black Jack opens the door and Hammer bundles Spike outside.

We sit down.

Mason, standing again, picks up his pear, which was the only part of his lunch to fall on the floor, sits, and reaches for another sandwich. Black Jack, going to his seat, pats Mason on the shoulder. Mavis is still shrieking in the kitchen – Ken goes to see what he can do, leaving Mason alone at the table.

Outside, Hammer's barring Spike's way and Spike's trying to push past him. Every so often there's a bump and a shudder on the plate glass. Mason's chewing his sandwich, watching. All dreamy, like some nut-case, he says, "If he gets in here and comes at me, I shall punch him. I'll clench my fist and hit him in the face with my knuckles."

"You want to, mate," says Bert, rolling up a fag. "He needs a bleeding good pasting, that boy."

"Aye," says Black Jack, "stick the nut on him. Gi' him the ault Glaswegian kiss."

Ken comes out of the kitchen and watches the struggle going on the outside. Spike's like a bulldog, he doesn't know how to give up, only how to get madder, but it's pretty unexpected when he kicks Hammer in the goolies. Hammer doubles up, letting Spike slip past him to the door; he gets it a foot open.

Mason throws a sandwich at him.

Hammer's right hand clamps onto Spike's neck, spins him around, and there's this heavy concrete thud, the type that you can feel even in your memory years afterwards, as Hammer's forehead butts into Spike's nose.

Ken shouts, "Oh no, Michael, for fuck's sake, son!" and rushes out of the caff to where Spike sits, dazed on the pavement, with blood pumping from his nose like shit from a sewage pipe. Hammer, holding his balls, his face pale, comes in and sits down.

Mavis's daughter, the punk one with the purple hair and massive bristols like her mum's, appears from somewhere to serve our food; she doesn't even look outside; she's seen it a hundred times.

Mason unscrews the silver cap of the wine sample and takes it over to Hammer. He sets it in front of him, goes back to his chair, peels his banana, and eats, watching Ken and Spike, then glancing back at Hammer. He keeps looking around like that, real nutty.

We're all getting sick of this when Spike pulls away from his dad and runs across the road. He stands by the oil drums, yelling. His nose looks bad. His T-shirt's covered in blood. Ken stands in the open door, looking at him, as the boy picks up a small piece of four-by-two and repeatedly smashes it against the oil drum as if to emphasize his words:

"You fucker, Hammer! You nutted me. I'll never forget it, you nutted me. You can fuck off, Hammer! Just fuck off to college with your mate, Mason. You think you're better than everyone with your fucking reading. You think you're bleeding God Almighty, you do. 'Hammer is God' you used to spraypaint everywhere. 'Hammer is God' painted on football grounds all over the country. You ain't no fucking god, Thorson, you're just a bastard that lets his mate down. Go on, fuck off to college and be a wanker like Mason. I'm done with you."

Ken, who's come inside, calls, "Michael, please. Calm down."

"You shut your mouth, too, you stupid old cunt. You're all fucking wankers in there – wankers!"

At that Hammer stands, but Ken shouts:

"Sit down, you, you've done enough damage," then steps outside again. "Now Michael, I want you to get in your car and go home. Go on, get out of it. No arguments. Now!"

Spike gives the drum one last bash before hurling the four-by-two at the blue wall. He stomps over the road to his car, gets in, turns the stereo on full blast, slams the door and roars away.

We eat without talking.

Mavis, her old man, and their other daughter, the fat one, are all nattering at once in the kitchen.

Poor old Hammer leaves Mason's wine untouched. He can't look any of us in the eye, especially Ken. It's odds-on we won't see much more of him. But we'll always remember what a good worker he was and how much he respected old Ken Cooper and what a mess he made of things here on the buildings.

Mason'll last about a week — him and his marinated bacon.

Meself, I don't know what the world's coming to.

SMOKING SECTION

He watched her swoop along the aisle in her black uniform. When she got to him she filled his coffee cup. Having done this she hovered a little, tilting her head sideways to see what he was writing. She had slightly stooped, rounded shoulders and wore the accoutrements of her generation: bobby socks, big earrings, penciled eyebrows, beauty spot; her graying blond hair was bunched into a loose ponytail, and, as she bent closer, he saw a small pink hearing aid clamped behind her right ear.

He stopped writing and smiled at her. His pen had quit working and his last few words were nothing but indentations in the paper. The smile she returned him was strictly professional: the mouth, which was full and pretty, that of a much younger woman, blossomed upwards at the corner, but the eyes remained emotionless and alert.

"You're keeping me well-supplied," he said.

She took her eyes off the blue scrawl in the notebook, looked him in the face and said, "It's just coffee."

"I've drunk more coffee in my time than a whale sucks sea water. I appreciate a constant flow — aids creativity."

"We're in the lull between breakfast and lunch," she said, "It's the best time for guys like you to come in here."

With his head cocked to one side, frowning humorously up at her and closing the notebook as if preparing for a long conversation, he said, "I know I look like a bum but I'm not. Story of my life, that. Eternally misjudged."

The spiralbound notebook was a nine-and-a-half by six inch college jotter with a crushed and folded orange cover, scrawled over with names, numbers, and lewd little sketches of women. The waitress shifted her weight, adjusted the position of her ponytail, and looking now at the orange notebook cover, replied, "So what are you? You sure ain't no cardiologist."

"Me, no. I'm a songwriter."

The waitress smiled. The man watched her mouth. Her lips were soft and full above a smooth little chin. Her teeth showed; they were clean and straight. There were lines and scars around her eyes and deep creases in her forehead. As she looked down at him she rested one hand on her hip, the other held the coffee pot. In the period of silence between them the man tapped out a cigarette from the pack by the ashtray, took a sip from his refilled coffee cup, and, pointing at the scratched name-tag attached to her lapel, said:

"Your name's Ericka, huh? Nice name."

She nodded, shifting her weight onto the other foot, observing him with her soft emotionless eyes. She did not say anything, so he continued:

"Mitch, they call me. For my surname, Mitchell. Only nobody calls me Mitchell. When I was a fat son-of-a-bitch back before I got sick, they called me Michelin, like the tire man, you know? That was down south where they're all assholes. I used to ride the trains a lot, from New Orleans to Phoenix, staying in the warm, chasing the dry seasons, writing my songs, playing my harmonica..."

The waitress looked over her left shoulder, back at the lunch counter and the entrance, then returned her attention to him.

"I had big dreams, then," he went on. "They called me Minnesota Mitch. And I've heard guys I don't even know singing my songs in the box cars. I guess they can't be the right kinda songs to make a guy rich because not even one got bought by a record company, and, boy, I hawked them all over hell. I got lazy though. It don't help any to be a lazy son-of-a-bitch if you want to make your mark on the world."

The waitress, Ericka, shrugged, backed away, saying loudly, "We all got broken dreams, honey. I gotta get back to work. Are you done with your hashbrowns? Do you want that plate out of your way?"

Minnesota Mitch looked at the plate he had pushed aside. Around the pallid strands of lightly fried potato were streaks of egg yolk and congealed fat. "No, Ericka baby," he said, "I'll work on it awhile. I have to eat real slow these days."

As Ericka walked away he opened the notebook, and scrubbed the ballpoint of his pen on the paper to get the ink flowing; it was all used up so he put it in the ashtray among the mass of cigarette butts. He talked to himself softly:

"And suppose I die soon, it wouldn't have meant much after all, would it, all this?" He swept his right hand in a miniature gesture from left to right. "Not even my chronic laziness would have meant anything – and all my ambition." He paused to think for a moment, then continued, "Hah, and how can you even prove you had ambition when you didn't do shit? You just kept letting it slide, letting it slide, easy through the grooves, along them bright shiny rails, always westward to the sun. Even now, you see, you're too lazy to develop that. Scribble it down, sure, but develop it, no. That's a nice idea for a song – rails, on the rails, railway lines taking you god-knows-where, where you didn't mean to go. See, you should borrow her pen and jot that down, maybe get a rhythm going like a train, get down some experimental stanzas. Society is like rails and if you get off them you're fucked and when you try to get on them again they take you straight to hell."

For several minutes Mitch stared down the lines of empty booths to the counter where a few old men in baseball caps sat reading newspapers. He held the coffee cup before his mouth with both hands, the handle pointing away from him, and the cigarette between the first joints of his index and middle finger, breathing in coffee steam and occasionally taking light drags from the filter which was never more than an inch from his lips.

The booths were dark stained, numbered with faded white stencil. To his right, a high yellow wall. Beside him, on the seat, a black plastic carrier bag with *executive fashion boutique* in red slash-script. Directly in front of him, right to left: pack of cigarettes, matches, ashtray full of butts and blue Papermate and a chewed toothpick, yesterday's *Tribune*, cold plate of hashbrowns with knife and fork set widely apart, brown coffee cup, spoon, sugar dispenser, salt and pepper pots, ketchup bottle, unused napkin, orange notebook. Immediate left: aisle, other terminal booth, plate glass, lobby, more plate glass, snowy parking lot, line of pine trees, freeway, some familiar neighborhoods, the Mississippi, Saint Paul, the East.

Sitting at the far end of the counter, an old man wearing a Twins cap was an inch and a half tall over the rim of the coffee cup. Opposite the counter, against the window, was a row of tables at which only two people could sit, each tight against the plate glass. Then there was the entrance with its *Please Wait To Be Seated* sign, and opposite that the swing doors of the kitchen and a recess that led to the restrooms. Then the cafe opened out into two rows of seven booths, a long scuffed linoleum aisle, massive plate glass windows looking onto the spacious lobby. The lobby had four elevators, a row of pay phones, a United States Postal Service counter, a Vision World, benches, potted trees, a janitor in a blue shirt, several bewildered senior citizens, and more plate glass windows beyond which was the packed parking lot – and, outside, snow fell heavily.

Mitch drained his cup and placed it on the table.

He smoked the cigarette almost to the filter then stubbed it out in the ashtray. He searched his pockets unsuccessfully for a pen. He examined the backs of his hands, attending closely to the fingernails.

An old fat man with a severe limp pushed a white haired woman in a wheelchair into the cafe and stood waiting beside the *Please Wait To Be Seated* sign.

Mitch searched again for a pen, then lit another cigarette and transferred it to his left hand and scratched his crotch. He muttered, "I must write all this down. All of it."

Ericka, who had been sitting out of sight behind the cash register, came with coffee pot in hand and menus under arm and escorted the old couple to a booth by the window, two from the end, booth number ten. When she had them settled, Mitch caught her eye, raised his eyebrow, lifted his coffee cup at an angle. She came and stood so that her black uniform blocked his vision of the cafe. She sloshed the remnants of the coffee pot into his cup, grounds and all, saying, "You sure drink a lot of coffee, fella."

"Yep," he said, "Happens when you're killing time."

"It's bad for you, too much of it."

Laughing, wide-eyed, waving his cigarette, Mitch said, "Hell, Ericka, you think it might make me ill?"

"Say," she said, "You're not one of these 'vulnerable adults' from the group home, are you?"

"No Ma'am. I'm just sitting here, smoking, watching it all happen."

"Well, I'll tell you, sometimes we get these mentally ill types in here. There's a big facility across the freeway. And they sit here for hours, right through the lunch rush, cutting into my living pretty bad, you know what I mean?"

"Sure."

"I dunno why they have to be out on the street. Some of them are dangerous."

"Reaganomics, honey. Late capitalism."

"There's one fool ought to be locked up."

"Reagan, you mean?"

"There's this one fool comes in here, calls himself the Ninja. Whatever the weather he goes around in one of those karate suits, and cuban-heeled shoes on his feet, and a red beret which he thinks keeps the Ninja power from leaking through the top of his head. Sits here for hours, right through the lunch rush, drinking all our coffee."

"I hope to meet him."

"Lunch rush'll be starting soon."

"Can I trouble you for a pen?"

"A pen?" She thought for a while, "I'll look. You can't use this one. I need it. I'll look." She turned around and stepped to the old couple, and, standing behind the woman in the wheelchair that partially blocked the aisle, asked them if they were ready to order.

"I don't know, sighed the old man, "soup and sandwich? Anything'll do for a pair of old stewies."

"Stewies?" smiled Ericka, "What's a stewie?"

"Why, a senior citizen that ain't worth nothing but making stew out of. Stew for dogs, that is. Dog meat. You know, the stuff you guys use for corned beef hash."

"Walter! Stop it!" said the woman in the wheelchair.

The old man threw up his right arm, said, "Jawohl, meine Liebling!"

Smiling, the waitress glanced at Mitch then back at the old people. "I guess you guys are gonna give me a hard time this morning," she said.

"Hell no. I gave Frieda here a hard time for nigh-on fifty years — put her in a wheelchair — but hard times are few and far between nowadays."

The old woman slapped the old man's hand and looked around at Mitch. Her eyes were bright blue, startled, outraged, full of laughter, but her mouth was tight, turned down at the edges. "Excuse us, sir," she said, "he is a dirty pig." She had a slight foreign accent. "I am so ashamed of him."

"He's a live one," said Mitch, toasting with his coffee cup. The woman turned hurriedly on the old man and slapped him again. "Teufel!" She said, "Alt schwine!"

A very tall boy in a ski jacket walked backwards past the plate glass window, chewing, holding a box of auto parts. He stopped by the cafe's entrance and shouted:

"Hey, come on, dude! Fucking-A!"

A short Asian kid in an overcoat and Twins cap ran up to the tall boy and feigned a kung-fu kick. The boys walked into the cafe and sat at the counter where they took out and lit long thin cigars, blowing volumes of blue smoke at the ceiling.

A stout blonde girl ran across the lobby to the entrance of the cafe, struggling to get her coat off. Under the coat she wore the same kind of black uniform as Ericka. Out of breath, she burst through the swing doors to the kitchen at the same time as Ericka, following, yelled, "About time. You can't have midterms every week. . . ."

Four women with short hair and white coats came and waited to be seated. Behind them a black man in a suit stood a distance from them and took a newspaper from his briefcase. Behind him came a couple with a child — a very heavy woman and a very short man who carried the child.

The young waitress burst from the kitchen as if she had been thrown. She got four menus from the counter and went to the short-haired women in white. They wanted no smoking so were seated by the door in number fourteen. A very large man pushed open one of the swing doors and watched the girl seat the women. With the door opened for a prolonged period it was possible to hear jazz playing in the kitchen. The man glared up and down the length of the cafe and disappeared. As the door swung back on itself, Ericka emerged with a tray full of food for the stewies in booth ten.

Ericka seated the suited gentleman with the newspaper in booth eight, the other terminal booth, and the couple with the child in booth six. After seating the family she placed a black Papermate on Mitch's table and was gone before he could offer thanks. He looked at the fellow in the booth next to him and said, "She's a pro that Ericka."

The man snapped his paper and read the sports page.

Mitch opened the notebook and wrote *What'dua do with an uppity black guy that won't give you the time of day? You treat him good, 'cos he wearing a suit, but he ain't foolin you none, he down on his luck, jus like all of us . . .* "Ah!" said Mitch, striking a line through what he wrote, "Garbage."

Then he wrote down the word *stewie.*

Then: *Ain't no good but for the making of stew.*

Then, in a rush: *Old seniors in the invalid cafe, vets of old wars, cold wars, danced with foreign whores in sleazy dives, their wives at home engaged in the pastime of combing kids' hair. Hashbrowns, hashbrowns, cheap as you got, I got me a dollar that I came here to spend. You want it or not? You want it or not? You want it or not?*

Mitch looked at what he had written, laughed and pushed it all aside. "If there's anything in it," he said, loud enough for his neighbors to hear, "I'll develop it later. I'll put it through the process."

The little man in front of him looked around. He had a permanent sneer on his left upper lip and stared at Mitch with curiosity. He looked pale and tired, his eyes were a watery blue and his stringy yellow hair stood up on one side and was plastered down on the other. The little man turned back and faced his companion just as Ericka brought a high chair for the child. With few words the woman and Ericka secured the child into the seat. The obese woman, wheezing asthmatically, moved slowly to adjust a pink plastic eye-patch that the child wore, then read her menu with a sad expression.

The little man got up, took off his coat and slung it in the corner of the booth. As he sat down again, he said, "Ah, fuck," and opened his menu. The woman gave the child a bottle of juice that it sucked solemnly. The man flipped the pages of the menu then closed them decisively with another "Ah, fuck." Then he lit a cigarette and and blew smoke in a jet toward the ceiling.

Dishes and cutlery clattered in the kitchen. Someone cursed, and, as before, the stout waitress hurtled from the swing doors.

Mitch lit another cigarette, and held up his coffee cup to Ericka who was seating two tall men with chiseled haircuts in booth nine. She glared at him with those nice teeth.

The big woman put down the menu, folded her hands in front of her and sat quietly, staring at her fingers. The little man sighed. Ericka came, wanting to take their order. The big woman slowly opened her menu and pointed. The waitress nodded, wrote, then said, "Anything to drink?"

Very softly, barely audible, the large woman answered: "A Diet Pepsi?"

"Coke okay?" said Ericka loudly, as if the woman were deaf.

The woman's head nodded an affirmative.

"And for you, sir?" Ericka said to the little man.

"Number eleven. Eggs overeasy. French fries. Regular Coke."

"Thank you. Anything for our little prince charming?"

"No," said the man. And when the waitress left, he said, "Stupid old fuck."

The lunch rush escalated.

The cold plate of hashbrowns remained on Mitch's table.

Ericka brought food to the family in booth six, including some crackers for the baby. She smiled at the large woman and said, "Just in case." The baby instantly tore open the packet and crammed his mouth full.

Ericka beamed at the child.

Mitch held up his coffee cup.

From behind Ericka's beam emerged a frown, but she went and got the coffee pot and filled his cup. Out of the side of her mouth, she said, "That's the last you get, buster. There's a party of four waiting for this table. Do me a favor, okay?" While this was being said the little man in booth six cut up all his food with a knife and fork, wiped off the knife on the edge of the plate, laid it out of the child's reach, switched the fork into his right hand, put his face close to the plate and began forking food into his mouth. His cigarette continued to burn in the ashtray. After eating for a while he stopped, muttered a single syllable, reached over his plate with his left hand to the ashtray and picked up his cigarette. He took a long pull on it, then a swig of Coke, and only when the glass was back on the table did he expel smoke from his lungs.

Mitch lit another cigarette and pulled the notebook into the writing position. "Somewhere a song in all this," he said so that the black gentleman in number eight would overhear him. "Some nice gutter-ass, downtown white boy blues about wage slaves treating themselves to a greasy feed at the tail end of capitalism. Invalid Cafe at the End of the World! The last feature at Deadbeats Circus! Lunch of the Living Dead!"

The man in number eight sighed. He had not been served yet. He put down his paper and said, "You're taking on too many themes, man. Concentrate on one, like this waitress's dirty white shoes. You know: *Dirty white shoes, dirty white shoes, strung-out waitress got dirty white shoes. I'm waitin all alone in boof number nine, watchin all the white dudes takin their time . . .* Something like that, man, know what I mean?"

"I hear you."

"Good. Be cool. You'll go far."

The black gentleman in the suit went back to reading his sports page.

Mitch put a line through everything he had written. He turned to a new page and wrote at the top, *Smoking Section: A Blues Opera*. Under this he wrote *Overture*: and the lines rushed out of him: *Lunch rush is coming and you sit here drumming your fingers to a newfangled song. This just may be, for you and me, the last . . .* "I'm feeling it. I got it coming. At last!" Mitch shouted as he wrote.

After a while he sat back and sipped coffee. The stewies were staring at him, the men with chiseled hair were staring at him, everyone, except the black gentleman and the family in booth six, stared at him.

At the counter, Ericka leaned over a customer and spoke to someone through the serving hatch. She nodded her head Mitch's way and her eyes were big and emotionless. In booth six the obese woman continued to fork small morsels of food into her mouth while her child sang quietly to himself. The little man finished his food, threw his fork and then his knife into the middle of the plate and pushed it away. "Ah," he said with a sigh of satisfaction, "fuck."

A huge man in a chef's hat came out of the swing doors and lurched up the aisle, keeping his eyes fixed on Minnesota Mitch. The huge man had the kind of legs that buckle inward at the knee. The little man moved into the corner of his booth, sat sideways and lit another cigarette. The black gentleman hid behind his paper. The men with chiseled hair put their scalps together and whispered. The two waitresses and the other customers went about their business of serving or eating with attention furtively directed on booth seven.

The big cook stood above Mitch, blocking out the view of the cafe with his white apron. He wore a scratched name-tag that said Mal. "Okay, bud," he said, "we've seen enough of your face in here today. Haul ass."

The little man watched, smoking with relish. The woman with him continued to eat daintily. The child sang.

Mitch said, "I was about to order lunch."

"You don't get no goddamn lunch here today, pal. You can goddamn bet on it."

"I was going to leave her a big tip."

"Bullshit. We know your type. Goddamn drifters. Get the goddamn fuck out of here before I snap your spine."

"You should know," said Mitch, "that I'm not a well man. I don't have long to live."

"You're damn right, about thirty seconds unless I see that scarecrow's ass of yours leaving my restaurant." The cook rested his knuckles on the edge of the table, pressing down on them so that they cracked. He had dark brown eyes, almost black, and his clothes smelled of fried meat.

The little man was very close to the action, but sat under it with fascination, his eyebrows lifted high as though he were about to make a humorous remark. Mitch looked back at the cook and said, "Okay, but you have to understand, Mal, that this kind of thing doesn't scare me anymore. It's just kinda ugly to my way of thinking. I guess it serves me right for patronizing cheap establishments."

"Just so long as you pay up and get out I couldn't give a motherfucking goddamn what you think." And with that the cook turned to go back to his kitchen.

"Excuse me, sir," said Mitch, standing, reaching into the corner of the booth for his coat and other possessions, "but you don't expect me to pay, do you? I mean, you're throwing me out."

"You'll pay."

"Well, no, I guess I won't.'

While the cook rotated slowly, his head lowered, the little man turned to the daintily eating woman opposite him and said, "Fuck. You ever seen such fucking shit?"

"You'll pay!" said the chef, punching his forefinger into Mitch's shoulder. A little off balance, Mitch replied:

"Nope. No way. Call the cops if you want. I'll wait for them."

The cook ground his teeth, picked up the bill lying on the table, and looked at it.

Mitch said:

"And besides, the hashbrowns were disgusting. Look, I had to leave them."

For the first time the cook looked at the little man. He jerked his thumb at Mitch and said, "Goddamn, what is it with these guys?"

The little man raised his eyebrows and shrugged, "I dunno, pal. But the service here sucks and I reckon I ain't gonna pay neither."

The cook narrowed his eyes at the little man, then looked at Mitch. The puffy skin under his eyes pulsated and his knuckles were white. By now, Mitch had struggled into his coat and gathered up his stuff. The notebook was put away, the waitress's pen clipped inside the spiraled wire. He could see himself in the glass above the black gentleman's head: he stood like a man about to be run over by a train.

The cook swung around and strode back to his kitchen with such rapidity that the waitresses had to leap out of his way. Once he had disappeared behind the swinging doors the eyes of the people of the restaurant turned to Mitch. He looked at himself, too, in the glass: tall, stooped, graying, ill — a strange bewildered thing in the army surplus overcoat, standing beside booth seven, holding a black plastic bag.

With the distortion of a smile, the little man, kneeling on the bench of booth six, held out his right palm for Mitch to slap. After several seconds Mitch registered the gesture and slapped the hand, then, slowly, held out his own, watching the palm intently.

The little man shook his head and slapped Mitch's open palm, calling emphatically, "Fuuuuuck."

Mitch was high fived and low fived by the patrons as he left the restaurant. No he wasn't — that was in a song he imagined. But the two young boys grinned at him as he backed into the foyer, trying to catch the eye of Ericka who hopped around behind them . . . he moved himself steadily backwards until his calves touched a public bench in the center of the foyer and he sat down.

Booth seven could be seen through the plate glass. The man in booth eight had his back turned to the foyer. The stewies, who blocked the view of booth six, laughed heartily and touched each other's cheeks with outstretched fingers.

The two waitresses bustled along the aisle with coffee and desserts, the men of the chiseled hair, like Siamese twins, were joined at the cranium, the cigar smoking boys stayed cool and nobody came to sit in booth number seven.

HESTA'S TALE

Although I sort of hope you'll never see this I'm writing it to you, Rodney, because at the same time as loving you for your incredible indulgence of my recent, shall we say, bizarre behavior I also expect that "the Otto thing" as you call it is going to come back and haunt our relationship in the future. You're basically a very possessive man and I fear that as we continue together Otto is going to eat his way into our love and make you hate me. I guess I won't blame you, I'd be pretty mad if I found out you'd done the things I have. You've been marvelous, you really have, and I'm yours now, completely, you don't have to worry about anything. But I must write this, it's the only way to clean Otto out of me. It's like recovering from a long period of insanity, a sort of prolonged hallucination, to which I hope you'll never make me return through jealousy or an inability to accept who I was when this all happened.

You remember, of course, last November – we've come a long way since then. I'll begin at the end – the furious beating tail of my hallucinatory monster: The telephone wakes me. I've no intention of answering it in case it's that asshole Bodo Haller from the language school, wanting me to work my day off – so I let it ring. I reach out for Otto, but his side of the bed is empty. I vaguely remember him fumbling in the dark several hours earlier, trying to be quiet in the kitchen, then kissing me goodbye and whispering that he loved me, toothpaste on his breath.

I yawn and stretch while that phone rings, feeling a pleasant ache in my hips and buttocks after a weekend of lovemaking. "Une fois de plus, ma'deesse," Otto had said, "J'ai noyé mes problèmes dans le vin et l'amour. Et voilà comment on setue à coups d'orgasmes!"

He liked making me climax. He faked some of his, I know, preferring to watch, to see how far he could push me. Sometimes I've opened my eyes and looked at him as my body's convulsing and I'm crying out, and found him staring at me, fascinated, with those big turquoise eyes — it was a bit spooky, now that I think about it, like he was some kind of demon. But he knew such wonderful things, like once when I had a raging headache he got two eggs from the refrigerator and put them on my eyes and when my eyes were numb with cold he took the eggs away and sucked my eye sockets very gently with his warm mouth so that my eyeballs were tugged slightly outward, easing the tension behind them.

I used to fantasize about this kind of man, long for him during those wintry Midwest nights. Mom would have brought in an exorcist if she could've seen into my mind. I imagined entrusting myself totally to someone who would take me seriously, help me learn. And it happened. When you find an Otto, someone who knows a woman's cycles, the workings of her body, her moods, you'll offer up your life, all your loyalty, to remain cocooned in his love. I understand it all now, now that I have you. You're my defense against these lovely old vampires.

It took some getting used to. Being the lover of an older man wasn't exactly what growing up in Minnesota prepared me for — but I had come to terms with it, I really had. I know you can't understand that, Rodney, but it's true. There's so much I want you to understand but you're so injured by the truth sometimes that I'm scared to tell you things.

So, back to the thrashing tail of the monster.

Otto was gone again and the bed still smelled of him and the incessant ringing of the phone was about to drive me up the wall.

I slither across the sheets and onto the bedside rug, looking for Otto's rugby shirt. It reminds me of him, it has that smell — deodorant powder, cologne, sweat. It's huge and comfortable. I hunt for it among the debris of his stay: books, magazines, lingerie pulled from the dresser. I groan, imagining the mess in the rest of the apartment. The bathroom: wet towels on the floor, hair in the sink, an unflushed toilet. The living room: international newspapers spread on the coffee table; records pulled from their jackets; books, shoes, candy wrappers, bottles, glasses, cups, plates, rumpled floor rugs, disarranged cushions. The balcony: poetry books lying open, wrecking the spines, among rock-hard bread and empty wine bottles that could roll over the edge any second and brain some passer-by.

He was out there a long time after we made love, drinking, hollering verses into the street — Baudelaire, Valéry, Mallarmé, Rimbaud. From the white apartment block opposite, someone got pissed-off and shouted:

"Du! Halt mal, oder ich ruf die Polizei."

"Ahhhhh, le Boche!" returned Otto, "Va te faire foutre!"

"Otto! Otto!" I laughed from the kitchen, "You'll get me evicted, you fool."

"Evicted? Then I buy you an apartment overlooking the Rhine – on the French side, away from the stupid Bosch. I tire of paying rent on this chest of drawers. Cheaper, I think, to buy you a palace."

"Get in here, Otto."

"No! I shall wake them all up. Réveillez-vous, bande d'abrutis. . . "

When Otto partook of the grape he became very Gallic; at work he was a Teuton; I later learned that he had Italian moods, too. He'd been on the balcony an hour and I was horny again, so I'd put on the red high heels, nothing else – it was one of our games.

"Otto, darling, I have a surprise for you."

That got his attention. We did it on the dishwasher.

The telephone was like Mother nagging for me to get ready for church:

I cover my ears and hold the hair out of my eyes as, in search of the shirt, I move things around with my toes. I search under the window, among the pile of shoes, boots and umbrellas.

The telephone chants.

In my mind, I hear Otto laughing: "Get away from the window, Liebchen, the perverts have their binoculars out."

I give in and look for the phone. It's under a big book on Gothic architecture propped up like an A-frame. As I reach into this little church for the receiver, I feel the mass of Otto's semen let go inside me, as if someone had been holding it between thumb and forefinger, and suddenly, gently, released it. I lift the receiver, shaking the hair away from my right ear. I feel him there, thick and wet, against the closed lips of my vagina, and reaching down to scratch, keeping my legs closed and muscles tight to hold him in, I say hello.

"Hesta, hier ist Hans Schulte."

"Grosser Gott, Hansi. Wie geht's?"

Otto's oldest son – his voice trembling: "Hesta, hör mich an. Papa ist tot. . .ein schrecklicher Unfall. . . "

My body recalls that moment's trauma: lips numb, muscles shivering, entrails writhing, skull covered by a wet, electrified wig.

Hans's voice was a wordless film in my head, all vision, all knowing. The Volvo motoring smoothly over slick winding roads in the Jura region that Otto prefers even though the autobahn is four times faster. . .a jazz station on low. . .Otto longing for sleep as dawn illuminates distant Alpine summits, the white peaks like cat's teeth. . .winding through shuttered villages and black clusters of forest, the valley below the road blacker than night.

Coming at him, filling the road, is the lumbering face of a truck. Otto's startled, swerves, and the Volvo smashes through the hillside barrier. Below is a deep valley full of trees, their tops getting the first glints of the sun. He's in air, coming out of the seat, the radio still playing. The car bounces over and over down the rocky cliffside, scattering debris, and what is left shatters the roof of an abandoned barn. The Italian truck driver continues on and reports the accident in Delemont.

I continually see him coming away from the seat, the look on his face — those few seconds agonize me: to be alone with no comfort in those seconds!

Hans says because the body's in such bad shape, the funeral will be on Wednesday in Bern. His family will be there and Hans isn't sure how I'll feel about coming. With exasperation, I say of course I'll come. He says it's rather awkward and that I must understand; he'll discuss it with his mother and call me back.

I hold my stomach and lean against the wall.

I hear myself ask Hans if he's under sedation.

"Was?" he says, "was sagst du? Was?"

He keeps making me repeat the question, but neither of us can grasp anything. I suddenly become angry:

"I only stayed here for him! The last three years, purely to be near him — God — in this boring shit-hole, hiding like a whore. I could've gone back to Minneapolis, I could've gone back. I had prospects, opportunities, there are men my own age there. Christ! Goddamn him, the son-of-a-bitch, I can't believe this. I'm his lover, goddammit, of course I'm coming to the funeral, you dumb little shit."

The phone line hisses. I'm sweating. A car starts in the parking lot below. I see the corner of the red formica countertop through the kitchen door, the eggshell-colored electrical outlet above the baseboard in the hall, the dark interior of the bathroom. The Spanish carpet in the hall that Otto brought me from Saragossa is bunched up outside the kitchen. Otto's stuff — sacred possessions entrusted to me — is out, scattered; his fingerprints on all things, his presence everywhere.

Hans, in English, says:

"Are you calm now, Hesta? I hope so."

"Yes, Hansi, I'm sorry. My temper, I . . . "

"I am a fool. Of course you must come to the funeral. We are all fools here. It is correct that you come. Mother and Grandmother must accept this."

"Can you imagine how it would feel to be left out? Can you imagine how I feel up here? God, I can't believe this."

"I must warn you. It will go hard for you . . . there will be surprises . . . it is difficult for me to . . . "

"I'll handle it, Hans. Okay? I was the closest one to him, I know what to expect."

"Ach, Scheisse. Hesta, bitte sei sehr diskret."

"If you think I'm coming incognito, Hans, you can forget it."

"No," he says, "but there are many problems, many other pressures. However, you are the last one with him and they believe that he speeds home so Mother is not shamed at breakfast. Do not give them opportunity to become hysterical with you."

"But he was going through the Jura. He could've taken the autobahn. It's not fair."

"Yes. But they say what pleases them. Who will reason with a grieving family?"

"He left in plenty of time for his goddamn granola and orange juice and all that other shit you people eat." As I say this I feel guilt digging into me like the talons of some massive black bird. So this was why he always left in the sweetest part of the night — he still cared about the woman, stupid of me not to understand: so that Francine wouldn't lose face at the breakfast table.

Hans says, "Hesta, I understand, but I am powerless. And what does it matter? The Devil has done his work. Now I ask, will you be all right?"

"I don't know if I'll be all right. Probably not. What about you, honey? You can't be doing very well."

There is a long pause, and then, quite suddenly, Hans is weeping — big falsetto sobs coming out of the plastic mouthpiece. That sets me off and we wail down the line at each other.

Any minute I thought Otto might emerge from the dark bathroom, drying his hair with the brown towel, and ask me what all the fuss was about. Was I flirting with little Hans again? Did I not learn my lesson that time we took him skiing at St. Moritz when he turned eighteen, and he had such a crush on me that my very presence on earth nearly broke the fool's heart?

I could see the boy's peach-down cheeks streaming with water and I thought of Otto again in slow motion, coming out of the seat, and I wondered if he called out to his son. And I had the impression that Otto watched from somewhere, seeing us all, our terrified, streaming faces; he was tapping frantically from the other side like a madman behind glass, pleading to come back.

Hans grows calm and excuses himself. I tell him to call back that evening when he feels better and has talked to his mother, and that when he calls he must give me directions to the service. He promises to call back tonight, after the evening meal. I expect him to break that promise.

"Bis spater, Hesta. Tchüss."

"Ja, tchüss, Hansi."

I hang up and lean on the cold wall, laying my left cheek on it, then my breasts, stomach and thighs, keeping my feet flat, the heels down. I fail to enter the wall, I fail to become plaster and stone. I've since tried several ways to enter walls but they remain closed to me; Galatea's dead but I can't return to what I was, I remain flesh.

I go to the bathroom, turn on the light and sit on the toilet with my hands over my ears. For me a bathroom has always been a place where erotic thoughts come easily. I go into a habitual reverie: I see myself in a post-coital languor, being pinned by Otto's weight, it pushes me into the bed; I feel flattened, my lungs are squashed, it's hard to breathe; in the meantime, he slows me down with gentle, ever lighter thrusts until his body becomes still; then, waiting for me to recover, he contracts his penis, twitching it inside me, as if it's gasping for air. I imagine all this as accurately as if it were real, but it passes quickly without the usual arousal, and allows my mind to shift to another thing that obsesses me: his wife.

I see Francine in bed, big plastic glasses on her nose, an intellectual reading her novel; this is how I always see her. At first, the habitual scene: him beside her, in white pajamas, studying a blueprint – Zeus and Hera in their misty boudoir. Then I remember, and Otto vanishes, and a new view forms. She gets out of bed and walks, a suffering old queen, to an antiquated window. She has graying blonde hair, worked into a French braid, and stands straight, holding hands against cheeks, staring out over the rooftops of a medieval town; the hands are long, red and shiny. . .

I shake her away.

In the right hand soap holder, next to the faucet, is a pile of dry nail clippings from Otto's fingers and toes. They are shaped like new moons but the way they cross each other reminds me of strange things: Turkish scimitars, boomerangs, misplaced American smiles. Leaning forward on the toilet seat, with the little finger of my right hand I brush them into the palm of my left, then sprinkle them into the toilet bowl where they spread out, moving to the edges of the clean water. Two or three cling in the crevice of my lifeline. I eat them.

My bladder aches, but I can't pee. I stand up and throw anything of Otto's that I can see into the trash bin under the sink: disposable razor (there are reddish brown hairs trapped between the double blades), shaving foam, clear brown English soap, Swedish face cream, steel comb, scissors, dental floss, deodorant powder. Then I stop, realizing that if I continue, everything would be thrown away and I would have to jump in on top of it. I sit back on the toilet and the pee comes, weakly at first, then in a gush.

Standing in my bedroom doorway, I let a bead of urine run down to my ankle. I wipe it off with my foot. The room looks as if apes lived there. My collection of shoes is spread out, scattered, all over the floor. Normally, they are arranged neatly under the window. As I gather them, joining pairs, I remember how they got so muddled: on Friday night he wanted me to model them all – for some reason it infuriated me. I hurled shoes at him. Then we made love. I wore a burgundy shoe on one foot and a pastel-yellow one on the other.

After picking up the bedroom, I do the living room, put it all in order. I organize magazines by language and date, then, using the teak tray, I bring everything in off the balcony. I straighten the Spanish rug, sit on it, and look at the open doors in the apartment. My hands and feet are numb. Of course, it is stupid to put off the kitchen.

I collect everything that needs to go into the kitchen – crockery, glasses, bottles, old bread, chocolate wrappers, cutlery – onto the big teak tray that Otto brought me from India. It was beautiful, despite the knife gouges in the middle. Its rich brown handles swirled with carved depictions of Siva's life. I set it by the wall between the bedroom and the kitchen. On Saturday, I had used the tray to bring Otto a sandwich, and he, filled with cognac, told me the tray was a wedding gift; all the things he gave me were wedding gifts – he said we had a marriage of the soul.

I guess, because a marriage of the soul wasn't enough for me and hadn't been for a long time, I got so mad that I ran into the kitchen, got the bread knife and went back into the bedroom. Naked on the bed, he bit into the sandwich with one hand and held the tray with the other. I lunged at him. I had no idea I was capable of such rage. It felt good, Rodney, it felt awfully good. I lunged again and again, chasing him around the apartment. He was a terrified, naked man defending himself with an antique tray of exotic design. I hope you'll never make me do this to you.

When my fury cooled we talked it over, but he couldn't understand what had happened to me, he couldn't understand that in releasing one of my passions he'd released them all.

I get up from the Spanish rug and take the tray into the kitchen, setting it on the counter beside the cooker. In the gloom of the shuttered kitchen I notice the blue ring of gas flame that Otto, as usual, forgot to turn off. When I raise the shutter, I see the mess. He had made a flask of instant coffee and a sandwich for the trip south. On the counter, beside a jar with the lid put on crookedly, is spilled coffee, breadcrumbs, discarded grease paper from the cold cuts and the infamous bread knife covered in mustard.

Blood has soaked into the smallest of the cutting boards; this reminds me of the faint smell of antiseptic plaster when his hand caressed my face in the night before he left. He always wandered around in the dark and was forever injuring himself. While tears blind me, I clear him up and put him away.

And there it was, in English, the thing I was frightened of yet longed for on a scrap of light green paper, the note that he never fails to leave, secured to the refrigerator with the magnet bearing the Masonic symbol of the sun. I copy it out for you here:

Darling,
   You have the most magnificent lips, the most magnificent breasts, hips, legs and bottom, you are a copy of the Goddess of Love, a fantasy of Jove. But it is four A.M. and I must drive south to the canton of gnomes. I love you and will most certainly telephone from Wien, Geneva or Milano – wherever I hide in midweek.
   Think of me and do not be tempted by that swine, Rodney Thorson. He is a stinking Englishman who wants to take you away from me. Ignore him.
   I kiss my hand every day where it last touched you. Please, sorry for the mess. However, I do not want you waking because we always have difficulty at the door because we will be apart so long.
   Moreover, you had a unrestful weekend. Please, no more carving knifes. I am your slave next time.

I wrote the recipe for that which I made on Saturday in the cookbook. Do not prepare this for Rodney.

I love you my darling,

Your own "Blotto"

I read this note, then reach up to the shelf and take that yellow cookbook from Mom's church down. It smells of stale spice, halloween, church basements. This file card drops out:

Hackfleisch des Ottos

- As much meat as you want
- A big onion, a big carrot, a big turnip
- A tin tomaten
- Some stock cubes (Oxo)
- Some white flour
- Whatever seasonings you like

Cut it all up and put it in your crock pot and cook it all day while you make love with an American girl, preferably Hesta Larson. Eat with fresh black bread and port wine.

I was cleaning the counter tops at one o'clock when Bodo Haller called from the language school. Everyone had let him down, all the instructors were calling in sick.

"No," I said, "I'm not coming in, a friend of mine just died. Forget it."

He was annoyed at first, but behind his voice is always a permissiveness that allows me anything I want. He's similar in some ways to Otto, only older and even less mature. The fool thinks if he waits long enough he'll get me into bed. He talked and talked about absenteeism but I soon stopped listening. I didn't think about it at the time, or I might have blown my top, but when I told Haller someone close to me just died he asked if it was Rodney Thorson, who wasn't merely absent but hadn't even called in. When I said, no it wasn't Rod, he seemed disappointed.

"Look, Bodo," I said finally, "I'm going to need a few days off. A week perhaps, to get things sorted out. I'm taking sick-time 'til I'm ready to come back."

"Ach Mensch! Das hat mir gerade noch gefehlt. Hesta, bitte, bitte. . . Mein Lieber Mann, noch eine Katastrophe!" You should've heard the receiver squeaking as I returned it to its cradle.

About three years ago, I tried to escape from Otto. It was while I was at Lausanne in my second year of graduate school, and met him during a shopping trip to Geneva. As you so well know I was pretty inexperienced with men. So I stood no chance against the wolf weapons of Otto. Brilliant, passionate, sophisticated, he understood the many processes by which the lamb lures the wolf. He recognized that I was a late bloomer with a self-esteem problem. You know what he did? He x-rayed me, saw my potential shape.

I was sitting alone in a cafe one wet afternoon. He sat several tables away and I felt his eyes on me. I had this tingling sensation. After a while I dared to look at him directly; those eyes, turquoise, like lakes, gazing into me, full of laughter. His face was round and ruddy with a thick beard, and his black hair, shot through with gray, was wild and unkempt. He wore a polo shirt and I liked his brown muscular arms. I dared to smile. He stood instantly.

My stomach quivered as he sat at my table.

Did I need an affair, was that what he saw? Had my sexuality been so criminally retarded that it was about to gush forth, uncontrolled? It felt like it, after ten minutes I was in love. He talked with his beautiful hands wrapped around a wine glass, gently touching my wrist with his forefinger to make points. We talked about everything, and did so in three languages. He told me I was a brilliant linguist and had a spectacular future. I can't express how flattered I felt that this older, wiser, man, this architect of dreams, took me seriously. I guess my up-bringing had starved my confidence rather than my sexuality, which was merely hibernating, waiting for the winter of my mother's religion to pass. Otto built my confidence and thereby, I firmly believe, unleashed my full potential. And although I recognize that this process, on both our parts, was unhealthy, I am grateful – I can honestly say that.

We first made love three days later and I was ecstatic for three months until he told me he was married. Then we were on and off for a time while he got me used to the idea. Like a fool, I just assumed he didn't sleep with his wife. When he admitted that he did, I wanted out, I wanted Minnesota.

And this was when he really got me.

My visa was almost expired and, despite the strongest attraction I had ever felt, and the fact that my body was now accustomed to being loved, my instincts – I now think of them as my old midwestern ones – were telling me to run.

One beautiful fall afternoon, we walked beside Lake Geneva, trying to decide what to do. We were miserably in love. I was so standoffish and bitchy that I could hardly walk normally. He was maddeningly reasonable:

"Of course you must leave me. You are young and I am old, and you are in the most vigorous time of your life. Perhaps I have helped you a little, taught you something. Find a nice young fellow, forget all about old Otto."

Walking and talking, angry as hell, ready to leave Europe forever, my feet blistering on the pavement, I came to the sudden realization that everything we did and said was lovemaking, that we were tangled together in an embrace that contained everything; love is not an adequate word – there is no word for this sickness, this forbidden joy. For when the tears sprang into his eyes and he ad-mitted that he couldn't imagine life without me, my resolution to leave scattered like a flock of doves. We went to a hotel and I gave up everything to him, ac-cepted everything the way it was, opened myself entirely.

My reward was also an entrapment.

I'm about to be blunt, Rodney, and I know you'd hate this if you read it, I know it would hurt you. I'm sorry.

I had an orgasm so intense that I tore the sheet and bit a hole in my lip and screamed so loud I was hoarse after. I was still shaking from it a half hour later when Otto reached for me again. It was the first I'd ever had like that, something, I'm sure, many women seldom experience. Otto was quietly pleased with himself. It was then that I learned how most of his pleasure came from watching me lose myself. I was wrapped in the ecstasy of self-imposed bondage. And of course he knew how to keep what I wanted in short supply so that I was always hungry for him. Even now I hear Mother saying such passion is unnatural, that the gift of sex is the reward of Satan. That made it even sweeter.

Writing this drives me nuts. Sometimes I think I'd be better off as a scholarly maiden aunt and do without men altogether.

Then what happened?

The apartment's tidy enough to win Mom's approval. And there's a knock on the door. I go rigid. There's a second knock. In my mind I whisper go away go away go away.

"Hesta, I know you're in there. Answer the door, it's Rod."

I hold my breath.

"Come on, you silly cow," you shout, "I'm looking through the keyhole at you."

I pull on Otto's rugby shirt, which I'd found earlier under the couch, and open the door. As I do this I realize there is no keyhole, you tricked me, clever old you. You walk past me, looking all around, patting my cheek, saying, "I lied."

You sit, smiling in the middle of the couch with your arms spread across its back. "So, has that sleazy old bugger slung his hook? Can a bloke talk to you now?"

Heavy with self-conscious irony, and already ashamed of myself before the utterance is complete, I say, "Yes, Otto's gone."

You say, "This is how I see it. I've got a couple of weeks to make you see that I'm the right bloke for you. Let's have a wild, romantic affair, all right? We'll go away to the mountains and talk abut babies and growing old together. And if I fail to persuade you to dump that old fuck, I'll do the noble and gentlemanly thing — beat the shit out of him."

I examine your big suntanned face with its blond eyebrows and crooked white teeth. I kneel in front of you and gaze deeply into your eyes. Your eyelids flutter suddenly and you frown. "What's the matter, Hesta?" you say, and boy do you ever get an answer.

You took care of me. We drove into France. You thought it was good for me. I felt guilty because this was what Otto was afraid of — that someday Rodney Thorson, the stinking Englishman, would be the one to look after me. Everything was cheaper. You bought me an apple from a roadside vendor, an old woman in black, who assumed we were lovers and gave us a whole bag for a franc.

We sat in your Mini, looking at the river and eating apples. It was a fine autumn day and the sun warmed my face. All the leaves had fallen and the light was rather harsh; it made me think of white blood which in turn reminded me of Otto's semen that had threatened to run down my leg that morning. Most of it, of course, would have leaked into my underwear by then, but I fancied that I retained a portion of it in me, I fancied myself as a kind of grail, holding to myself the last living cells of the architect of love, Otto Schulte.

It was past nine when you got me home. I wanted to be alone for a while so you left. The apartment was cozy and tidy but the shutters were up and the cold darkness looked in with its stars and street lights. I could smell Otto. I drew a bath, crying the whole time. Then the phone rang and my skin jumped. That's when I first started to lose it.

"Otto," I thought, "it's you and you've faked death to escape Francine you have a new identity a secret bank account we're going to run away to Sweden oh God please please please I'll believe in you forever please God."

"Hesta, hier ist Hansi."

"So. What then?"

"Yes, come to the funeral, I have fixed it. But it will be shocking. It will be big, everyone comes. Try to avoid confrontation and stay away from the children, they know nothing of his affairs."

"I'll want to speak to your mother."

"Nein! Unmöglich."

"Hansi? Be nice to me."

"I will be nice," he says, "but today I am sorry for Mother. She takes it very badly."

"I've never even seen a photograph of her. He didn't want me to ever think of her but I do, all the time."

"She thinks you're after his money. Stay out of her way. She will slap your face."

I'm about to scream at him but he cuts me off, "If you come down by train, I can meet you at the railway station on Wednesday morning. Visitation is at two o'clock. He will be cremated in the evening."

"It's all so fast," I say.

"Yes, yes," he says, "it is how we do such things."

That night the bed smelled of Otto. I searched the pillow case with my nose until I found the faint smell where, behind his ears, he usually forgot to wash; and I found the wiry smell of his beard; and the scent of his farts were hiding between the sheets, their gastric ingredients easily identifiable – strong cheese, cognac, port, numerous lighter wines, fine sausage, asparagus. I found tiny specks of skin, mine and his, mixed together in the sheets.

I tried to sleep with the shutters up but the sight of the white apartments opposite gave me nightmares. I took a blanket and lay in front of the door where I have so often waited for him when he was late or simply didn't come. Even now, when I'm alone after a little too much to drink, I'll go to a door and scratch on it like a cat.

I dreamed of avalanches. Avalanches of mothers, mothballs, Victorian furniture, great white hotels crashing down mountains into lakes, nets full of salmon and trout being dumped into my kitchen, great choirs of babies crying in the mountains then bursting from the valleys onto the plains as roaring, invading barbarians with wild blue eyes and tangled beards. The night was a long surrealistic miasma, packed with the life of the world, but at dawn it suddenly calmed and Otto appeared to me. He was a silhouette standing in the bathroom doorway. "Otto," I said, "Otto." He didn't answer, just shifted his position, crossing his arms like a boy in a funk. I had the sense that there was some sign in the movement, some articulation that I should know. "Otto," I whispered, "have you survived?"

He seemed to tense himself, to bunch up the way weightlifters do. "Yes," he said, then walked the few steps to our bedroom where he stood with his back to me in the doorway. The bedroom was alive with light and when he turned to look at me his eyes were luminous within the silhouette. Again, I had that sense of some great articulation that was beyond me.

There was a knock on the door. I kept my eyes on the silhouette. The apartment was filling with light. There was a second knock: "Hesta. Hesta, it's me, Rod."

"Come through the keyhole."

"Very funny. Open up."

The silhouette leaned casually against the left doorframe with its toes turned up at the base of the right frame. A black right arm reached out and a black finger beckoned me to come.

"Hesta, open the fucking door."

Unsteadily, I stood. The apartment was all atilt, all the angles were wrong, distorted; I had to clasp the door handle to keep from sliding into the living room. Otto started toward me.

"Open it, Hesta!"

"I can't."

Blackness suffocating me, no air, my hands grasped at black liquid, no up or down, no way out, being smothered.

There's a crash and I hurtle from the hallway into the living room. I clutch the couch and my life spins before me. You're in the doorway, rubbing your shoulder, and the apartment begins to right itself. I look for Otto but he's gone — he was always afraid of you.

You walk forward and get your feet tangled in the blankets. You fall on your face and I laugh, say something idiotic like, "You're a dream clown, make me laugh again." I'm in quiet hysterics, absolutely freaking out. You were a dream saving me from a nightmare.

You untangle yourself from the blanket and come over to me, putting the blanket around my shoulders.

"I don't care what anybody thinks," I say, "that wasn't a dream. I don't exactly know what it was, but it was no dream."

I'm on the couch with the blanket over me while you make a pot of tea. The phrase *nervous breakdown* keeps repeating itself in my mind. Mother had one once you know, during that first trouble I told you about, when she and Dad nearly split up. I was quite young, but I remember her shaking uncontrollably in church, surrounded by ladies with blue hair who clucked and flapped around her like buzzards. I see her and myself shaking, I see the walls of the apartment shaking, I see myself and Dad and his sexy little girlfriends. Dad and Otto as one. Mom and Francine. . .the old mothers set for betrayal.

You sat beside me and forced me to drink that sweet milky swill that you call tea. I told you about my night and then you fixed the damage to my door lock.

We went to France again, crossing the Rhine in a downpour, and lunched at an empty cafe that you'd taken other women to in a suburb of Mulhouse. We ordered scrambled eggs, black coffee and baguettes with butter. As we ate, the rain strengthened and beat against the window. Ghastly French music played in the kitchen and the waiter had a big nose. The cafe echoed if we scraped chair legs against the dirty brown floor.

While we eat, I tell you of my intention to take the train to Bern on Wednesday. You finish your food, wipe your plate with some bread, and say:

"Over my dead body – not after what I saw this morning."

"I'm going."

"Not by train you're not. I can just see you acting nutty like that on the train. The way the Swiss are they'll lock you up in a second."

"How shall I go then, ambulance?"

"I'll take you. I'll take a couple more days off. Bodo Haller can fuck himself. You're not going alone."

"Why're you being so domineering?"

"If you haven't sussed that one out, you're a half-wit."

I avoid commenting on this, say: "All right, but back off a bit, will you? Anyway, you drive like a maniac, we'll never make it."

"Fine, but you're not going alone, you're too daft."

"Okay, okay. Pass the bread. I'll have to call and ask Hans for directions. He'll be relieved not to have to meet me at the station."

"That little pansy."

"Stop it."

"I hate the Swiss."

"You hate Otto, that's all. Don't blame the whole country. Now who's acting crazy?"

"You're right, but that little pillock, Hans, I'll tell you, he'll grow up just like his old man, thinking he owns the place and everybody in it."

"Hey, come on, your class hatred's showing. Switzerland isn't England."

"Oh, sod you, what do you know about class?"

"Not much. Pass the butter."

After a long pause, you say, "I'm cleaner than these rich old businessmen, Hesta. I think you know that. I can give you a real life."

It was another of your declarations that I stupidly took so long to take seriously. I butter a piece of bread and dip it in my coffee – taste the smooth butter, melting on the bread in my mouth as I gaze out of the window at the jumping rain.

We left early next morning because I wanted to take the same route Otto took, I wanted to see where he crashed.

You went home briefly on Tuesday afternoon to get some clothes and stayed over that night, sleeping on the couch. I slept well with you there. When you woke me you had gray suit pants on and a white shirt with rolled-up sleeves and a loosened red tie. It was still dark out.

I don't know why, as you know I've never been in the least extroverted, but I wanted to stand out at the funeral. I wore the black lingerie Otto bought me last time we were in Luxembourg, black stockings from Copenhagen, a red blouse we bought in Saarbrücken, the tight charcoal suit he bought me when we were in Paris, black high heels from Milan, black purse and beret, both from our trip to Portugal, black cotton gloves from god-knows-where that he made me wear a few times while we made love. If I'd had black lipstick and nail polish I would have worn it, but I didn't, so I wore red. Your comment was:

"What's this, the Dutch dominitrix look? And for Christ's sake comb your hair, you look like something out of *Last Tango in Paris*."

"I told you not to boss, leave me alone."

"Fine, but you look a right old tart."

"Maybe I am a goddamn tart."

"Steady on."

"Don't say *steady on*. I hate it when you say that."

"Steady on."

"You son of a bitch."

It was tedious getting out of Basel during rush hour and I fell asleep. I woke with a shiver, the taste of lipstick in my mouth. It seemed that I'd only been asleep a few seconds but it had been nearly two hours. The windshield wipers were on and you were hurtling around a rocky bend. We were deep in the Jura.

I watched you drive for a moment, then said, "Hey, steady on, Jackie Stewart."

You grinned and said, "I thought I'd make some headway before the Sleeping Dominitrix woke and started nagging."

"Where are we?"

"Just passed Courroux."

"I wanted to see the whole route."

"It's very misty, not much to see."

"It happened somewhere between Moutier and Reconvilier."

"We're not far off. But I doubt if you'll be able to see anything."

I shrugged, then looked out of the window at the drenched terrain that was visible only where the mist thinned. Here and there harvested cornstalks grew right up to the curb on one side of the road while opposite was a sheer face of rock. The route turned into a meandering valley road, cut into the side of the old mountains, that roughly followed a little river. The road surface was greasy and treacherous but you, as always, didn't slow down. I was about to insist that you do so when I suddenly knew, with absolute certainty, that around the next bend I would see the place where Otto went over the edge.

"We're coming to it now," I said.

As we rounded a massive rock abutment I saw the road rise up into the mist. Beside the road grew tall dank trees that hung naked in the gray air. A blue tractor, hauling three trailers full of hay up the steep hill, was slowly entering the thick mist.

"It'll be up there, Rod."

"More than likely," you said, "Are you going to be all right?"

"Yes. Don't worry."

I needed some time to adjust, to get ready, but we were accelerating up the hill within moments of rounding the abutment. It was very steep but we soon caught up with the tractor. The dense mist ahead, coupled with the steering wheel being on the right side of the car, prevented you from overtaking. You shouted:

"Fucking bloody swine, move that shit over."

"Relax."

"Bloody swine."

I started to cry. I knew it would upset you even more, but it just came. It must have been hard for you, poor darling, seeing someone you love pining after a dead lover.

You slammed the car into second gear and blindly swung around the tractor, laying on the horn. We passed slowly, all the time risking a head-on collision with anything coming the other way; the farm worker, for his part, went as fast as he could. I knew that when we drew level with the driver something would happen and sure enough you gave him the finger and the man grinned and waved. It was Otto's grin.

"It's him, it's him, Rodney! Stop the car!"

"What the hell are you on about?"

"It's Otto. In the tractor."

"Don't be so daft. It's just a little farmer of about sixty with rotten teeth."

We roared up the hill, laboring the engine, while I told myself to relax, to remember Mother's nervous breakdown. The little man, of course, looked nothing like Otto. I tried to see Otto's face in my mind's eye, but it wouldn't come, I couldn't get the details.

After a few minutes we emerged from the mist into an expanse of blue sky and green plateau. In the distance, in a wide circumference, the familiar white cat's teeth of the Alps pricked the gray underbellies of the clouds. The valleys were filled with mist that was being drawn off in long ghostly wisps by the morning sun. The road descended slightly toward an acute curve; there was nothing beyond the curve but mist. As we approached I saw the temporary orange barrier thrown across the breech in the safety wall.

"This must be it," you said, and pulled into a scenic overlook just beyond the barrier.

As I walked back I was surprised that my imagined picture of the crash site was so completely wrong. I had him plunging over the east side of the road; the skid marks went over the west side; and the terrain was nowhere near as mountainous as I'd envisaged. I went in front of the orange trestles, leaned over the shattered wall and looked down.

The mist was lifting rapidly, and what at first seemed just a ravine was gradually revealed as a small valley or glen. It was mostly wooded, with some scattered pastures. I watched as the wreckage of the green Volvo emerged from the mist among sheer, razor edged rocks: a hub cap, a door, a wheel, a seat, pieces of plastic and green metal. Then the shape of a wide roof appeared: orange tiles with a gaping black hole slightly off center to the northeast corner. I was wincing at the sharpness everywhere.

Gently, holding my elbows, you eased me away, saying, "You're been standing here a long time. Come back in the car and get warm."

I'm in the car.

You mumble, "Do you want to go down? Would it help?"

I say yes and we're back down the hill, passing the blue tractor, parked and empty by the roadside. And you somehow find your way into the little glen where big trees, dark conifers mostly, with their deciduous companions holding rags of mist in place with spikey, hoar-frosted branches, stand brooding like frozen ghosts. You stop in a badly rutted lane, before a rusted iron gate.

"He would've been conscious until he hit that roof."

"No, Hesta. That's a hell of a rocky drop, he'd have been knocked out on the windscreen when he went through the barrier. He wouldn't have known anything."

"He wore his seat belt, Rodney. Not like you."

"Still, there's an awful lot of wreckage. I bet he didn't know much."

"I feel it. He called out my name just before he died."

"You're being silly again."

"Leave me alone. He thought of me."

"If you say so."

"He thought of me and he looked at the stars. The stars were lovely that night. And he called out the name of his son as he plunged into the abyss."

"Look. Hey, look at me, Hesta! Get a grip on yourself, all right?"

"Fuck off."

"Look love, I've been watching you make up all this stuff and I think there's something sick about it. I'm sorry the geezer's kicked the bucket and everything, but you've got to keep things in perspective. There're things you can't know and there's no sense in trying to know them, just let it rest and stop torturing yourself."

"You son of a bitch, who do you think you're parenting?"

"You don't get it, do you? Has it ever crossed your fog-bound little brain that I might care about you? Has it? And I wish you'd cut out the swearing, it'd make a sailor blush."

"He loved me, me. Not Francine, me. You're not half the man Otto is. You're a boy, a mere boy. Don't think you're going to wheedle your way into my bed by doing me a few favors. I'm on to you. I bet you have a fiancée back in England, a wife even, I bet you've got a goddamn wife."

"Hesta, this is stupid. You're making me angry."

"Leave me alone."

"Leave me alone."

"Don't mimick me, you creep."

"Grow up then."

"You grow up!"

Your knuckles go white on the steering wheel. I want you to slap me so I can hate you forever. After a while you shake your head and say, "Life goes on, for Christ's sake, life goes on." I sit on my hands to keep from scratching out your eyes.

Soon you got out of the Mini and opened the rusty gate. You drove beyond the gate, got out again and closed it, then we drove through a steep meadow and into a dense copse that nestled below the hillside. You stopped abruptly and a spray of gravel shot into the ditch beside me. "This is it," you said, pointing, "Your barn."

I could see the barn up a narrow track of gravel in which a heavy vehicle had recently made deep ruts. You were sulking and it annoyed me, but I apologized for being a bitch while all the time my eyes were on the great stone barn as we carefully approached, scraping and revving in the ruts.

It was all that remained of an abandoned farm complex that by the looks of it had suffered a bombardment of minor avalanches after the road above it was built. The barn was surrounded by deep brown mud. We parked by the north wall. I was about to get out and trudge through the mud but you said wait and fished around behind my seat, producing a pair of your soccer boots, you still have them, the ones with yellow laces. I took off my heels and put the boots on, lacing them tightly. Then I stepped out of the car and walked to the barn door in the slippery, churned up mud, feeling like a clown with huge feet.

Looking into the barn, fascinated, I called, "Rodney, it doesn't look at all like a Volvo. You can see why he didn't survive. Nothing's intact. Only the chassis with a few things twisted around it."

"All right," you said, "Go in. Go all the way in."

You spoke in your usual soft voice but we were in a kind of amphitheater so that you sounded strange, oracle-like.

The compressed car had smashed through the roof and onto the flagstone floor. Roofing, rocks, branches and splintered beams were entangled with the wreckage. There was the smell of oil, then other smells: petroleum, urine, dung, rust, plastic – and finally all the smells mingled and there was the smell of blood. Water dripped somewhere.

After a while you stood beside me.

"Rod, I can't move."

"Go on."

"I'll faint."

"Go on, you're no fainter."

Once inside the circle of wreckage it became clear where the steering wheel and driver's seat were. Tiles, glass, plastic and the multitude of shaped metals that go into a car cracked under my soccer boots. Above, birds sang through the hole in the roof, the white air was visible, and so was a bit of mountain, and a few overhanging branches. Foolishly, I sought the color red.

"Rod, there's no blood anywhere. He could've survived."

Very gently you said, "It's all around you."

It is. Like spilled gravy. Dried where it's thin, wrinkled and tacky where it lies thick. Like rusty motor oil everywhere, over everything. Wretching, I cover my mouth, swallowing the bile that comes in spasms, while the wreckage, the hole in the roof, the yellow laces, the flagstones, the dripping water, the barn walls spin and spin and spin. Then there's your face and pressure under my armpits.

I sit in the Mini with the door open and my feet in the mud, breathe cold wet air. . .long drips fall through the trees and smack the forest floor. . .bird song. . .a truck up on the highway. . .underwear uncomfortably tight. You cough as you unlace the boots, knock them against the back wheel, put them in the trunk. Spots of cold water touch my face. Your hands on my legs, smooth through the nylon, putting them into the car, closing the door, then your door, sitting beside me, starting the engine. . .just sitting staring with the heater blowing and rain hitting the roof.

To yourself you say, "Poor bugger."

I say, "It's horrible how you blend in and disappear. He's blending into everything and I can't remember his face."

"You going to be all right?"

I could only shrug.

"I suppose we'd better get going."

"Yes. Get me out of here."

The rain falls harder. I want to move, I sense danger, a predator on my tail. There comes a sudden deluge of rain, making the mud thwack all around us like flailing fish fins. You rev the engine, spinning the wheels out of the barnyard and through a pair of rotted gateposts. The windshield wipers go smear clear smear clear smear clear smear clear, and, coming up fast, a man stands in the track, appearing and disappearing with the smear-clear of the wipers.

"Otto! Rodney, it's Otto!"

Otto's covered in mud, wet through, but you roar over him so fast there's scarcely a bump.

"You swine, you ran him down."

"Get a hold, will you?"

Through the back window, in the jumping mud, I see disjointed body parts quivering and writhing, squirting blood and viscera, pink intestines and purple organs steaming, the face half buried upside down with its mouth gaping like a drowning fish. My seat belt won't undo.

"Hesta, what're you doing, what's the matter?"

"You killed Otto, you ran him down."

"There's no one. Get a grip."

"Stop the fucking car, will you!"

You stopped and backed up as far as the gateposts.

"Satisfied?"

"I saw him."

"It was just somebody wandering around or something. That little farmer on the tractor perhaps." You put your hand around the back of my neck and turned my face to yours. "Otto is dead, Hesta. You can't bring him back with fantasy. It's over."

"I know. I'm not nuts, despite what you think. But I saw him. Seeing is seeing."

"Okay. Okay. I'm the one who should calm down. Okay. Seeing Otto, who is grisly dead, is not nuts but is hallucination. Agreed?"

"Sure. But I still saw him."

"No one there though."

"You're a bit thick, Rodney. A bit too technical. Seeing is seeing. It means stuff."

"Now you're giving me the creeps."

"Don't be silly, Englishmen can't get the creeps."

"You must be at least partially sane."

"I'm glad this is over," I say, "Drive to Bern."

111

"Marvelous. We can continue our day of psychic masochism?"

"Drive on."

I can no longer separate dream and reality.

Driving down the Aargauerstalden, in what should've been the driver's seat but wasn't, toward the Bern Altstaat is more like a dream in my memory than something I actually experienced. I put this down to being nuts; I was, after all, existing in a kind of fog. The events surrounding the death of Otto have brought home to me the peculiarity of memory; how do we keep track of the difference between things we've seen and done, things we've imagined and things we've dreamed? If one could project them all onto a big video screen, there'd be only one person, oneself, able to distinguish history from fiction. It mostly seems to depend on a coding of images, a remembrance of remembrances. I'll make a study of neurology one of these days but I don't suppose it'll help much.

And the image I hold of our descent into the old part of Bern is reflected back to me more like something I conjured myself while dreamily reading some epic romance. In the distance, to the south and east, there are mountain peaks brilliantly white against a gray moisture-loaded sky: the Bernese Alps. "Oh look," you say, gazing over the splendor of Old Bern as if the place had never existed, "the Jungfrau to the right and then the Mönch and the Eiger to the left, see? I've been up the Jungfrau. It's brilliant when you get high up, you can see everything as it really is."

I'm not much interested in mountains, my eyes are on this forbidden city. Forbidden to me because the ancient Schulte family resides here, has for centuries; but that doesn't matter, what matters is that Francine lives here. Otto insisted that under no circumstances was I to visit.

But here I am.

The city juts high out of a loop in the River Aare. Its modern suburbs cluster around but the magic, the romance, remains within the river's loop.

"Where to now?" you ask.

I'm consulting the back of an envelope; directions I took over the phone from Hansi – it's an utter mystery, the strange hieroglyphic scrawl of a psychotic. Something about *Crossing the Nydeggbrucke – on the corner is the bear-pit. Can't miss this turn, is main bridge into old town, park near Cathedral. On foot to. . .*unreadable.

You turn at the tourist-engulfed Barengraben. You turn against the law-abiding traffic, answering the blasting horns, "Yes yes yes, keep your bloody hair on," and we rocket over the bridge to the cobbles of Gerechtigkeitgasse, swerving around monuments and trolley cars, fools on bicycles and oblivious tourists until we jolt into a parking place in Kramgase, right in front of the clock tower. I get out and look at the famous Zytgloggeturm with its twelfth-century jesters, bears and kings, parading like corpses four minutes before every hour around an astrological clock face.

We walked along the arcades, dodging crowds of people, stepping over street musicians, stepping down into the road where the crowds became impassable, and somehow, I don't know how, you found the romanesque building where the funeral service was to be held, prior to the cremation – it was almost as though you knew the way – it was somewhere west of the Münster in a little dark alley, and was, to my surprise, a Masonic temple. I got a feeling that a lot had been kept from me. I have that feeling even now, about everything.

Stepping inside an enormous oak door onto worn flagstones I'm suddenly cold. My heels scrape harshly. A gloomy reception area gives way to a circular room, illuminated by four round stained-glass windows, placed symmetrically in the high walls, depicting, with great ostentation, various acts by shepherds and maidens against the ancient symbols of an astrological cosmos. The walls are white; there are no chairs or pews. The ceiling, supported by thick oak beams, is corbeled and oat-colored like the inside of a judge's wig. The floor is an intricate mosaic in the same style as the windows.

I feel inexplicably illiterate.

A plain walnut coffin with silver handles rests on wrought iron trestles as thin and black as spider legs. A small black-clad figure sits on a stool with her back to the door. She sits with the coffin at the center of a pentagram within a circle of twelve unlit candle-stands that match the trestle legs.

The old woman turns and frowns. We come forward until she hisses something in what I take to be Romansch. Then she repeats it in French: *"Vous arrivéz trop tôt. Pour l'instant, seule la famille est admise. Il vous faudra revenir à deux heures."*

Everything's red before my eyes, there are little black bouncing flecks in my vision, black stars.

I've exchanged places with the old woman; I'm on the stool, leaning against your stomach with the old woman patting my hands while I stare at the kaleidoscopic swirling of the floor. The floor soothes me as if it's the generator of all natural things, as if, at this moment, everything's relative and I'm just a small part of something colossal; the fight's over, it says, you can relax.

I try to see Otto but can only conjure the vaguest outline of his big head and beard shot through with white, his barrel chest and heavy limbs. . .no, the limbs had grown rather thin since Geneva, and his buttocks were flattening out and sagging. I work hard for clear vision: skyblue or turquoise eyes, at any rate very changeable; and his big teeth, gold-filled and coffee-stained, but strong enough to gnaw down trees; then I see his penis at rest across his thigh while he sleeps – very unintimidating like that, the head nestling back in its foreskin, encrusted with the dried residue of our love. I inspected it once, its detail was magnificent: its wide pink mouth breathed with him as if it had a tiny cardiovascular system all its own. How many gallons of urine and pints of semen had it spat into the world? How many women had it been in, how long would its potency last? I touched it with the tip of my tongue and its mouth opened like that of a blind snake.

With some effort I can feel again that delirium I sank into, that floating chaos, that tortured tangle of languages, a frenetic confusion of grammars. Hell must be like that: no stability of meaning.

I must have been babbling out all that I saw because you were shaking my shoulders, trying to quiet me. The old woman obviously picked up the gist of whatever I was saying because she suddenly slapped me very hard.

The slap shocks me: Otto's coffin looms from the shadows of my peripheral vision into the center of this strange place, and I think it's breathing, or rather, quaking as though it could burst open and engulf me.

I'm up and walking towards the door. I can hear my shoes. Your hands hurt my armpits, you're hissing instructions into my right ear. From the door you call out, "Oui, Madame Schulte, nous reviendrons a deux heurs. Elle se sentira mieux. Eh oui, vous comprenez...elle est tres émue."

The old woman said, "Elle devrait manger un peu en attendant."

I felt more in control as we walked through the crowds looking for somewhere to pass the time until the service or the visitation (I'm still not sure exactly what it was). We ended up at Zeughausgasse outside the Hotel Metropole, so we went in.

My mind was full of the coffin and the blackness of Otto's mother, and I began obsessing upon the possible survival time of spermatozoa, minute amounts of which, I presume, were still lingering in the recesses of my body.

The restaurant ceiling of the Metropole was very high and cream-colored, the walls had a pale gold and blue floral pattern as far down as the wood paneling, the carpet was maroon and the table cloths starched and white. The maître d'hôtel us next to a grand piano that was polished into a black mirror. I became fascinated looking into this black mirror piano; it recalled the atmosphere of my dreams, the music of the subconscious, the deadly, polished outsideness of a coffin.

I listen: there's a muffled buzz of traffic, not enough to counter each click of a fork or knife hitting a plate or the carefully modulated converstiaon of the well-to-do, inclining their heads graciously to each other, inclining their heads graciously to the waiters who served them; the old men and women who sit alone, incline their heads graciously to their own unexpressed thoughts, staring at white tablecloths.

"Rod," I said in a carefully modulated tone, inclining my head, "What's the survival time of spermatozoa?"

I sipped water as you looked at me.

"God," you said, "you have no mercy."

They brought coffee and the gâteau de jour which was made of chocolate, almond and raspberry, but I could hardly taste it. Then there was a paperclip. It was hard to see against the white cloth next to the water jug. I unwound it, made it very straight and placed it in the clean glass ashtray. I said, "God, Rodney, am I okay?"

"Of course you're not," you said. "But you will be."

When the waiters periodically came through the kitchen doors there was the hiss of kitchen activity, accompanied by a blast of Italian which was itself followed, thirty seconds after, by the aroma of delicacies being prepared for the evening menu. My stomach rumbled. For a moment it was possible to forget the feeling that Otto was still inside me.

"Perhaps I could eat something," I said.

"That's my girl. Have a steak. Some port. Put some iron back into you."

"Yes, okay. You're been right all day — order me a small steak. Take care of me. I'm going to the bathroom."

"You need a bath?"

"Don't start that."

"Well, for crying out loud, why call it a bathroom? It's a toilet or a lavatory. You Yanks are so bloody puritanical."

I laughed, "Am I puritanical?"

"Of course you are. You weren't designed for all this muck you've got yourself into. And now with old fuck-face out of the picture you're up against a muddle you're not equipped for."

"How can you speak of the dead like that?"

"Alive or dead he pisses me off."

"Surely he's no threat to your conquering ego now — as you so tactfully put it, he's grisly dead."

"Yes, but he's still got you, hasn't he?"

"No one's got me. I'm my own person."

"Bullshit."

"All right, fine. Now can I go to the bathroom?"

"Toilet."

"Bathroom. We have more warheads."

As I got up you grabbed my hand and held it to your mouth. "Hesta," you said, "are you really going to let me go to my grave without having the chance to love you?"

You looked so sweet gazing up at me. I touched your nose and said, "We'll see. But anyway, thanks for trying to distract me."

The ladies room was immaculate: white tile, mirrors, a heater, a bidet. I had been having sensations, intestinal shooting pains, ever since I saw Otto's coffin. I still had spermatozoa on my mind. I imagined the presence of a homunculus inside me; I was convinced of its presence. I went into the stall, took off my underpants and shoes, put the soles of my feet against the door and tried to examine myself. I had a good feel around but the little runt was hiding. I stayed in that position and began thinking of Otto, trying to see his face. I found that if I stroked myself the images came clearer. By doing this I went deeper and deeper into reverie until I could actually hear the coffee maker gurgling in the kitchen as we made love in the bedroom. Every detail of him came back to me.

I hadn't intended to masturbate, it just happened. And then I looked around, still hot in the face, wondering if I'd made a noise.

I smiled at you when I got back to the table.

"Blimey, you took your time."

"Sorry, I had to masturbate."

You should've seen your face.

The steak came. While I ate I examined the other women in the room. One in particular had been glancing at you whenever I wasn't looking, she averted her eyes when she saw me looking at her. She wore no make up. Her face was pale, her eyes and hair black; she was tall, aristocratic, with a large full-lipped mouth and straight white teeth.

"Look," you interrupted, "I know you're having a rough time. I'm trying to help because I care about you, but I think you're being a bit of a bitch and I'm warning you now that I have my limits. It's time you showed me the same respect I show you."

"You're right," I said, "I'm sorry. I'll try."

The woman looked Italian. She was alone, dressed all in black. I tried to ignore Otto as I ate the steak. He was buzzing around inside me again.

Hans Schulte appeared at the door, speaking with the maître d'hôtel. I knew him instantly although he was much taller and broader than when we went skiing together. He was shown to the Italian woman's table and greeted her soberly, standing with his hands behind his back until she invited him to sit. He began speaking in low tones, his body rigid with restraint, his head shaking a little, then nodding, then shaking again. She put her left hand up to her cheek and closed her eyes. I was eating and watching. I could hear the meat grinding in my mouth. Suddenly Hans swung around and looked directly at me. His lips moved and he turned back to the woman, said a few more things to which she inclined her head graciously. Hans then stood up, straightened himself, and came over.

When you towered over Hansi to shake hands I was struck at how contemporary the two of you were; same style of clothes and haircuts. As far as I knew you'd never met but you were immediately cordial to each other as if some bond were already in existence between you – something to do with this ridiculous Masonic thing of yours, I guess. While you exchanged a seemingly endless string of pleasantries, I noticed the Italian woman watching us.

At last Hans sat and touched my left wrist with his right forefinger, and looking at me with the same moist alpine eyes of his father, said, "I must warn you, Hesta, that there may be trouble. I cannot keep all the sides apart. I don't even know all the sides." This was someone quite different from the boy on the phone.

I said, "Who's she?" and pointed at the Italian woman.

Hans rubbed his eyes with the thumb and middle fingertip of his left hand and blew out a long stream of air.

"My father had many secrets. He had secrets from secrets. Now they converge on us like a gang of harpies."

"Is she one?"

"Fedora a harpie?" scowled Hans, "Of course not, I've known her all my life. It was a thoughtless metaphor, I should avoid them when speaking English."

We were quiet until Hans continued:

"If I were to stay with Greeks, I would have to say she is one of the goddesses."

My body went light. Already full of knowing, I whispered, "Which?"

He searched my face before shrugging and saying;

"Aphrodite."

He wasn't intending to be cruel, he was in fact laying things out for me, but I couldn't help saying, "So what am I then, according to your metaphor, a wood nymph?"

And without looking at me, sensing my shrinkage, he said, "What can I say?"

I sat back in the chair for several minutes, listening to my heartbeat, while you and Hans muttered. In my despair I glanced over at Aphrodite and we looked at each other. She had watched it all; her eyes glistened and she sat erect, solid and immovable at her table. We said everything in those seconds, it was a massive act of comprehension: I knew no facts but I felt all truth. The moment was only broken when a waiter stood between us and I felt Hans take my hand as he stood to leave. He gave a stiff little bow, kissed my fingers, said, "Dann bis spater, Hesta."

Two older men in dark suits met him at the door, his uncles probably, Lucian and Florian, and he left with them, scratching his head. I took my last bite of steak, chewed it, and despite the disgusting taste of cold blood, swallowed.

The Italian woman opened her purse and took things out. Holding a tiny lighter up to her face she tried to light a cigarette, but her hand shook so badly that a waiter had to do it for her. She blew smoke and stared at the wall, leaning on her elbows and clasping the cigarette with both hands. The tobacco smelled strong. A gray ash formed, the smoke streamed by her face in a blue plume; she hardly blinked – she was in a room somewhere with Otto, making love to the gurgle of a coffee pot, utterly lost in his presence, or perhaps it wasn't sex that obsessed her as it did me, perhaps it was some little thing, the way he regulated her drinking or nagged her about smoking. Hans had known her all his life. It was a strange kind of jealousy I felt, it was mostly curiosity devoid of malice, perhaps because it seemed to me that she must love him far more than I.

As we arrived, a little early, it was starting to rain and it seemed to me that we were ourselves no more than raindrops. The narthex (I have come to think of the Masonic temple as a kind of church and will therefore use ecclesiastical terminology to describe its contours) was now filled with tall people wearing

117

black. I stood beside you, holding your arm. I may by then have been certifiably nuts. I said, "How did these buzzards all get here at once?"

You said, "He's a bigger wig than you ever realized."

The rain intensified. People ran to the door under black umbrellas, and once inside, gave off an odor of ozone and damp wool. I wandered into the middle of them. There were a lot of middle-aged men accompanied by young women. They spoke in discreet low tones. Some of the women were alone. After a while I realized that we were in a line that was slowly filing into the sanctuary. Once in the sanctuary, the line became more defined and at its head, at the center of everything, was the coffin.

I was assigned only a portion of Otto and had no great part to play in the mourning. We were a congregation of demons, mourning the passing of one of our own. I looked around for Aphrodite and spotted her, alone, a dozen demons back, still in the narthex. She nodded at me, and I smiled; we exchanged a knowing show of fangs.

The scrape of my heels on the mosaic floor sounded like the gates of Hell opening inch by inch. Those who had already filed past the coffin were ushered, by Hans and one of his uncles, into either side of a large semicircle, according to whether or not they were family. I knew this because the mother, the woman in black who slapped me, stood in front of a group I took to be the Schulte clan. There was nothing special about this mother, no particular likeness, she was like any old woman. Several males looked like Otto though, and also one woman, whom I took to be his oldest daughter, Greta, who is a year older than I.

My throat dried when Hans led a weeping woman to the family group. Everyone stood still and watched her taking small steps with her face in her hands. She was thin and attractive from the back, and had streaks of white in her brown hair. A man in a brown suit came on her other side and helped her to a place among her children. Damn her, I thought, she's a saint – but a prude in bed, I know that much. For an agonized moment I couldn't prevent myself imagining Otto making love to her. Then I saw myself banging nails through her children's temples.

I stepped nearer and nearer, opening Hell with my feet. One moment the casket's closed, nailed shut, now suddenly it's open, revealing Otto's white, bearded face. A beautiful sheepskin's pulled up to his chin. I smell formaldehyde.

The face is false. For a moment my heart jumps; it's not him, this is an imposter, a bogus Otto! A ploy to collect insurance and unload all the demands, begin a new life!

Of course it was Otto, and as I stood over him I saw the demonwork of the mortician: embroidered nylon hair almost like his, brilliantly applied plastic make-up, but through all this the pulverized and disarranged facial bones were obvious. I restructured his face in my mind, watched him brushing his teeth, grimacing in passion, reading a poem, saying goodbye – those big stained teeth grinning.

Others before us had been whispering things to the head so I bent in close and did the same. "Otto," I said. "It's Hesta. I dreamt that you visited me after the accident. What were you doing? You scared me. You're not angry with me, are you? Who are all these women?" He was about to reply, I could tell by his eyes, when you took my arm and moved me on.

Hans put us as far away from his mother as he could.

With interest, I watched the lovely Aphrodite come closer to the coffin. She held herself regally, utterly controlled. Then a noise came from the narthex: a blond woman with two brown-haired children walking nervously behind her, pushed her way by someone who sought to stop her entering. She argued in whispers with a large man, probably Otto's brother, Lucian, who barred her way.

My attention returned to Aphrodite: she was looking into the coffin. She gazed, frowning and purse-lipped, for a half minute, then moved on. She came and stood close to me, close enough for me to smell her perfume.

An elderly demon and his mate sobbed over the coffin when the blond woman burst in and rushed along the line of mourners, crying, "Otto, Otto!" The children ran after her. A old woman said, "Mein Gott, seine französische Hure."

"Nein," said another woman, "Es ist die aus Genf. Aber sie ist genauso schrecklich, ganz schrecklich."

The woman fought her way through the mourners and charged the coffin with her wild blond hair flying and the ripped sleeve of her blouse hanging off. She was caught and held before she could get to it by the other brother, Florian, who led her calmly to the coffin. She looked in and sobbed and sobbed with the two children, a boy and girl aged about five and seven, clinging to her skirt. It's not at all like an hallucination, before being led away, I hear her crying, "Pauvre Otto, tout le monde se l'arrachait. Il en a fait des heureuses! Seigneur, il va bien nous manquer. . . " and she's scratching her face with her fingernails, and her children look embarrassed.

Of course you'll tell me this didn't happen, you'll tell me we witnessed a perfectly normal visitation hour, drank coffee afterwards, then drove on the autobahn back to Basel. But that is not what I remember. I remember a sudden shriek, the blond woman broke from Florian and launched herself at the coffin. Otto's mother tried to stop her but the woman was too fast, she hit the coffin with all her weight and sent it flying off its trestles, slamming onto its side on the floor. The lid came off and white objects scattered along the floor under the feet of leaping mourners.

I and Aphrodite stood still as one of the objects rolled between us. Whatever it was, it was well bandaged, but even so, a small brown stain revealed that it must have been freshly wrapped. It lay between us as if it expected one of us to pick it up and pet it. I looked at Aphrodite and found her gazing at me with dark, terrible eyes. All around us, the demons screamed and leaped about, trying to avoid the rolling body parts that were now slowing down, finding their places on the mosaic floor, and stranding everyone in terrified clusters. Aphrodite looked at the package at our feet and addressed it in English, the significance of which was not lost on me:

"And look how it all turned out, Otto — pandemonium, you silly boy. Listen to the trouble you have caused. Listen to all your screaming children, we are all your screaming children." Then she turned to me and said, "You seem like a nice girl. You are lucky to have escaped him. Go away now and have a normal life. Stop being a fool."

She began to back away into the crowds of demons.

"Wait," I said. "I have things to ask you."

She sighed, "There is nothing I can tell you. I must go. I hope never to see or hear from any of you again. This has always disgusted me. Now I am free. You can have that." And she pointed to the package on the floor. I looked at it for a second, when I looked up she'd gone.

The blond woman, who had continued to flail beside the coffin on the floor, stopped screaming and started looking around at the mourners. I could see why Otto liked her: she had no restraint, she was a powerhouse of emotion. She grinned suddenly, then pointed at the shocked faces and started laughing. Her children helped her up; the little boy straightened her disheveled clothing, and the little girl led her toward the narthex.

Hans righted the trestles while other men lifted the coffin and set it back in place.

Francine Schulte walked out of a cluster of people, holding Otto's head. It was heavily bandaged at the neck and the eyes had come open. She gently placed it where it should go at the top of the coffin. She looked at it for a moment, stroked the hair, then turned to nod at the gaping mourners.

Francine walked toward the narthex, stepping over the other pieces of her husband. When she came to the blond woman from Geneva, she stopped and said, "Contrôlez-vous, Nanette. Pensez aux enfants. Vous n'avez aucune renue!" And with that she left the sanctuary.

Nanette looked around, blushing and grinning, and ran the palms of her hands over her clothes. She picked up the package that lay nearest her and took it to the coffin.

Another woman, then another and then all of them, picked up pieces of Otto and put them in the coffin. Soon it was my turn. No doubt I was in shock, behaving oddly, but I wasn't going to be upstaged. I picked up my package and walked to the coffin, summoning, perhaps for the last time, all the coquetry that Otto had coaxed from me for three years, and placed the package where I thought it should go — in the anatomical location associated with one such as I.

The spectators gasped. The demons hissed.

As I drew my hand, empty, from the coffin, I felt as though, having deposited the package, I'd relinquished the bondage I'd so stubbornly remained in, and, dressed as I was, I became suddenly embarrassed by all the eyes upon me, especially those mountain eyes of Otto's mother.

Madame Schulte waited until I was back in my place and then picked up her package. She watched the rest of the pieces get picked up by the mourners and placed in the coffin. As old as the Alps, Madame Schulte passed across the mosaic floor with its occidental symbols to the coffin's edge. She held her package out in front of her and placed it where a heart should go. She stood looking down into the coffin for she was his oldest lover and had brought him into this world for love.

MACHINE

There were three of us around Dorothy's bed but we were all the spouses of her children, not her own kids. I suppose we were all in need of a mother and thought we'd found one in Dot. We were trying to keep her spirits up, but it must have seemed like a queer sort of deal to her, this presence only of in-laws. It was the kind of thing she'd take as a bad omen, and probably had the same feel to it as the recurring dream she'd been telling us about: her wandering around in her house and finding all the rooms empty.

There were other bad omens. This was the same bed in the same ward as last time. And William hadn't called. She was blessed before; the Lord guided the hospital staff, but sometimes it was touch-and-go, and in the dangerous period, when she was on the ventilator, she heard voices in the machine — angels chattering. She had acute mylogenous leukemia so no one was surprised that she was back on the eighth floor. I knew she was hearing those angels again, they were all around her, but she didn't mention them, not with me there anyway.

In a few days she'd be fifty-one and Doctor Sorensen had scheduled her for a bone-marrow transplant on her birthday. This was a good omen and if William would only call her her luck would turn. That's the way she thought.

She brought the red wig from last time.

It was an excellent match to her real hair which was falling out again with the renewed chemotherapy. She had kept her hair cropped as a precaution. The wig was a good prop, she liked arranging it at odd angles to amuse us.

The bedside phone rang often, but it was never William, it was always well-wishers from church. She was the most popular of parishioners, highly respected for her exceptional devotion to Christ and the heftiness of her tithes.

Margie, my sister-in-law, Billy's wife, had brought a plastic bowl of fresh rhubarb puree which Dot was consuming ravenously – it was a family favorite made from the rhubarb patch at the bottom of the yard at the big house. Dot had never stopped praying for William to see sense and return to her, but she was comfortable with her weight now and had long since given up the indignity of diets. Sitting propped up with pillows, she kept pouring heavy cream from a small carton into the pudding, and as long as she kept pouring and eating I don't suppose she felt so conscious of her chattering angels.

I might've been coming down with a cold or something; I had a touch of fever. I shouldn't have been there but I was needed as bouncer to control the host of simpering gloaters from her church. At one point a dozen of them, led by Dot's best friends, Arthur and Elizabeth Hemsley, wanted to gather around her bed, ignoring the need for masks and gloves, and heal her themselves, there and then, with the power of the spirit. Dot was nice to everyone, but she didn't protest too much when I sent them out into the hall.

Keeble Hawksfeather, my ponytailed brother-in-law, married to my wife's sister, Karen, is one of those self-educated types that's good with his hands. He used to be called George Keeble. He decided to change his name to Hawksfeather after seeing it written in the clouds during a vision quest. He's a motor mechanic, a Jaguar specialist, and on this day, when we in-laws sat around the bed together, he'd just gotten off work. He's a follower of New Age religion, makes jewelry weekends in his basement, and he'd made Dot a crystal necklace with healing power. Earlier, with great ceremony, he'd placed the leather cord over her head but couldn't help knocking her wig crooked. As she ate her pureed rhubarb and heavy cream, the crystal, hanging down and swinging like a pendulum, kept thudding against the plastic bowl or clinking against the gold strap of Dot's Rolex. She held the bowl in her left hand with the fourth and fifth fingers delicately fanned out. On the fourth finger was the huge diamond William gave her years ago, looking much more likely to heal cancer, if anything could, than the piece of junk hanging around her neck.

Keeble likes to pretend he's so spiritual, but as he sat by the sick bed, pretending to look at his fingers, he was actually looking up through his eyelashes at Margie's breasts.

I liked Margie. She told me later that she knew I was running a fever and that it crossed her mind to suggest that I shouldn't get too close to Dot. It was good of her to try and take some of the blame. I miss her, too. She liked it that I was kind of the family bad boy, the token atheist. We were allies because Billy, her husband, her ex-husband now, well, to put it kindly, he's living on another planet from the rest of us – he's even more of a fanatic than his mother was, without her humor and flexibility.

I'll never forget how Dot looked. Intravenous tubes disappeared under plasters on both of her arms. There were yellow bruises where the nurses had failed to find good veins in her big arms. She was covered by a sheet and wore a white hospital gown patterned with small blue flowers. And that unruly red wig. The room was a constant temperature; always too warm, as she spooned in that rhubarb pudding. It was a critical period, essential that she acquire no infection, because the chemotherapy, a beautiful gold mixture hanging in a plastic bag above the bed, was obliterating her immune system.

So it was a shock when I sneezed.

The sneeze was so powerful that it blew off my blue mask, and, in the good afternoon light from the windows on two sides of the room, the motes of nasal moisture could be seen drifting on the warm air.

"Jeez, Dot," I said, "I'm awfully sorry."

With her mouth full, she said, "Gesundheit," and kept eating.

I used to cause discomfort to that family at holidays by looking around the room and yawning during grace. I only did it for Margie. She enjoyed the paradoxical relationship Dot and I had. "You and Dot adore each other," Margie'd say, "She loves to fight with you over religion. She loves to be scandalized."

That had always been the case, but after she came down with the illness things became a little awkward. At Easter, just after they'd got her into remission, we had a fierce debate at the dinner table which wound up with Dot being uncharacteristically direct and, with a kind of glassy look in her eyes, asking:

"I'm not going to live much longer, so with that in mind do you maintain that when I die, with all the devotion to Jesus I carry in my heart, with all my love, that I will just end, that there'll be nothing, no reward?"

We stared at each other over the hambone.

I rubbed my face with both hands, feeling awkward and said, "Dot, darling, you're putting me on the spot."

"That's the way of the Lord."

Now that's the kind of remark that infuriates me. *The way of the Lord* indeed. I said, "All right. I've thought the same since you've known me and I've not changed my opinion just because someone I love — and I do love you, Dot — is going the way of all flesh."

The color drained from her face. "So say it," she insisted, "Let me hear you say, in your own words, that there's no salvation, no redemption, that when Satan finally trips me there'll be no one to catch me, no reward for all my sufferings and I'll be a blank, a nothing — no consciousness."

I said, "I wish we hadn't got into this."

Dot stared at me, her eyes wide and luminous. "Well?"

"What do you want me to say? You know what I think."

"But you can't bring yourself to say it. The Lord won't let you. He's trying to protect you from a great sin."

"You're sinning, Dot. You're sinning against reality. Look, I'll say this — the only life, the only consciousness we have, is this one. It's all there is. I know it, always have, and on some level so do you. Humankind can't progress while we maintain this infantile terror of the dark."

"No!" she shouted, "Absolutely no. It's pearls before swine is what it is, pearls before swine."

After the sneeze Margie got up and moved around that unplugged ventilator of porcelain-dimpled beige, and stood behind me where I sat at the foot of the bed, mortified and guilty, and gently massaged my shoulders. Then she withdrew to the window and looked down at the freeway. I went and stood behind her.

"Look at all that traffic building up," she said.

She was trembling. Keeble was engrossed in Jaguar grease under his nails. Dot continued to eat while the uncombed hair of her wig flew up from her head like flames.

A few days later Dot had a virus. Doctor Sorensen said he was about ready to throw in the towel. She was on the ropes. It was inevitable under the circumstances, and there was only a slim chance a miracle would occur, but he'd seen miracles, they had seen many miracles on the oncology ward, you could never tell, they were doing all they could.

Doctor Sorensen was very tall and wore spectacles with clear plastic frames. He wore plaid shirts, knitted ties, loafers. He never wore white like the nurses who did all the work. When he talked intimately with people smaller than himself he leaned over them with his hand on one of their shoulders and turned his ear toward them as if he were hard of hearing.

I went to the hospital after office hours on Monday afternoon and found the doctor looking over charts in the nurses' station. I leaned over the high counter and asked quietly if I could have a word with him. He looked up and I realized that despite a number of previous conversations he didn't recognize me. This was annoying because Sorensen affected a certain familiarity.

"I'm Dorothy Larson's son-in-law."

"Of course, I know you. What's up?"

"A private word?"

The doctor looked around, "I'm not sure if I can . . .Oh, what the hell, I need a break."

We went into a small office with a television and a coffee pot. Doctor Sorensen sat in a plastic chair and sipped coffee from a styrofoam cup. "Boy," he said, "It's good to get off my feet. Your mother's quite a gal, she cracks me up every time I'm in there. Help yourself to some java. The things she can pull off with that wig. She's hilarious!"

I asked as directly as I could if my sneeze had caused Dot's lapse. The doctor laughed and said that was extremely unlikely but that it was possible, but what did it matter? The world is germ infested, that's why we have immune systems — no, the stuff's right in the air all the time and her chances of not contracting something were slim. But, yes, it could've been your sneeze – honestly though, what's the difference?

I left the doctor sipping his coffee and walked along the carpeted hall to the room at the end where Dot was. I pushed open her door; the room was filled with people. It was them, the dingbat contingent from Dot's church, doing a laying on of hands; dirty hands all covered in germs, those bastards. The room was so full I could scarcely squeeze in. I couldn't even see Dot's bed, but I spotted Margie standing by the window, looking down at the traffic. I watched her until she sensed my presence and turned to look at the doorway. I gestured with my head about the crowd of goons. Margie just shrugged, shook her head.

The Hemsleys were leading the twenty or so elderly people in prayer. Reverend Rowan was not present. This was a spontaneous action on the part of the Hemsleys and other church friends. They had arranged it during the coffee hour after Sunday's service. They did not know how serious Dot's condition was until Reverend Rowan asked everyone to pray hard for her recovery. The Hemsleys were so successful signing people up to come and heal Dot that they had to limit participation. They believed that when the Lord saw their outpouring of love, provided of course that it did not disturb his divine plan, He would heal Dot and let her continue her work at the church.

As soon as the amen was pronounced I pushed through the people at the end of Dot's bed, making quite a point of putting on my rubber gloves and mask. "Why aren't any of you wearing these?" I shouted.

Beth Hemsley smiled in her crazed way, her extraordinary blue eyes gleaming with love. "Welcome," she said. "The nurses say those precautions are no longer necessary."

I felt a bit stupid. They knew stuff that I didn't. I may of gotten a little mad, I said:

"I think you should all get the hell out of here."

No one moved.

"I think you people should have your goddamn prayer meeting in the hall instead of using up all the oxygen in the room and filling it with germs. Come on, out!"

Beth Hemsley looked, still smiling, at her husband, Art, who very patiently said, "Easy now, son. We know you're upset, but the Lord is at work here. . . "

A weak voice from the bed said:

"It's all right, they're my friends." Dot was lifting her head from the pillow. She had had to remove an oxygen mask from her mouth to speak and her speech sounded strangled when she repeated, "It's okay. Really. Friends."

"No, it isn't okay," I said, and went to her bedside, pushing Art Hemsley out of the way.

"Sweetheart, this is insane. They're crowding you out."

"I need help. I need prayer. I don't know what to do."

"Let me get them out of here – I'll pray with you."

"Oh, yes," she murmured, "that would be wonderful, yes."

"You heard. Out. Now!"

Margie was the only one left, she sat gaping on the window ledge; I looked at her until she stood up, squeezed around the machine which, of course, was now plugged in, humming and sucking. She said, "I'll go and calm down the Hemsleys."

I knelt beside Dot, helped her put her oxygen mask back on and straightened up her wig. And do you know what? I did it, I prayed with her.

Margie told me later how she felt as she walked down the carpeted hall with the private rooms leading off it. She realized suddenly that only the two rooms at the end of the hall, her mother-in-law's and the one opposite, were singles, the others were all doubles. The parishioners were haunting the halls and nurses' station, waiting for an opportunity to get a private interview with Dorothy. When she got to the nurses' station Margie saw Keeble taking to Doctor Sorensen. They were laughing. Keeble smiled at her and said hello. She was annoyed by their joviality. Keeble said, "A coincidence – I serviced his Jag this morning – piece of garbage."

Sorensen laughed and turned to Margie, saying, "I hear your brother-in-law's taking over the ward."

"He doesn't like bullshit," she said.

Keeble's expression changed. "Neither do I," he said, "But life goes on, Margie. Life goes on."

That night the family gathered at Dot's. It was a big wooden house on two lots. William Larson Senior was due in from Wisconsin around 7:30. Margie got there early and laid everything out. Billy was to follow soon with liquor. Margie made four quiches, different varieties, French bread, pickles, cold cuts, Wheat Thins, different cheeses. She put a white cloth on the table and set out Dot's best plates, glasses and silverware. Then Billy arrived with three jugs of cheap California wine. "No," she told him, "that won't do, why are you such an asshole? I'll do it myself."

She told me how she drove, inexplicably mad, to the liquor store. She had a long talk about wines with the manager. He helped her select half a dozen good French and German bottles. She told me how she liked his clean hands and neat beard. He wanted to make a dinner date with her. She said he had shiny eyes. She gave him her work number.

As she drove back to Dot's, she admitted to herself that she was, and had been for a long time, waiting for Dot to die so she could dump Billy. She wanted to say to him, "Look, I want a man who isn't guilty all the time. I want a man I can make love with till my nose bleeds."

When Margie got home Keeble's rusty VW bus was in the driveway and he was unloading baby Amy. Karen, the daughter that most resembles Dorothy, was taking in homemade pies wrapped in tinfoil. Karen's cooking was always very unrefined, according to Margie, it was always thrown together and unattractive – no class. Billy's BMW had been moved into the street and this overtly considerate gesture of making space for others further irritated Margie. She went in and put the French wine on the table, laid out corkscrews, then tried to find room in the refrigerator, which was loaded with health store products, for the German wines.

Hesta and I arrived about then. Billy had built a fire. William Senior was late so we opened a bottle of beaujolais without him.

After his second glass of wine, Billy announced that there was to be a surprise and he hoped his father would arrive soon because it was due to arrive, the surprise, at eight o'clock.

"Stop being an asshole, Billy," said Karen, "and tell us what's up. I hate this shit."

Billy blushed. "Yes," said Hesta, "Tell us. It's no time for boy scout games."

Margie poured her third glass of wine, and as she poured more for me, I said, "Oh, for Christ's sake tell them, Billy. They don't appreciate you."

He shrugged. "All right. Reverend Rowan's coming over."

"Oh, hell," said Hesta.

"Shit," said Karen.

"How did that happen?" said Hesta.

"Shoot, I though you'd be pleased. Mom worships him. He's her best friend."

"It'll be okay as long as we can keep this character off the subject of religion," laughed Keeble, shoving me on the shoulder. He'd been glancing furtively at Hesta's breasts since we arrived, and his overly hard shove almost made me bust him one in the mouth.

"No way," said Billy. "Sidney likes a good theological debate – Rod won't get it all his own way."

Margie said, "Sure he will," and pushed my knee with hers. Without looking at her I smiled and gave a small laugh. Hesta didn't like Margie getting so close to me. She got up and stomped over to the fire where she took her pumps off and laid them on the hearth. There was no love lost between Hesta and Margie. Hesta thought Margie was a stuck-up, domineering bitch, and Margie thought Hesta a pretentious little neophyte who was always talking about writing a romance novel that she never let anybody see – including me.

Karen was saying, "Jeez, Bill, this was supposed to be a family affair. We've been deluged with strangers for a week now, and we're all uncomfortable with Sidney except you. And besides, Dad's coming."

"I called Dad about it. He was enthusiastic."

"He's always enthusiastic," said Hesta. "He makes a fuss about everything, then never turns up. I'll be surprised if he comes at all."

Keeble said, "Can't you guys just have a quiet drink and stop arguing?"

We opened another bottle of red wine.

At eight o'clock the doorbell rang. Billy answered it. He ushered in Sidney Rowan, who strode across the parquet flooring in his leather-soled shoes. He was tall, thin, and had a mop of gray hair, sideburns, a jutting jaw. He knew all our names, shook our hands. He was good at small talk. Soon the discussion turned to Dot and someone offered him a glass of wine which he accepted gratefully, draining the glass quickly then helping himself to another.

William was still absent and Billy found it necessary to announce: "My father continues not to arrive."

"There he is again at the door, gone!" said Karen, referring to some old joke.

"Oh no," groaned Keeble, "Don't start those stupid word games, please. I'll throw up."

We played stupid word games for a while.

By ten o'clock, William had continued his unarrival and we were finishing the last bottle of good wine. The food was all eaten. Margie went and pulled a jug of Billy's cheap chardonnay from the refrigerator and with it came a shower of brown vitamin bottles rolled across the kitchen floor. "I'm trashing Dot's kitchen," Margie called. She left the vitamins on the floor, and brought the chardonnay into the living room where we sat around the fire listening to Sidney Rowan tell a story about someone's miraculous recovery from a fatal illness.

During a lull in Sidney's talk, I couldn't help saying, "Well, Reverend. Did you hear about the mummy they just dug up? Very well preserved – two and a half thousand years older than Christ. By those standards, Christ's a relatively new phenomenon, almost a cult, wouldn't you say?"

"A cult?" smiled Rowan, "Well, I don't know about that."

"That Egyptian religion," said Hesta. "I forget what it was called. It was around a lot longer than Christianity has been."

"Was," stated Rowan.

"It's hanging on in odd places, probably," I said. "Religion transmutes."

"Alive where?" said Keeble, "California?"

Rowan laughed, "Undoubtedly."

"I don't know how you guys can keep up this claptrap," I said. "For years, thousands of years, there's been guys, nearly always guys, espousing afterlives in the materialistic image of their own cultures. We worship this desert god, Yahweh, even up north here. We're a forest people. . . "

"My husband himself is a worshipper of Bacchus," Hesta interrupted. She often says this to shift things onto a lighter note when I'm spoiling for a row. Rowan laughed heartily.

"I mean, look at it," I continued, "It's basically a desert religion with medieval European attachments. Take Hell for example, it's a horrific value-laden version of Hades, designed to frighten the masses – an ideological tool, yes – of patriarchal oppression."

Rowan smiled, "You may well be right. But you see, anthropological or historical theories don't alter our faith."

"Screw anthropology, Sidney, I'm talking psychology."

"You're talking gibberish," said Hesta. I smiled, put my head on her shoulder and closed my eyes.

"How did we get onto this?" said Karen, "It's boring."

"He started it," laughed Keeble, probably trying to prod my arm again, but missing.

"Well, it should be opened up," I said with closed eyes. "It should. Materialism dictates rationalism."

"But rationalism's so boring," said Rowan. I opened my eyes to see him winking at my wife.

"I'd rather be bored than have these awful wars that have been fought in the name of religions and cults and things," said Karen.

Rowan shrugged, "We need it – we need reason. We need heaven and most of us, though not all, need hell."

"The system fails utterly if it sends me to hell," I said.

Rowan didn't rise to the bait, but continued staring at my wife's ankles. "There can't be a hell," I pressed, "because if you send me there I'd be eternally in heaven simply knowing heaven existed. Knowing a few of you righteous folks were up there – although I expect most of you will be accompanying me. Even in Hell I'd be in Heaven knowing Dot was okay."

"Supposing hell is not knowing there's a heaven. . . " said Rowan. He was looking at Hesta's legs, he hadn't really heard what I'd said, he was speaking automatically. It annoyed me, I leaned forward and pointed at the tip of Rowan's nose and might well have given it a good poke, but the phone rang and Hesta got up to answer it.

Her back went straight.

"Yes. You did. Why? God. Oh, God. No, never mind that. Oh, God, yes. Of course, right away."

We all looked at Hesta.

"That was Dad," she said. "He went to the hospital."

Then she cried. She sat in a chair with her hand on the phone and cried.

It turns out that William got into town early so decided to swing by the hospital instead of going to the old house. He went to Dot's room and found the doctor and two nurses leaning over her. They looked up, startled. She'd deteriorated suddenly and Doctor Sorensen was about to call the family.

"Are you her husband?" asked Sorensen.

"Yes, I've come to see her."

"That's fortunate," said the doctor, "I know she'd been wanting to see you."

All the machines were blipping and Dot lay in their midst, heaving great lungs full of oxygen through the clear plastic mask. William told us that he went to the edge of the bed and saw terror in her face. He took her hand and she gripped it. She could only speak with her eyes.

The staff withdrew and William sat with her for a long time. She was burning up. The nurse had been rubbing her with cold towels to try and keep her cool. The heat of her hand made his sweat. She didn't once take her eyes off his face. After a while, he said, "I'd better go and call the children," but she tightened her grip on his hand.

She wore the huge diamond ring William bought her when he was rich. It was a guilt present because he had given her gonorrhea. He called it a second engagement, a new start, and she believed him. They went on for another eight years until he left her for a collegiate girls' volleyball coach, and moved to Wisconsin. Dot, of course, forgave him. She always believed he would come back. He was the love of her life.

From what I understand Dot's kind of love infuriated William. After years of being angry at her, she was dying, and she was still fat. He hadn't seen her for months, since they got her into remission, and she was still fat. Now he felt like a swine for despising her obesity. He said, "Do you remember our first car, that old blue Chevy?"

She squeezed his hand, closed and opened her eyes.

Then he sat with her while she slipped slowly into a coma. The nurse was always there. That's about when William called us.

Billy, Hesta and Karen went together in Reverend Rowan's Cherokee. Hesta sat beside him, Billy and Karen in the back with little Amy who was irritable at being woken up. Margie drove Billy's BMW. I sat beside her, Keeble was in the back. She wept as she drove and I squeezed her neck with my left hand.

The cars arrived together at the hospital's entrance. We all got out and stood around. Then Billy and Rowan drove the vehicles to parking places and the rest of us went up to the eighth floor in the elevator. At the nurses' station William was bent over the counter with his face in his hands. Doctor Sorensen was beside him, leaning over him, talking.

When we were grouped around him, William told us how he had been holding her hand and she was taking bigger and bigger breaths and suddenly she just stopped sucking one in and, right in the middle of a breath, died. He said it was like a stone dropping. It was only moments ago, he said.

"The virus just overtook her," Doctor Sorensen said. He tried to stand in the way, to somehow prevent anyone going down to the room until he'd finished explaining. "She just didn't have the reserves to fight it off. . . " and he began an incoherent postmortem, using a vocabulary that clattered at our feet like a spilled tray of surgical instruments.

Billy and Rowan arrived. Without saying hello to his father Billy ran down the hallway to his mother's room. His father walked after him, followed by Margie who held a handkerchief to her face. Then Hesta and Karen with little Amy, and Keeble walking behind them with his head bowed and his hands in his pockets. Rowan followed but stayed outside the door, sitting on the windowsill. I stayed with Doctor Sorensen who talked faster and faster, making very little sense. Finally I said to him, "It's all right. You did the best you could. She liked you. She had faith in you."

"I liked her," Sorensen said, and turned away, swallowing repeatedly, shaking his head.

I passed Sidney Rowan at the door, he patted my arm as I went in.

The thing lying there was no longer Dot, but it still wore a huge diamond ring and a Rolex watch that continued to tick. The wig was on the night stand, half covering the crystal necklace. The machines were still switched on, although the big beige one, the ventilator, had stopped sighing and wheezing. It infuriated me and I began picking it up. All the wires snapped out of the wall as I hauled it toward the window.

"No — please," said Margie, "No, please," she said, gently restraining me. Rowan came in then, and helped move the machines away from the bed. I feel foolish about it now, I remember saying, "All this paraphernalia around her, it breaks my heart. Somebody for God's sake take her watch off."

Rowan said a little prayer and then asked us if we'd like to sing a hymn Dot had been fond of. It was this one:

> Now the light has gone away,
> Father listen while I pray,
> Asking Thee to watch and keep
> And to send me quiet sleep.
>
> Jesus, Savior, wash away
> All that has been wrong today;
> Help me ev'ry day to be
> Good and gentle, more like Thee.
>
> Let my near and dear ones be
> Always near and dear to Thee;
> Oh, bring me and all I love
> To Thy happy home above.
>
> Now my evening praise I give;
> Thou didst die that I might live.
> All my blessings come from Thee;
> Oh, how good Thou art to me!
>
> Thou, my best and kindest friend,
> Thou wilt love me to the end.
> Let me love Thee more and more
> Always better than before.

The others had the words by heart, but I didn't so I went and stood by the window and watched the sparse traffic zoom by on the yellow-lit freeway.

Later, a nursing assistant in blue scrubs, wearing an earring and a neat hair-net, came to remove the diamond ring from Dorothy's finger. The job took thirty-five minutes.

DADDY'S EYES

It was early dusk, and the man had worked against a deadline all day while his three-year-old son waited to be taken to the playground. The man still had much text to generate before he could begin editing, but he had been distracted and uncomfortable since lunch, and the promise made earlier, that "If you're a good boy and don't bug Mommy I'll take you to the swings," began to nag at him above all his other concerns. He sighed suddenly and hit the save command on the computer, then stood and groaned at the disorder of his project: it was spread about the room as though a great wind had passed through.

He shut the office door and locked the mess inside, undisturbed. On the way downstairs he stopped to look at the family photographs hanging in the stairwell. The colored ones were mostly of his life in America; the black and white ones were of his parents and his early years growing up in England. In recent weeks he found himself lingering longer and longer in the stairwell, examining every detail of the black and white photographs, particularly the one of his high school cricket team. He could recall only half the names of the other boys, and the big boy crouching in the middle with the sarcastic grin, wearing the pads and gloves of a wicket keeper, seemed as strange to him as someone he might have been in a former life.

The man's wife sat reading a fat autobiography under the floor lamp by the window. She looked up when he appeared, then dropped her eyes back into the book. She had made a fire and the three-year-old played on the hearth rug in front of it. He drove a cardboard box, using a Frisbee for a steering wheel. The

134

box was surrounded by puzzles, coloring books, building blocks, and small plastic superheroes. The rest of the room was very tidy, all the mess being contained on the hearth rug. The child made skidding sounds with his mouth as if he were permanently going around a bend on two wheels. Stretching and yawning, the man said, "Righto, little chap, on with your tennies. We're off to the swings."

"Wings! Wings!" said the little boy, struggling out of the box. He rolled off the hearth rug, spilling superheroes across the hardwood floor, and ran down the hall to his room to find his shoes.

"You've left it too late," said the man's wife, looking up but keeping her forefinger in the book to save her place, "it's going to be dark."

The man rubbed his hand over his eyes and forehead.

"Look, honey, being out in the dark won't do him any harm."

"It'll soon be his bedtime and he didn't nap today."

"Bloody hell," said the man, "why is everything so awkward with you? I promised him, okay?"

"You always do this kind of thing," the woman said, carefully draping the open book along the armrest of her chair and then standing facing the man with her hands on her hips, "You're so unreasonable. Why are you trying to undermine the way I raise him?"

The man spun away, threw his hands in the air, and as if in pain, moaned, "Oh, for Christ's sake, what the hell's the matter with you?"

Then they quarreled about everything. As usual, they began by denigrating each other's parenting skills, then escalated to the man's long work hours, the woman's obsessive neatness, the uncut lawn, household chores, and then finally money – the focus being a restrained but nasty contest about excess water usage. To punctuate her points the man's wife picked up superheroes and threw them in the cardboard box.

The little boy came into the living room, having found his hightops under the bed. Holding a shoe in each hand, he looked at his mother and father, and during a gap in their talk, said, "Wings? Wings?"

"Yes, chappie," said the man, "we're going to the swings."

The mother, who had picked up her book again, threw it on the sofa and stalked into the kitchen where she yanked open the utensil drawer, then slammed it shut. The man went into the front hall and took the boy's red coat off the hook and called, "I won't be long, okay. Don't worry."

The man listened for an answer as he helped the boy to put on the coat and shoes. When he opened the door, the boy leapt down the steps and ran along the garden path, shouting. The man put on an old black leather jacket, turned the collar up and went out, slamming the door.

There was a richly colored sunset taking place, most of which was obscured by the heavy growth of trees in the neighborhood. The little boy chattered all the way to the main road and after a while the man understood a few words; the effort it took distracted him so that he was able to stop thinking about his angry wife and the unfinished work. No one else was on the street. The man wondered what they looked like: a little boy in a red tunic and a big man in a black leather jacket, walking slowly along the sidewalk.

They had to wait at the main road for two buses and some cars to clear the junction, then they crossed and entered the tree-protected trail that went by the duck pond and into the woods. The man noticed fish rising in the pond. He couldn't see any ducks. A few crickets, survivors of a recent cold snap, chirruped laconically, as though conserving energy. The little boy tried to copy them, and the man laughed, saying:

"What are you up to, you little twerp?"

"Carwy me, I want hup," said the boy, holding his arms up, "dadda carwy Harwy."

"No. You've only been walking five minutes. And your name's Harry not Harwy. Say *Harry*."

The boy stood in front of the man, hopping and squeaking, "Harwy want hup, Harwy want hup."

"Oh, all right," said the man, and swung him up. As he carried him along the trail he could smell the boy's milky skin and soft hair. He sensed, after walking for a while, that the boy was nervous and looked at his face: the boy gazed back along the path as though something followed them.

"What's up, matey?" said the man, "Frightened of the cockerlooloo, are you?"

"Dark. Monshters."

"No," said the man, "no monsters here. You're all right."

And there was a light touch, no more than the brushing of a whisker on the man's consciousness, no more than the landing of a cricket on a leaf, and it was really the voice of his own father, speaking from a great distance, that said:

"This is fairy territory. The darkness protects all the little animals, and the fairies keep an eye out for good little boys."

"Fairwies?" said the boy.

"Yes, sir."

"Where's fairwies?"

"Fairies, not fairwies. They're everywhere. Under the roots of trees, high in the branches, hiding in the long weeds."

"Fairwies in dree, dadda? Where's fairwies in dree?" said the child, pointing to an oak whose gnarled branches and roots made a sort of tunnel of the trail.

"They're everywhere, but you need special eyes to see them."

"Eyes?"

"Of course. Special eyes."

Then the boy caught sight of the swings beyond the two tennis courts and wanted to get down and run to them. "Walk, don't run, little chap!" shouted the man and the boy slowed to a fast, buttock-rolling walk.

They passed the empty tennis courts and baseball diamond. No one was around except an overweight teenager with a cowlick, walking a very old Labrador on a leash. The man stopped to pet the dog while the teenager waited, sullen and embarrassed. "Come and pet the doggy," called the man, but his son's heart was set on the deserted playground and he sprinted delightedly into it, scattering a flock of sparrows as they preened themselves in the dust.

He picked up a grimy condom and said, "What dis?"

He used all the rocking animals first, furiously, then climbed the tallest slide but was too afraid to slide down and also too afraid to come back down the steep ladder so that the man had to go up after him.

"All right, little man, I'm coming."

Then he sat at the top of the slide with the boy in his lap.

Sitting up so high it was clear that before the park existed the oaks surrounding the playground were part of a much larger wood. They were just now catching the last light from the sunset in their topmost branches and, for a moment, the leaves were pink. As the light faded the trunks turned black, and the man imagined them twisting into magical beings – their exposed roots became knobbly feet with long toes that curled around those of their siblings, thatching themselves stubbornly into the earth. "Where did that impression come from?" the man murmured. And then he remembered, felt that whisker-touch of his father's influence again: oaks were very old people that had lived in the world since the beginning of time.

Streetlights came on. A yellow Jeep went by and the driver put on his lights before he stopped at the corner.

"I used to do this with my daddy," said the man. "I had a red jacket, too, not quite like yours, we called it a blazer. And I had a white cap so he could see me in the gloom. Where I grew up the winter days are much shorter than here so I often went to the swings in the dark. I loved it."

"Fairwies?" said the boy.

"Yes," laughed the man, "there were fairies – plenty of them."

The little boy only knew that it was getting dark and that when he was with his mother darkness was a signal that fun must stop. Orders came abruptly and without compromise which made him mad at her. With his father fun was easier, he could stay at the swings as long as he liked provided his father's office door was closed for the day. He could see the baseball diamond through the trees, and he just wanted to sit still for a long time on his father's lap at the top of this slide and watch the light go. He could feel his father's breath on his neck and he sensed that his father was crying privately again, and he instinctively sat very still until his father's sadness went away.

The man's left hand was on the boy's chest so that he felt heartbeats against his palm. The boy's back was pressed against the man's chest and the man wondered if the boy could feel his heartbeats, too, because his heart was pumping so hard. The man was thinking of another oak-surrounded playground — Old Deer Park, near the river, where he grew up. He knew he was being ridiculously sentimental. "But it's not a crime," he said, "I'll be as sentimental as I please. To hell with it!" He was choked up by the thought of the soccer fields where he first played in those huge football boots that smelled so strongly of leather, and then he remembered the Great West Road and heard again its thundering traffic, and felt again the trembling air as big four-engined airliners flew in to Heathrow. And that crafty old river slipping by with its secrets — even as a boy he wondered about it, how constant it was, like a rapacious dragon, pilfering the years and decades, hoarding its booty in the sea. When you dug around in its silt you were as likely to find a Celtic sword as a Nazi bomb.

And he saw his father, the glow of his cigarette at first, then a huge bald man, looming out of the shadows to push him higher on the swing or save him from the brutality of some bigger boy.

"Dad?" he said, then muttered, "Where's it all gone?"

Time erodes fathers, he thought. London and the old miasmic river were from another life that may as well have existed on some far away planet, and had been replaced by this new city and this new river with its absurdly foreign name. Goddamn them, thought the man, why can't they have decent names for their rivers? This might be the river little Harry'll grow to love. Each man has his river and once he leaves it he's in big trouble. Rivers are the dragons of memory, the filterers of time.

The man laughed at himself, but he felt the same inside as the day his father pointed out a brown fairy hiding in a wet pile of autumn leaves. It was a foggy evening by the river and his eyelashes dripped. "See the fairy, laddy?" his father pointed, "She's keeping an eye on you so you'll remember to be a good boy and think about everything." The man felt the same inside as then, his soul felt unaltered — but there was always the pricking knowledge of what had happened later, how everything had become spoiled with his father. He tried to avoid thinking of that.

Tonight, with his hot-hearted little son for comfort, he could forgive his father all the dreadfulness that came later. And he desperately wanted to share something with the little boy, tell him a story or something. But the boy was young yet, had the attention span of a sparrow.

He held the boy too tightly.

"Dadda, don' hurt me."

"All right, matey. Sorry."

"Look," said the boy, pointing, "star!"

"I think that's a small airplane, actually."

"No. Star. Nice star."

"Okay then. It's a plane old star."

The slide was cold, and the man, remembering his wife's constant warnings about chills, said, "Shall we slide down now?"

"Des."

They slid down and the boy laughed when they fell in the sand at the bottom.

It was dark. The man sat on a swing seat, holding the chains, while the boy dug a hole in the sand. He often tried to see things from his son's point of view, it helped his parenting to remind himself as often as possible what childishness was like. When they looked at each other, man and boy, they were nothing but black shadows, the one sitting, swinging slightly, the other scooping sand.

A night bird called. A few crickets, under a death sentence, tried to get a miserable chant going. The boy abandoned the hole and ran frantically to the roundabout, then the swings. The man knew what it was like to want to squeeze in as much play in as possible before fun was terminated. He remembered this well, how your protector, who made the darkness bearable, would have an inexplicable change of mood, and suddenly, irresistibly, take you away.

The man looked over his shoulder and was startled by a sliver of light in the lower branches of an oak. It was what his father liked to call a Turkish moon — shaped like a deeply curved scimitar with space enough to enclose a star in its belly. And he thought of his father's song about the man in the moon who came down too soon before the pub was open and when the landlord got to work he found the doors all broken. And his mind roved around the lexicon of his father's songs and stories until there came to him the one about the leopard, and he longed to be able to tell it to the little figure digging in the sand, but for now he had to be content with thinking it through to himself.

It was a tale his father, Henry, told about great-granddad William, who was renowned for taking his grandchildren to dangerous places like the darkest parts of Bombay where cut-throats and lepers lived, or to ruined Hindu temples in the high country outside the city where the spirits of discredited deities thirsted for the blood of Christian children who wouldn't go to bed. It was during World War I and old Robbie, Henry's father, a very sober head of the household, was fighting in Europe, so old Willie, who drank rather a lot, was *burra-sahib*. When it got really hot in Bombay old Willie would take the family to the hills where it was cooler, and the men and boys would sleep all night on the roof of the bungalow under mosquito nets and marvel at the extraordinary sky.

The man understood how his father told that opening part of the story to set the scene, but also to create a sense of who everyone was in the family and when it was all supposed to have happened and to teach from where they all came. And then he thought about the way his father told of the moonlight hunts old Willie took him on in the jungle where they saw pythons and elephants and leopards, and once even a tiger. When the old man was sober he preferred to hunt at night, Henry told, because his eyes were so pale that night was the only time he could see properly.

One night a very troublesome leopard took a baby from a local woman, and the villagers came to the bungalow to get old Willie to deal with it. It was his duty, part of being *burra-sahib*.

This was a peculiar leopard, it had taken children before and seemed to know exactly where they would be. It had gone into buildings, even into bedrooms, to get them. It preferred succulent little boys and prowled hungrily during bright moonlit nights.

The man registered a concern of his wife's about such stories, that they were too disturbing, and he had to admit that he had himself spent many a wakeful night convinced that a snarling beast lurked beneath his bed, waiting for him to fall asleep. But it was nothing compared to what the kids today saw on television, and sitting in this cold playground in the dark he was stirred by the prospect of one day telling his son this story, perhaps in front of the fireplace with light from burning oak logs glinting in their eyes.

He remembered lying in bed with the sheet up over his mouth as his father sat beside him and told of how the villagers had chased the child-snatching leopard, with its prey between its jaws, into a wooded area at the bottom of a cliff. The man remembered how it felt to be transported, to no longer be in a cold London bedroom, to have forgotten whatever ailment had him bedridden, and to be there in India among sweating, squabbling villagers who had surrounded the wood but did not dare enter it. It was the wood of the ruined temples, of course, stuffed with malevolent spirits.

If Willie had not been full of whiskey when the villagers came Henry would never have been permitted to accompany him on such a dangerous hunt. As it was he had to plead and plead until the old man gave in. All the men of the household came along, but old Willie had the only gun.

The man saw the wood as he had seen it in his mind's eye as a child, it had not changed a bit. It was a wood perhaps no bigger or denser than this one here in Minneapolis, but it was big enough for a boy-eating leopard to hide in. Old Willie had learned to hunt with his father, James, in South Island, New Zealand, where James's father, Magnus, an Orkney Islander, had settled on account of whaling enterprises – so he had the hunt in his blood. And the man could see himself telling his son: "Which is why the men of this family have been keen hunters in their time . . . "

Once he got to the wood old Willie quickly understood how to get the leopard out, but – and the man saw again how his father's eyes took on a look of alarm when he told this part – Willie had a feeling he had never experienced before: he was afraid.

Nevertheless, he organized the villagers into teams of beaters and ordered them to penetrate to the wall of the cliff and then close in so the leopard would have to leave its cover and escape where the wood turned to brush and then gave way to a dry stream bed.

What were his actual words, thought the man, how did he actually say it? And he strained his brain to make a moment of the past return.

"I sat with my grandfather and two houseboys while the eerie sound of the beaters came closer. The moon was very bright and I saw the leopard's head above the brush very clearly. I didn't see any baby. It looked around for a moment, its eyes like blazing torches, before bursting out of the brush and into the stream bed. It happened so suddenly that Pops didn't get off a good shot, it seemed to only graze the leopard's flank and spin him over, so that he got up and bounded away. Well, the old bugger fired again and the animal somersaulted and lay still in the moonlight with dust rising around it."

But no, this was not the man's father, not the real Henry, it was an actor made from snippets of retained knowledge. His father was gone – for the most part, even from memory. So he relaxed and let the rest of the story come to him naturally, in images, the residue of a dead man's speech.

Old Willie, an incredibly wide man with a long white beard, looking very pleased with himself, snaps his gun onto his shoulder with a gesture of authority. No sooner has he done this than the leopard gets up and runs off again. Many of the villagers are gathered along the stream bed, staring at him in wonder. It's a large caliber hunting rifle and he apparently hit the leopard twice. The shock of one round should have killed it. But it got up and ran off.

There's a trail of blood, however, that's flowing so strongly that it can be followed in the moonlight. The trail of sticky moonlit blood leads the great host of terrified people back to the village. They are nervous lest the leopard is some kind of god who will now be even angrier with them. But the trail leads to the poorest section of the village and into the shack of a pariah, an untouchable who for some years has earned a few rupees carrying water.

Willie and the head man of the village enter the hut. Henry must stay outside with the servants. Inside, they find the water carrier, tended by a very old woman with yellow skin, lying on his charpoy with gaping wounds in his shoulder and side. The wounds bleed heavily despite great wads of sacking the old woman has wrapped around them. The untouchable has huge demonic cat's eyes, but as he grows weaker the yellow drains out of them and he turns all the way back into a man. And by the time he is dead and the villagers are about to toss his carcass in the river, he is nothing but a limp piece of rank flesh shot through with bullets.

The man could not remember what happened to the old woman. There was something vague about her being stoned to death, or perhaps they let her go unmolested back to the wood of the ruined temples.

"Yes, that's it, back to the wood with her," he muttered as he pushed on the swing chains slightly and strained his eyes to keep control of the silhouette of his little son. He tingled all over, he felt himself connected to London and Bombay and New Zealand and Orkney – all the places of his psyche – the places of Henry, his father, and Robbie before him, and Willie before him, and Jamie and Magnus and back and back and back where the stories don't reach unless you reinvent them. "We're all the same," he muttered, "we're all one. And this is what it is to be alive. It's what life is, this connection, all it can be, beautiful."

The man gazed through the branches at the moon and reminisced haphazardly until his past and present flowed together as though the Thames and the Mississippi were one oily time-slick, slipping and sliding to some distant sea mythical of dreams. The reverie ended with a surprising image that he found comical: three old men sat in a pavilion at a cricket match – his father, himself, and his American son, nursing glasses of beer, watching the bloody paint dry – England were following on, batting for a draw on the fifth day of the fifth test – and there was a great multitude in attendance at the match, and they were all his forefathers with white beards and pale blue eyes.

God, how he longed for some decent beer.

It was a relief that his son would be one of the chain. And he sighed as if a weight had lifted because this was his son's place and his son's place would be a haven for him and perhaps he could stop longing for a home he could no longer have. But still, leopard men were rare in Minneapolis, it was not what you'd call an exotic place. But perhaps there's a wolf man hereabouts, he thought, or a bear man, or even a raccoon man who, at this moment in his basement, is shape-shifting for a night of raiding garbage cans. This idea of a raccoon man amused him – he know lots of men who were like overgrown rodents.

He watched the little darting shadow flit like a bat from apparatus to apparatus, chattering happily.

"I'm happy too," muttered the man, "I'm happy to be sad that my dad's gone and to be with the little boy who knows nothing yet, only how to have fun or be sad or to get away with being a scallywag. I'm happy to be with him and I ought to work more effectively instead of such long hours so I can be with him more, and I ought to try harder with her otherwise she's going to get even meaner, and, unless I can take it, I won't be able to be with him anymore, at least not like this."

The boy looked at the silhouette on the swing to make sure it was not standing in the time-to-go attitude. He set all the baby swings going at once and spun the roundabout as fast as he could. Then he realized he was done, there was nothing else to play with, he was satisfied. He ran up to his father, who was looking at the sky, and said, "All done now, Dadda."

His father's eyes were full of moonlight which the boy thought of as lanterns inside his father's head. "Dadda's eyes," laughed the boy and jabbed with his forefinger.

The man evaded the jab, then stood up, laughing:

"Yes, Daddy has eyes, and he would like to keep them."

The boy asked his father if having lanterns in your eyes made it so you can see fairies and could he have some too please, but his father didn't understand, and said, "What on earth are you talking about, you little twerp? Come on, time to go home and see the momma."

The little boy grasped his father's finger and walked quietly as far as the baseball diamond, then he looked at the tall shape beside him. He sniffed his father's hand; it smelled of leather and soap. The boy suddenly realized that the father was looking at him, he couldn't see this at all because of the darkness, but he felt it: his father was looking down at him, smiling. This made him happy – he let go of the finger and charged three times around the baseball diamond until he was dizzy and exhausted and had to be carried through the woods.

The little boy was asleep with his head on the father's shoulder when they got back to the house. He woke to the opening door, the taste of drooled-on leather, the sound of television, and his mother's face as she took him from his father to get him ready for bed.

He wanted his Batman pajamas.

His mommy made cocoa. Then mommy and daddy were quiet and nice to each other. Daddy wrote in his notebook in the story-chair by the fire. Mommy read. The little boy sat on the hearth rug in his pajamas and sipped his milky cocoa, watching his mother read and his father write.

"Dadda," the boy said.

"What, little man?"

The boy sipped cocoa, and smiling, said:

"Daddy."

His father lowered the notebook, leaned forward, said:

"Whaty?"

"Dad-dads. Old daddydada."

The mother laughed and put down her book. Looking calmly at the father, she said, "Bedtime."

"Yes," said the father, "he's sozzled."

"Are you going to go to bed tonight like a good boy?" said the mother.

The boy yawned, drank the last of his cocoa, and stood.

"This is a first," the mother said, surprised at his cooperation. "What did you do to him out there?"

The man frowned, said, "We just had fun. No big deal. He's tired, you said yourself he didn't have his nap today."

The mother sighed, "Okay, I was just asking." Then to the boy she said, "Kiss the dadda goodnight then, Harry."

The boy did this, then went with his mother down the long dark hall to the bathroom where he peed and cleaned his teeth before going to his own room with the Sesame Street wallpaper and getting into bed.

Tonight the terrifying black bird with red eyes would not stare in the windows at him. He didn't think of the unnamed horrors lurking in the crevices of his room. He was sleepy and lay quietly in the soft atmosphere of his house. After his mother turned out the light he kept his eyes open and his chest squeezed with a kind of happy-sad joy.

He heard his mother call from the kitchen:

"Cal, honey, you ready for some more cocoa before I fix supper?"

"Cal?"

"What?"

"I asked if you want more cocoa."

"All right. Thanks."

And the little boy thought things were indeed all right after all and that the world was a lovely warm place for him to be in and gradually he fell asleep, smiling in the dark.

GLOSSARY
OF UNFAMILIAR TERMS

A13 – a highway from East London to Shoeburyness ("Piggybank")

"Ach Mensch! Das hat mir gerade noch gefehlt. Hesta, bitte, bitte...Mein Lieber Mann, noch eine Katastrophe!" – "Damnation! That's all I needed. Hesta, please...for the love of man, another catastrophe." ("Hesta")

"Ach, Scheisse. Hesta, bitte sei sehr diskret." – "Oh, shit. Hesta, please be discreet." ("Hesta")

aggro – aggravation; violent trouble ("Bottles and Bricks")

"Ahhhhh, le Boche!...Va te faire foutre!" – "Oh, the krauts...go fuck yourself!" ("Hesta")

Amor fati – an annoying Latin phrase meaning love or embrace your fate ("Bottles")

Anobiid – a grub that eats its way through dead wood for a number of years before emerging as a beetle during mating season, then dying ("Anobiid")

Anobium punctatum – the common woodworm ("Anobiid")

army greens – army surplus trousers ("Bottles")

bairns – children

"Bis spater, Hesta. Tchüss." – "Until later, Hesta...goodbye." ("Hesta")

145

Black and White – a rather sweet, blended Scotch whisky, very popular with alcoholics ("Bombay," "Wounded")

blarney – Irish bullshit ("Anobiid")

bleeding – from "bloody" (God's blood) or "bleeder" (a woman) ("Bottles")

bleeding good pasting – a damn good hiding ("Bottles")

Bloodynora – a meaningless exclamation ("Bottles")

Bobajee – the cook ("Bombay")

bollocks – testicles, sometimes spelled "ballocks" ("Bottles," "Greenacres")

bonce – head ("Bottles")

bonkers – insane, nuts ("Bottles")

bonnet – hood of a car ("Piggybank")

boot – trunk of a car ("Piggybank")

borstal – a corrective establishment for young offenders ("Bottles")

bumf – stuff ("Bottles")

bundle – juvenile word for a flight ("Piggybank")

Boudiccea – Queen of the Icinii, a powerful tribe of ancient Britons who defied the invading Romans ("Piggybank")

Brentford Football Club – a usually unsuccessful soccer club with very mild supporters ("Piggybank")

bristols – breasts, from rhyme-slang: Bristol Cities = Titties ("Bottles")

burra-sahib – the boss of bosses ("Bombay")

caff – Café ("Bottles")

cha – tea, usually with milk and sugar ("Bombay")

Charles Laughton – a fat English actor with pompous pronunciation ("Bombay")

charpoy – a little collapsible bed ("Bombay")

chavvy – guy, fellow; probably from "chappie" ("Greenacres")

chips – French fries ("Piggybank," "Bottles")

clapped out – referring to a run-down car; a beater ("Bottles")

Cockney – someone from East London; the dialect originating in that area ("Piggybank")

"Contrôlez-vous, Nanette. Pensez aux enfants. Vous n'avez aucune renue!" – "Pull yourself together, Nanette. Think of those children. You're a disgrace." ("Hesta")

coreblimey – from "God blind me" ("Bottles")

crisps – potato chips ("Piggybank")

cunt – derogatory term, nearly always aimed at men; among friends, a meaningless put-down ("Bottles")

Cutty Sark – a old clipper, dry-docked in the East End of London ("Piggybank")

dander rising – a tantrum coming on ("Bottles")

"Dann bis spater, Hesta." – "All right, until later then, Hesta." ("Hesta")

dhurri – a rough cotton rug ("Bombay")

dirk – a little knife carried down the socks of Scotsmen ("Anobiid")

dosser – someone who "dosses down" at night; a tramp ("Bottles")

do you in – kill you ("Bottles")

"Du! Halt mal, oder ich ruf die Polizei." – "You! Shut your mouth or I'm calling the police." ("Hesta")

"Elle devrait manger un peu en attendant." – "See that she eats a little something." ("Hesta")

faece – the excretia of wood-boring grubs ("Anobiid")

fags – cigarettes ("Bottles")

fishing fleet girl – middle class Englishwomen who sailed to India with the intention of finding husbands ("Bombay")

fried egg rolls – slit open a fresh crusty hard roll, spread it with butter and slip in a hot fried egg – much better than those boring Oriental things ("Bottles")

Geordie – someone from the industrial northeast of England, famous for their funny accents ("Bottles")

git – slightly offensive term deriving from "whore's begat" ("Bottles," "Piggybank," "Greenacres")

gob – mouth ("Bottles," "Greenacres")

going spare – getting frantic ("Bottles")

goolies – testicles ("Bottles")

Gordonbennet – a meaningless exclamation ("Bottles")

gormless twats – stupid fools; brainless, unattractive ("Bottles")

got the hump – depressed and taciturn ("Greenacres")

governor – the boss ("Bottles")

"Grosser Gott...Wie geht's?" – "Good day...how's it going? ("Hesta")

groyne – a tide breaker, breakwater ("Piggybank")

Guardian, The – famous for its bad copy editing and a more middle class newspaper than *The Daily Mirror* or *The Sun* ("Bottles")

gymkhana – a sports festival, mostly for Europeans, usually with pomposities like polo and croquet ("Bombay")

Hackfleisch des Ottos – Otto's Hamburger ("Hesta")

"Hesta, hor mich an. Papa ist tot...ein schrecklicher Unfall ... " – "Listen to me, Hesta. Dad's been killed...a terrible accident" ("Hesta")

high cockalorums – originally, getting crazy in the officers' mess; partying with alcohol-induced extroversion ("Bombay," "Piggybank")

hob – top of a stove ("Anobiid")

hod carrier – a laborer, specifically assigned to a gang of bricklayers, who carries bricks and mortar in a hod ("Bottles")

Home Counties – the posher counties within commuting distance of central London ("Bombay")

honk – to vomit ("Piggybank")

Howa-khana time – having a rest ("Bombay")

juldi – hurry up ("Bombay")

karsi – the toilet ("Bottles")

knackered – tired out; emptied or bruised testicles ("Bottles")

krait – a very beastly little snake ("Bombay")

Laurence Olivier – an overrated English actor with pompous pronunciation ("Bombay")

lemonade – lemon soda pop

Liebchen – darling ("Hesta")

maisonette – a two-storied apartment above a shop ("Anobiid")

mali – the gardener ("Bombay")

Marathi – the predominant language spoken in Bombay ("Bombay")

masala – a kind of curry ("Bombay")

"Mein Gott, seine französische Hure." – "My God, his French whore." ("Hesta")

memsahib – lady, from "madam-sahib" ("Bombay")

Millwall Football Club – more famous for its unruly supporters than for its success on the field ("Piggybank")

motor – automobile, from "motor car" ("Bottles")

muck – wet mortar ("Bottles")

nattering – talking incessantly; rabbiting ("Bottles")

navvy – a Irish ditch digger, derived from "navigator" ("Bottles")

"Nein...Es ist die aus Genf. Aber sie ist genauso schrecklich, ganz schrecklich." – "No...it's the one from Geneva, but she's also terrible, absolutely awful." ("Hesta")

"Nein! Unmöglich." – "No! Impossible." ("Hesta")

Newcastle United – famous old soccer team, the pride of Geordie land

nicks – steals ("Bottles")

nig-nogs – derogatory for Blacks or Asians, or in some cases the population beginning at Calais ("Bottles")

noggin – drink of liquor, dram, peg ("Bombay")

nutter – a "crazy," someone who gets violently irrational during conflict ("Bottles")

office-wallah – a minor bureaucrat; anyone who wallows in paperwork ("Bombay")

old bill – the police ("Bottles")

"Oui, Madame Schulte, nous reviendrons á deux heurs. Elle se sentira mieux. Eh oui, vous comprenez...elle est tres émue." – "Yes...we'll return at two o'clock...you understand, she's very overwrought." ("Hesta")

"Pauvre Otto, tout le monde se l'arrachait. Il en a fait des heureuses! Seigneur, il va bien nous manquer..." – "Poor Otto, everyone wanted you. You kept everyone happy. My God, how can there be no Otto?" ("Hesta")

peg – measure of liquor, dram, noggin ("Bombay," "Piggybank")

pillock – an idiot ("Greenacres," "Bottles," "Hesta")

Players – British cancer sticks ("Bombay")

plimsolls – the original tennis shoes ("Bombay")

plonk – to plunk something down ("Anobiid")

plonker – a big penis, someone who does not need brains ("Bottles")

ponce – a mild insult; a pimp; someone who gets something for nothing ("Bottles")

pong – usually a bad smell; in the case of "Bottles and Bricks and Walking Sticks," an inappropriately good one ("Bottles")

pratt – not quite as stupid as a "plonker"

prop forward – front right and left positions in a rugby scrum requiring players of some heft ("Anobiid")

punters – the paying public

purse – specifically, a woman's billfold or coin purse ("Piggybank")

Queens Park Rangers Football Club – not famous for anything ("Piggybank")

rabbiting – talking incessantly ("Bottles")

ramjani – dancing girl; prostitute ("Bombay")

"...Reveillez-vous, bande d'abrutis..." – "Wake up, [loosely] you boring, goosestepping squareheads" ("Hesta")

Roedean – the most prestigious British public school for girls about which numerous songs and limericks have been composed ("Bottles")

rumble-tumble – scrambled eggs ("Bombay")

sahib – sir; any European; boss ("Bombay")

scarper – runaway ("Piggybank," "Greenacres")

scoff all that nosh – greedily eat all that food ("Bottles")

scorcher – hot; hot day; nasty argument *et cetera* ("Bottles")

shandy – mildly alcoholic drink, consisting of beer and lemon soda pop ("Piggybank")

shufti – a quick look ("Bottles")

singlet – sleeveless undershirt ("Anobiid")

skiving – inventing ways to avoid work ("Bottles")

Smoke, the – a regionalistic term for London ("Piggybank")

snogging – kissing ("Greenacres")

sod – meaning has derogatory expression deriving from sodomy but is considered a mild insult or curse ("Bottles")

spunk – semen; courage ("Greenacres")

stick the nut on him/Glaswegian kiss – a head-butt

stone – fourteen pounds ("Anobiid," "Bottles")

stroppy – belligerent, pissed off ("Greenacres")

susses – from "to suss out'; to figure out ("Bottles")

take the piss – to ridicule or razz someone ("Bottles")

teapoy – a portable tripod table ("Bombay")

trainers – tennis shoes, plimsolls ("Bottles")

truncheon – a policeman's night stick, billy club ("Piggybank")

try – a touchdown in rugby where the ball actually has to touch the ground in the end zone ("Anobiid")

tum soor ka butcha – you son of a pig ("Bombay")

turps – turpentine ("Anobiid")

"Une fois de plus, ma'deesse. . .J'ai noyé mes problèmes dans le vin et l'amour. Et voila comment on setue à coups d'orgasmes!" – "Once again, my goddess. . .I have blotted out my troubles with wine and love. And we kill ourselves with orgasms, don't we?" ("Hesta")

vindaloo – a meat and potato curry, spicy enough to give you hiccoughs and make your head sweat ("Bottles")

"Vous arrivez trop tôt. Pour l'instant, seule la famille est admise. Il vous faudra revenir à deux heures." – "You're much too early. Only family are admitted at present. Everyone else has their turn at two o'clock." ("Hesta")

wally – someone who is conspicuously uncool; a buffoon ("Bottles")

wanker – someone enervated by excessive masturbation ("Piggybank," "Bottles")

"Was. . .was sagst du? Was?" – "What. . .what did you say? What?" ("Hesta")

wazzock – who knows? Probably something sluggish and useless; a gormless pillock ("Bottles")

Xestobium refuvillosum – the Death Watch beetle. ("Anobiid")

yobos – backslang: boy, then pluralized normally from "boyos" ("Bottles")

yomp our clobber – carry our equipment ("Bottles")

IAN GRAHAM LEASK

Ian Graham Leask was born in Twickenham, West London and has spent the rest of his life attempting to breathe clean air. He has lived in Southend-on-sea and Brighton & Hove where the air was nice; Saarbrucken, Germany, where it was nearly as bad as London, and now Minneapolis, where it seems to be getting worse. Leask has taught fiction writing, literature, mythology, and composition for the University of Minnesota, the COMPAS Writers-in-the-Schools program, and the Loft, a non-academic institution for the advancement of literature in Minneapolis. He is also a private editorial consultant for fiction writers. Leask is currently at work on an advanced textbook on the art of fiction writing, and a second collection of short fiction, entitled *The Blue Flame Club and Other Stories*.